all this useless Beauty

G.S. Hentschel

Tate Publishing, LLC

"All This Useless Beauty" by G.S. Hentschel

Copyright © 2006 by G.S. Hentschel. All rights reserved.

Published in the United States of America
by Tate Publishing, LLC
127 East Trade Center Terrace
Mustang, OK 73064
(888) 361–9473

Book design copyright © 2006 by Tate Publishing, LLC. All rights reserved. No part of this publication may be reproduced, stored in a retrieval system or transmitted in any way by any means, electronic, mechanical, photocopy, recording or otherwise without the prior permission of the author except as provided by USA copyright law.

Scripture quotations marked "NIV" are taken from the *Holy Bible, New International Version* ®, Copyright © 1973, 1978, 1984 by International Bible Society. Used by permission of Zondervan Publishing House. All rights reserved.

This novel is a work of fiction. Names, descriptions, entities and incidents included in the story are products of the author's imagination. Any resemblance to actual persons, events and entities is entirely coincidental.

ISBN: 1-5988621-3-8

Chapter 1

"... And I believe it is possible to fulfill the promise of a general unified theory that would transform the twenty-first century. We have it within our grasp to finalize this revolution of understanding and technology . . . to bring to humanity a new way of thinking . . . a new reasoning that reaches beyond the errors of the past and unites the natural and physical sciences.

Let me be clear; it's preposterous to think that we will ever reach unanimous consensus in every detail of science, but humanity deserves a more productive and a more rational framework of knowledge. We will never stop the discussion of conflicting ideas and theories; it is how the story of science has been written, and we wouldn't have it any other way. But, there is a difference–a difference when the science itself has an agenda. From the very beginning of organized thought and sadly to this very day, we suffer from artificially generated sciences that try to manipulate ideas in attempts to justify agents of exploitation and control. Propaganda sciences based on nothing more than myth are a constant and ever-growing obstacle to this quest for verifiable knowledge of our world. For centuries, man has been taught to fill the Earth, subdue it, and rule over it. It is a crime to which humanity has paid dearly.

And the punishment for this is evident. Instead of thriving as a species in balance with the universe, we have become its enemy, its ultimate parasite. We are only now beginning to understand the sad truth that we are no match for its wrath. The environmental effects alone resulting from this false dominion could eliminate life as we know it in a relatively short time. No matter our constant medical advances, it seems that our reliance on fossil fuel energy production, pesticides, and flawed food production methods continue to make us vulnerable to diseases that aim at the very heart of our being."

On the campus of the University of Texas, Dr. David Levin challenged the faculty and graduate assistants of the School of Natural Sciences. The cavernous auditorium's bright spotlight projected onto the lone speaker behind the ornate wood podium. As he reached the summation of his talk, some of the younger students began to assemble around a single microphone in front of the stage in hopes of posing a question to the renowned scientist.

"I believe that it is this flawed view of nature that has thrust the natural sciences to the forefront of our society. We, as scientists, have an unending obligation to change this paradigm of self-destruction. Political and religious forces that stand in the way of scientific discovery must themselves be revealed for what they are and put to an end. As this new semester begins, it is my hope that each one of you, whether you have been a member of this faculty for years or are just beginning with us, will approach this quest with a renewed sense of purpose and pride. Thank you, and I will take any questions that you may have." Dr Levin gathered his notes and texts together as he stoically received his applause. Shading the spotlight with his hand and squinting in to the dark aisles, he motioned to the group of students at the microphone. "Yes, you there."

A graduate student stepped up to the microphone. "Yes, Dr. Levin, I was wondering . . . how you think one's personal spiritual beliefs play a part in the pursuit of science?" The question was greeted with turned heads and quiet mumbling. Dr. Levin stared quietly at the student who spoke up once again. "Or I guess what I mean to say is, *do* you think that plays a part in the pursuit of science?"

David stood silently behind his podium as the crowd's rumblings grew slightly louder and the skin of the young questioner paled. A range of emotions began boiling within David as he stared at this nervous graduate student. The anger that still burned from the recent events mixed with the contempt for how the question silently mocked him.

"Again, I say no." David paused as his squinted eyes scanned the audience, wondering how this student could have missed his message the first time. "Faith in the unseen or unobservable has no place in the pursuit of science. Hunches and gut feelings are crucial to develop ideas, but should not be confused with established fact." David spoke firmly, his resolve becoming more palpable with each word. "But, I also know that many here in this room have differing levels of faith in varying forms of religions . . . or belief systems, and it is not my intention to belittle these. So practically, I'd say yes, one's faith does play a part in what some must consider when making judgments or conclusions about evidence stemming from their particular inquiries. But it is the duty, then, of the scientist to eliminate these biases, if they be biases, to ensure the purity and integrity of this ever-broadening understanding of established fact." David's gaze went out across the sea of faces in the auditorium. "Do I think that faith has a part to play in the pursuit of science? I think that it may have a part to play in self-realization or self-actualization of the individual, but I don't believe that faith has a place in explaining the how and why of nature . . ."

At the same moment in a small town in Oklahoma, a small choir donned in fading gold gowns trimmed in green harmonized along with the vibrating tones of an ancient pipe organ. The animated music director pinched quiet the last note and the final echoes of the music died down. Pastor Charles Wilson stood up and headed for the pulpit. The morning sun shone through the stained-glass windows and provided its warm glow to the small sanctuary. He gazed out across the congregation, cleared his throat away from the microphone, and began to speak.

"Good morning. I appreciate the opportunity to stand here and talk to you today. This church, this congregation has always been a friend to my family and our ministry. I have many great memories and stories of friends in this church, and I want to share one of them with you.

"It was a few years back. I was talking with a man, a particularly colorful fellow from your congregation who will remain unnamed, after one of your beautiful worship services. We discussed the usual things, you know, the weather and so on. He then looked at me and asked me a question. I'm still not exactly sure what he said, but what I heard was, 'Charles, why are we here?'"

Pastor Wilson paused to allow the question reverberate among the temporarily attentive crowd. "Obviously, it took me by surprise as I suppose it would any of you. I truly wait for these kind of moments though, and I'm sure I smiled as I began to think of all the ways I had tried to answer this question in my own mind. Though surprisingly, it was the first time that someone had come right out and asked me. It's a big one, you know, for people in our profession. People sort of expect us to be able to answer it.

"So, I began to roll it over in my head, the ideas of companionship for God, the participation that we have in His creation, the recognition of the one who created us and the act of acknowledging Him.

"Once I had gotten my bearings and the explanation all mapped out in my head, I began to speak. I had rehearsed so long for this moment that the words seemed to flow out of my mouth, like a sort of poetry. At least to me they did. Not even a minute into my monologue, I looked at my friend who stood there obviously trying to understand what I was saying. Immediately, I thought my explanation was going straight over his head, until he interrupted me.

"'No, no, that's not what I'm talking about at all,' he said.

'What I mean to say is why are we here on Sunday? Someone told me this morning that the Sabbath is Saturday. If that's true, then what the *heck* are we doing here on Sunday?" The hall of the sanctuary filled with a low roar of laughter as Pastor Wilson over-emphasized his re-enactment. After the congregation quieted, he began again. "As you can probably tell, I was embarrassed a bit and I'm sure I had a look of disdain on my face as I changed subjects. It's a question not as profound or significant I guess, but when I began to answer it, I found it almost as hard to explain."

"These two days, Saturday and Sunday, have an almost transcendent meaning to a lot of people, though maybe without a full understanding why," Pastor Wilson's sermon began. "Saturday *is* the Sabbath, at least on the Roman calendar that we find ourselves with today; the seventh day of creation. The Jewish people . . . that is, the descendants of Abraham, Isaac, and Jacob, know this day as the day of rest. They believe that this is the day that God rested after creating everything that we know as our reality. The day God authored from the beginning of creation to be set apart from every other day.

"Who knows how many creative processes God has been through? But as for the one involving 'man,' God included a day of rest at the end to be as much a part of creation as any of the other. God even wrote in His own hand how important the Sabbath is in the Ten Commandments. Honor and recognition of the Sabbath is the fourth commandment. I read from Exodus, chapter 20:

> Remember the Sabbath day by keeping it holy.
> Six days you shall labor and do all your work,
> but the seventh day is a Sabbath to the Lord
> your God . . . For in six days the Lord made the
> Heavens and the earth, the sea, and all that is
> in them, but he rested on the seventh day.
> Therefore the Lord blessed the Sabbath day
> and made it holy.

"Jewish people all over the world celebrate or recognize Saturday with different festivals, rituals, and prohibitive laws in temples and synagogues with a tribe of priests carrying on a tradition from a man named Levi. Interestingly though, as I've learned, if you were to ask the average Christian what day the Sabbath was on, they would say Sunday.

"Sunday is the Lord's Day. Sunday is the day that Jesus of Nazareth was resurrected from the dead to prove that he was the long-awaited Messiah from the ancient prophecies contained in the Book of the Law and the Prophets of the Hebrew people. For some reason, we Christians find it easy to forget that God has been dealing with people for much longer than this Roman calendar has been counting.

"In the twentieth century alone, Christians have constructed enough deep-rooted cultural traditions and real-life experience around Sunday to almost erase the thousands of years of Jewish history from the collective world memory. Sometimes I think it has become nothing more than fable and legend on par with the likes of Mother Goose.

"Not to be outdone by the Jews, we Christians developed Sunday into our own, with our own festivals, rituals, and prohibitive laws with our own tribe of priests carrying on a tradition from a man named Peter.

"To further complicate these religious differences, a mere 500 years after Jesus claimed he was this Messiah of the ancient and holy scriptures, a man named Mohammed sparked another faith from these very same roots that has rivaled any religion ever conceived.

"Islam, like Judaism and Christianity, is derived through Abraham, though it traveled a far different path. Before Isaac was born, Abraham had another son named Ishmael. Ishmael was born to Abraham's Egyptian maidservant, Hagar. Born into an immediately hostile environment, Ishmael was forced to flee with his mother from the safety of Abraham's tents. At Abraham's wish, God blessed Ishmael to become fruitful and the father of a great nation. As we can see, this blessing came true. Arabia, Persia, Babylonia, Egypt, and many other Middle Eastern, African, and Asian kingdoms are now ruled by Islam. As you probably know, the tenants of Islam are contained in a book called the Koran.

"The Koran all but rewrites the history of the Jewish nation to the extent of saying that this Ishmael, not Isaac as the Bible says, was the son that Abraham was willing to offer as a sacrifice to God on Mount Moriah, and the eventual heir to the many blessings promised Abraham." The excited preacher looked out at the confused faces in the sanctuary. "Stop me if I'm going too fast here," he chuckled.

"Abraham, from Ur of the Chaldeans, seems to be at the center of all of this confusion. If you think about it, he is responsible for virtually all of the monotheistic faith in our world today: Judaism, Christianity, and Islam. He lived in a time where legends and history collide, so it is very hard for serious historians to recognize him as a reality. Think about it; he lived only one chapter away from Noah in the book of Genesis. To truly believe in the story of Abraham, I suppose one would have to believe in the story of Noah and the flood. The oral traditions of Abraham's family must have included this story, the story of Cain and Abel, the Tower of Babel, and so on. Even the story of the Garden of Eden was a fresh one; not so far removed as most of us see it today. According to Biblical texts, he would also have been witness to the drastic decrease in the human life span of the time. Though Abraham supposedly lived to be 175 years old, the generations that came before him were said to have lived for three or more centuries.

"More important than any of this, Abraham began a relationship with God and a spiritual bloodline that would forever change the world."

These words echoed far away from the perception of Allison Wilson, the beautifully awkward daughter of Pastor Charles Wilson. As she walked into her first day of class, a chapter of her life was coming to a close. She had made it to the final semester of her senior year at the University of Texas in Austin. Her college career was coming to an end, and only years later would she realize that this time would be monumental and forever missed. She had come alive, developing into a strong, young woman during these years in a place so different from her hometown. Growing up, her weekends were spent helping with Pastor Wilson's revival crusade in towns all around Oklahoma and North Texas. If one were to go below the skin, Allison's desire to learn medicine probably came from helping the endless parade of souls seeking healing from these evangelical events.

As she sat down, Allison read the unique name of the professor written on the chalkboard. Ramana Punjabi would be teaching her three times a week for the next four months. He sat at his desk shuffling through papers and looking through his briefcase as he watched students filter into the classroom. He was from India and had lived in America for three years now. Though most of India was Hindu, Ramana was raised in the Islamic tradition. He spoke English well but retained the typical Indian accent that most Americans had grown accustomed to and loved to imitate. Allison noticed that he stood up as a man in a sport coat walked into the room. Dr. David Levin had come to sit in on the first day of one of his doctoral candidates and personal research assistant. David had taken Ramana under his wing three years ago, helping him get to where he was today. David had spotted Ramana's untamed intelligence early and knew that with the right training, this raw talent could become a powerful asset. Through David's advice and prodding, the naturally shy Indian was about to begin his teaching career.

After talking to Ramana, David walked to the back of the classroom and took a seat. He pulled out his palm computer and began to tap his stylus on the small face to confirm his schedule for the day. David was from New York, raised in an orthodox Jewish family with six siblings. He had come to Texas ten years ago as a teacher in the Biology department and had moved up into the administration. David was not an orthodox Jew, far from it. He had lived through the agony of all of the strict practices of the Jewish faith and escaped to a world where the rules were yet to be discovered.

As the clock hit 1:00 p.m. and the syllabus for the class was passed out, none of the three realized the work that had begun. Originating from the very beginnings of time, the tapestry of religious history was preparing a dramatic stage for a miraculous birth. The history of this world was unwritten up to this point and was still unsure if this would be noteworthy, but it stayed and watched as these three religions set to confront each other. "How apropos," it whispered, "Biology, the study of life."

Chapter 2

As the classroom began to quiet down, Ramana knew that this was the moment of reckoning. He hadn't quite figured out how he was going to get past the next several minutes without looking like the frightened man that now began to quiver inside him. It wasn't necessarily the cultural differences that made him queasy; he knew he would be feeling the same way if he were teaching for the first time in India. Fortunately, there was one hope, one undeniable principle that shy public speakers around the world relied on to get them through the anxiety.

"Good morning," Ramana said. "Welcome to Advanced Biology 304, I am your teacher Ramana Punjabi." He got through the sentence without a stutter or a stammer and with very good diction. The truth is he had now practiced that line for about four weeks.

As he looked up and around the class, he saw everyone looking at him and his throat began to tighten, his vision slightly blurred. Ramana knew he had to act quickly to keep their attention and not look like he was losing it. The rest of the script that he had practiced now began to erase from his memory, and he knew the next words out of his mouth would be shaky at best. He took a deep breath and went back to the comfort and honesty of who he was, "I am a Muslim from India . . . and I would like to tell you a joke."

David sat motionless in the back of the classroom expectantly, knowing the feelings that Ramana was experiencing.

Although they had not talked about it, David grinned as Ramana attempted the old trick that even he had used as a virgin professor.

"A Jewish rabbi was talking to a Catholic priest, and the priest asked, 'Is it true that you had to give up pork to become a rabbi?'"

The room echoed with a few soft laughs in mere acknowledgment of the depth of his set up, giving him the power to continue. Quickly the room quieted as the collective attention drew to Ramana.

"'Of course,' the rabbi replied."

"So the priest asks, 'Just between you and me, have you ever tried pork?' And the rabbi says, 'Oh sure.'"

Again, laughs spread through the room at the multitude of directions the joke could go.

"So the rabbi asked the priest, 'Is it true that you had to give up sex to become a priest?'"

"The priest replied, 'Yes.'"

"The rabbi asked, 'Just between you and me, have you ever tried sex?'"

The room gripped in anxious laughter. The response itself would have been sufficient for the punch line of any joke in this situation. Ramana caught David's uneasy stare and it made him wonder if he should leave the joke unfinished.

"The priest said, 'Oh sure.'"

Ramana tried to duplicate the proper accent, "And the rabbi said, 'I must tell you, it's bedder dan powk!'"

The quiet classroom erupted into laughter. David was startled at the completely unexpected reaction and found himself laughing too. The once silent room filled with the noise of laughter and words as the students used the break to relieve their tension. Something about this obviously shy Muslim telling a joke about Catholics and Jews on a university campus was hysterical. As Ramana playfully tried to get order restored in his classroom, a warm feeling of confidence that started in India and ended at his chest began to lift him off the ground, where he stayed for the remainder of the class.

David's laughter soon turned to disapproval for the success of the punch line. He immediately discounted the fact that Ramana had turned this situation in his favor using a comment that quite possibly could have offended someone and find its way back to his desk. *I can't stay for this*, he thought to himself as he let out a scoffing exhale. His patience with colleagues had grown to razor thin since his latest promotion. *I need people with metal*, he thought as he attempted to get a feel for how his large investment in Ramana would pay off. He was newly aware of how he would now be judged by the people who represent him. His thoughts were interrupted by the beat of his cell phone as it sounded from his pocket. Ramana quickly scanned the room, annoyed at the almost commonplace occurrence. David reached and answered the call as he headed for the door.

Allison noticed the man leaving the classroom and could feel the tension that emanated from him. Pulling her own phone out of her purse to turn the ringer off, her attention went to Professor Punjabi. Although the words he spoke were filtering through her mind, she was concentrating more on the way they were spoken and the person who was speaking them. In her spirit, she could feel something strange about this man. The way he spoke, even though cloaked in a thick accent, was different than anything she had heard before.

"Biology, as all of you already know, is the study of life," began Ramana as he moved forward and sat on the corner of his desk. "It is the study of how life forms function, how natural forces affect those life forms, and the interdependence of the many parts of a life form to function in a specialized manner for its survival. I must say, in all humility as a biology teacher and as a student, that we now stand on the shoulders of giants of biology and science. Giants who have given us the ability to know what we know today and paved the way for all of us. Men like Pasteur, Newton, Galileo, Mendel, Kepler, Pascal, Darwin,

Watson, and Crick; women like Curie, Goodall, and many others have dedicated their lives to certain aspects of the study of science and life. These icons of science have opened up the doors to help us uncover virtually every secret that lies hidden in the natural world. The biological sciences are more exciting than they have ever been, and I would encourage each of you to pursue it as a field of study, even if it is not your major.

"Science, especially the science of life, is an essential part of one's thought process. Science is and has always been powered by the engine of observation. Once nature can be observed to act a specific way, it can be predicted. Once we can predict nature, we can begin understand how it works, watch it, and in some cases, begin to manipulate nature. As we have found over these many years, this thing we have decided to call nature, is a bastion of compounds . . . and processes . . . and physical laws that can be manipulated to basically create anything that the mind can imagine.

It is my belief that anyone who ponders these things and puts them to use is a scientist. I think we forget that sometimes and see scientists in a different light than the rest of society. Sure, some scientists are more educated than others, but it is not the degree or education that makes the scientist, necessarily. It is the dedication to the unbiased pursuit of truth that makes the scientist."

Ramana stood up and continued his inaugural lecture. "But back to our main focus: biology. In the last few decades we have uncovered more secrets about how life works than all of history. We have begun to understand the unseen forces that control the many functions that make life possible. Molecular biology studies the processes of life down to an atomic level. Genetics has mapped out miles of DNA code that dictates how carbon-based life develops and functions. The human genome project has given us our very own recipe. Evolutionary biology has given us a picture of our true origins, and the road map of how these life forms have changed. Medical biology has given the world vaccines and treatments for countless afflictions. Just like a gigantic puzzle, the biological sciences have built precept upon precept to gather the knowledge of life and attain the importance that they hold in our society.

"Incredible discoveries are now commonplace that begin to tie all the various fields closer together, to the extent that the world now waits . . . in some ways impatiently, for the natural sciences to cure the latest devastating diseases and rescue the weakening environment." Ramana was so worked up that he gasped for air after the last sentence and quickly wondered if maybe he was overdoing it. Without realizing it, he had walked into the center of an isle in front of his desk, right in the middle of his 40 students. Before the tension of the situation returned, he quickly turned back toward his desk. "Well, enough of that crap, let's take a look at the syllabus." Again, the classroom filled with laughter and smiles as Ramana continued his triumphant teaching career.

After the class was over, Allison sat and waited for her chance to talk with Mr. Punjabi. She had worried about this class and knew that it would be a tough ending to the slow decline of her grade point average. She also knew that it didn't hurt to befriend the teacher to increase the sympathy factor in determining those all important differences between A's and B's and C's. She remained seated until most of the class had left. Then she gathered her books and her confidence and made her move. As she walked up to Ramana's desk, he looked up and noticed her then quickly glanced away as a natural reflex. When he realized that she was coming to talk to him, he allowed his eyes to take her in fully. Allison had a simple grace to her. Her sandy brown hair seemed to shimmer to blonde as she moved closer. Her eyes stood out more than any other feature on her face, and Ramana was swimming in them as she said her first words.

"Hi, Mr. Punjabi. You really did great for your first day," Allison said. Ramana slightly turned his head. "It was your first day, wasn't it . . . I mean to teach?"

"It was obvious, wasn't it?" sighed Ramana.

Allison retreated, "No, that's not what I mean, I . . ."

"It's okay, hopefully I get better," Ramana interrupted.

Allison pursed her lip as her hand raised to her hip. "Hey, wait a minute, I'm serious, you did fantastic. I was listening the entire hour, everyone was. You really believe in what you're doing and it comes across in how you say it. I am really looking forward to this class."

Ramana sat a little straighter in his chair and said, "What is your name?"

"Allison Wilson," she said.

Ramana looked down at his class roster and spotted her name, "Ah yes, what can I do for you, Miss Wilson?"

"Oh, nothing really, I just try to make it a point to get to know my professors," Allison said semi-truthfully.

"I see. Are you interested in biology?" The more questions Ramana could think of, the longer this lovely vision would be talking to him.

"I'm thinking of becoming a nurse or if . . . uh yes, I'm very interested in biology," she stopped herself before she repeated her career mantra once again.

"If what?" asked Ramana.

Allison shyly smiled, "Well, if everything works out right, I'd like to become a doctor."

"Well let's hope that everything works out right." Ramana paused, then raised his brow. "We are always in need of lab assistants, do you have any interest?"

Allison panicked inside as she thought about how to answer without ruining her first impression. She hesitated and said, "Um, that does sound interesting . . . though, you know, my days are pretty full right now. What does that entail?"

Ramana recognized the hedge. "Well, maybe I can take you to the lab sometime and show you." As he finished that sentence a feeling came over him that seemed to take over his thoughts.

There was only one thing that Ramana had not accomplished on his list of milestones since he had arrived in America. He practiced constructing phrases in different ways to hear what it sounded like coming out of his mouth. He knew sooner or later he would have to practice them in public. To this point it was restricted to the shower, in front of his mirror, only in safe places. He had not gone public with these requests yet, but things were going so well and he wasn't going to feel any luckier than right now. He slowly lifted his head and said, "You wouldn't like to meet sometime . . . with me . . . somewhere . . . for something to eat . . . would you?"

Allison's eyes widened and her head cocked as she was completely taken by surprise, "Huh? No!" Allison's head shook as she tried to regroup. "I'm sorry, I mean sure, whatever."

Ramana quickly began to feel faint as his head twitched, "I'm sorry, that was out of line. I meant only in the most professional terms. I have a lot to learn about this art of teaching and I thought that it might . . ."

Allison interrupted him, "No problem. I'm sorry, I know what you mean. You just took me by surprise."

He paused as a feeling prodded him to take it further. "I mean I didn't think a girl like you would . . ." His words stopped.

"Um, well, I don't know what you know about a girl like me," Allison wondered how men could bury themselves so quickly.

As Ramana's anxiety rose, his sense for tact hid far from his grasp. "I could show you fun time," came out of his mouth like some kind of wartime whore. He had never uttered those words, let alone imagined that they would ever come out of his mouth.

Allison stared at him with her mouth and eyes agape. "What the heck is that supposed to mean?"

Oh my God, thought Ramana as her reaction communicated beyond words. *I've gone too far.*

Words came fumbling out of his mouth, "No . . . no, I'm sorry, I . . . I, that's not what I meant, I . . . was just . . . Oh God. ." His face, even through his dark complexion, was instantly flushed. He scanned the room and saw students whose wondering faces turned toward them at Allison's reaction. His thoughts were on how he would explain this to David . . . to his parents. Suddenly, he felt his hand being touched.

"Don't worry about it," Allison chuckled as she could see the weakness of his situation ooze through his pores. "The things that come out of guy's mouths."

Ramana's pulse, which had reached the mid 100s, slowly began to come down as he looked at Allison in confusion and defeat. He made a mental note not to explore this territory without a little more thought on the strategy game that accompanies it. Ramana's chest was heaving like he had just sprinted a race, and he blinked his eyes to try to refocus on this strange creature.

"Allison Wilson?" He paused to regroup. "I believe I will remember that name. Please let me try that again, if you will allow me."

Allison closed her eyes and graciously nodded her head.

"It is very nice to meet you, Allison; I am very pleased that you will be my student for the next four months."

Allison responded with a big smile on her face, "Why thank you, Mr. Punjabi. I am very excited about this class and hope to be one of your best students."

As she turned around and walked out of his classroom, Ramana dropped back in his chair in exhaustion. "Man, what came over me?" he asked himself as he looked down to his lap and ran his fingers through his hair. Ramana tried to get his breath back as his thoughts went back over his eventful day. "Just throw away everything you've worked so hard for . . . you idiot."

Chapter 3

Inspiration is the name that we have given the unseen hand that bestows creativity upon man. The word itself implies a kind of supernatural influence. Insight seems to develop instantaneously from nowhere, bursting into the thought process like an unexpected wind to the face. Such inspiration must have its origin in some invisible, unknowable realm whispered by angels or laid upon the human brain in wispy sheets of woven linen.

Other ideas come from a struggle born solely from the human spirit, a thorough contemplation of a specific problem or equation. Calories burn and sweat forms along the brow as the unseen machinery of the brain grinds monotonously over theoretical concepts until thoughts are forced together into an invisible mental puzzle.

David's latest research project had taken this long, grueling route to where it stood now: standing on the brink of being a real possibility.

Generally, most ideas at inception only have a miniscule chance of even becoming a real possibility. They never reach paper, or if they do, they quickly find their way into the same landfill that buries tons of junk mail, soggy diapers, and other inspired ideas. Once an idea had reached the stage of being a real possibility though, the chances of achieving reality skyrocketed to just a little above a slight likelihood.

The thought process for David's idea to evolve into the current project took about six months and started at about the same time he was installed as Director of Research for the University. Although David now used some of the most sophisticated and complex computers and machinery in the world, he himself was not well versed enough to feel that he was using these assets to their full potential. As with all geniuses who had yet to become computer geniuses, David knew what he wanted done but was unable to fashion it with a keyboard, mouse, and so much computer code. His first desire was to create an algorithm that would simulate the thousands of variables that determined adaptation and natural selection in living things. It would be a huge equation that calculated minute changes and mutations to show how time and environmental changes affect different animals and plants. The sheer magnitude of all that information in one equation was too much for David to fully conceptualize, so he attempted to compartmentalize the idea.

The revelation came as he was looking at a chart of amino acids. He realized that a computer program, in the right environment, could be made to function just like a single amino acid. Only a relatively small number of amino acids were needed to build every protein that make up living organisms. Computerized amino acids could be written to react in a graphic environment to show the interactions on a monitor. Depending on their realism, one could actually see the atomic reactions as these programs combined and built proteins. The more he thought about this computerized creation, the more David realized the other compounds and elements that could be written as a single program entity. Hundreds of small programs knit together to form a cellular membrane as well as the inner ingredients of a cell. Each cell was fully dependent on a set of instructions in its nucleus in order to react properly with other cells, compounds, and its environment, and most importantly, trying to keep itself alive.

If everything went as David had planned, time factors could be manipulated to send these creations millions of years into the future or into the past to try to duplicate the evolutionary process and gain insights as to how life changes over long period of time. As the programs would be created with more complexity to duplicate real life, new standards of understanding and observation could be reached. If he could create the basis for computer-generated life, it would revolutionize science as we know it today. Once he broke it down to this level, he knew that this was the right type of project, even if it turned out to be impossible.

Since David had the prominence and resources as the Director of Research, the only thing he needed was a strategy to involve the tremendous resources of the computer sciences department. Collaboration of these sciences was tricky, so obtaining the proper approval from the right faculty required a well-planned strategy.

The only people who knew about this project to this point were the head of the natural sciences department, Dr. Wallace Green, and Professor Ramana Punjabi. Ramana had begun documenting the exact structures, functions, and properties of amino acids and other compounds for the past year. Ramana was also very accomplished in programming languages, so he had already begun the process of converting these properties into a computer code.

David was working at his desk when Ramana knocked on the open door of his office.

"Hey David, you left right when it began to get interesting. You didn't want to stay around for the fireworks?" Ramana smiled.

David looked up from his folders, "Huh? Oh, I saw plenty of fireworks. You pretty much had the class in the palm of your hand when I left. I hope you survived through it."

"It went well," Ramana said. "I appreciate your help. The students were very friendly. I guess some of them could tell it was my first day."

"That joke was pretty gutsy. I'm not sure I can condone something like that," David said with a wondering smile. "Somehow, I don't think I could get away with a joke like that."

"Anyway, I think I am very close to presenting our project to Jim Meyers over at the computer science department," David said as Ramana took a seat. "Do you think you're ready to start working with some real programmers?"

"Absolutely," answered Ramana trying not to take offense. "I have virtually all of the amino acids written or at least mapped out, and the environmental control program . . . well I've got a preliminary form of it. You'll need to take a look at it. I'm not sure I'm going in the right direction."

"I'm sure it's a good start," began David, "I am hoping to get four or five programmers from Meyers to speed up the work and bring some ideas to the table."

Ramana thought for a second as his head nodded. "If we get some programming help, it wouldn't take long at all to develop a working model. I could actually concentrate more on the biological information, with the help of some research assistants . . . that is, as soon as we can go public with it." Ramana paused, then asked, "How soon until we can go public with the project?"

"It shouldn't be long. I've talked to Dr. Green about accompanying me on my visit with Dr. Meyers," David said. "I've set up a meeting for the first of the week, but who knows?"

"That will sure be a relief," Ramana said. "Not just the secret part, but getting other minds and opinions involved should give me some help in some of the problems areas."

David turned his head as he looked at Ramana. "What areas are giving you problems?"

"Well, I have begun to run into some blind areas, where there is very little microbiological study," said Ramana. "We know generally what happens but we are unsure of exactly which proteins are causing it. You know, in some cases, the proteins that are present could be the cause of the process or the effect. Sometimes it is unclear."

"Yeah, I knew we would run into some uncharted territory," David started. "I guess it's our job to figure those problem areas out. We will have the ability to simulate these processes; we can figure it out."

David continued, "Once I have wrapped up the logistics and have the grant approved, I can spend more time with you solving these things . . . I would say two to three weeks. Anything that you have problems with, go ahead and describe the problem to me in a memo and I can start taking notes and doing some research."

David stopped for a second. "By the way, you are working some serious hours, especially now that you are teaching. Do you think you can handle both teaching and heading up this project?"

Ramana grinned as he nodded his head. "David, I just had one of the best days of my life. I am teaching advanced biology at the university level, and I am working on a revolutionary biological simulation program that will not only help me to get my Ph.D., but will ultimately help me teach biology. Right now I feel that I am blessed with everything I have wanted. You know, from Allah and everything." Ramana shuttered as he realized what he had blurted out.

David chuckled at the innocent enthusiasm that Ramana had and said, "Well, way to go Allah." He tried to not noticeably shake his head and laugh.

"I will have to cut back on my indulgent social life, though," Ramana joked. "You know how girls are attracted to us laboratory nerd types."

"You better watch out now that you are a professor," David warned. "Some girls, and I should say some boys, have figured out that the way to a professor's grade book is through his heart, or pants I should say." David paused then continued with a smile on his face. "I've found myself in some interesting positions. You really have to watch what you say and how you say it."

Ramana bit his lip and thought about his earlier scene with Miss Wilson. "You would not just be whistling Dixie."

David laughed. "What?"

Ramana shrugged his shoulders and laughed with David. David thought to himself that Ramana, for better or worse, was becoming Americanized.

David changed the subject back to work again. "I've been looking for any articles or papers published in this area. I've run searches through the *Journal of Molecular Evolution*, the *Proceedings of the National Academy of Sciences*, and any books written on the subject. Almost all of the work has to do with the analysis of genetic information. There are a number of mathematical models that have been developed to attempt to mirror the molecular processes or interpret protein sequences, but nothing to the extent of what we are trying to accomplish."

Ramana smiled at the thought of their revolutionary work. "I am documenting all of the work that I have done so far in a journal. I am hoping to publish my perspective on this work at some point in time. That is, in addition to my eventual thesis."

"Good, I'm sure if this works out like I hope, there will be plenty of perspectives published regarding this work." David continued, "Again, that reminds me, even when we open this project up to others, we still need a continued discretion on the part of any assistants until we are ready to go public in a peer sense. And one thing I want you to remember; I want you to be very selective in who we trust to be part of this project. This is an extremely sensitive project. I want the best we can get to assist us."

"Agreed," said Ramana. After he paused, his eyes looked straight into David's. "You know David, to make this work we are going to need an incredible amount of storage space and computing speed. Each program is of significant size, and we will need thousands, if not millions, of them. I can't imagine that this will be possible with any ordinary computer."

"I know, I know, that's why I have to sell Meyers on the project. I've targeted a computer that they have assembled down in the basement of the science lab. It uses a different type of memory storage that they have been experimenting with for a while. They've had a lot of trouble with it, and they have spent a ton of money on it. It takes up too much space to be practical for commercial purposes so they just use it off and on for different experimental projects."

Ramana's eyes lit up. "I think I know the one you are talking about. I've heard some of the information systems grad students talking about it, but I've never seen it. It's the one that uses a silicon gel core to store the information three dimensionally?"

David smiled and nodded his head.

"I have been intrigued with the idea. What's the computing speed like?" Ramana asked.

"The last I heard they had gotten the Technology Consortium trying out their latest processors on it," David said. "They are having a hard time relating the time and space coordinates with information location. It uses an incredible amount of energy to run this thing; I'm not sure anyone really understands it yet. You should go down there and find out what you can."

Ramana thought about the computer as he sunk back in his chair. "That computer definitely has the storage space that we need. We could house multiple cells in that space."

"You know what they have been calling that computer?" David asked.

"Um . . . I think I remember them referring to it as the beast," Ramana replied.

"That's the funny part," David started. "That's the tentative name that I have come up for the project, the Bio-Evolutionary Algorithm for Scientific Testing."

Ramana laughed nervously. "Wow, that could really scare some people."

"It should scare some people," David laughed. "It could change the world. Anyway, you don't believe in that kind of stuff, do you?"

Ramana just smiled and slightly shook his head.

"Well again, it's just the tentative name. The more important thing is getting the computer, the programmers, and the funding." David looked down at his watch. "And we are not there yet."

"No we are not," Ramana agreed as he looked at his watch too. "Well, I know you have a lot to do, just as I do, so we will talk more tomorrow. Again, I feel I have you to thank for getting to this point in my career. I appreciate the guidance and the opportunity."

David smiled and waved to Ramana. "Okay Ramana, you have yourself to thank. You've done amazing work so far, but we are not there yet."

Chapter 4

What am I doing here? Allison thought to herself. She had been thinking that a lot lately. Sometimes, she felt like everything was falling apart, in between the crying. She couldn't really point to the one thing that made her feel this way. It lasted about thirty minutes or so, and then she could convince herself that things were going to be okay. This one, though, was lasting a little longer than the others.

I should really be happy, she thought. She was graduating in less than a year with a pre-med degree and four years worth of good friends and good times. She was so lucky in the big scheme of things to be living in this beautiful sorority house and know hundreds of new people in her life. She had learned so much in the last four years that she felt nursing school would be a breeze, and medical school would not be such a distant dream, except for the monetary considerations. She still never knew where the money for the last four years had come from. She knew that her parents couldn't afford it, but the bills always seem to get paid. Was all this putting an unnecessary burden on her family back home?

Maybe she thought about things too much. Allison would find herself in daydreams, going over thoughts and problems in her mind, oblivious to the world until she could emerge from the vastness of her own consciousness. Only rarely did she actually come to some resolution. It took four years of these journeys, but she had just about figured out college.

College was such a strange lifestyle. The final level of formal education coupled with the first time to be absent parental control, it combined two diametrically opposed options to her. One was to build a solid foundation on education and career for the fulfillment of her own personal dreams. The other was to go absolutely wild finally, without any parental figure to answer to. Just about the only permanent results were measured by report cards, and sometimes, police records. If one were to combine the two and come out with high grades and a clean record, that seemed to be the ultimate success.

Allison had seen both sides of the spectrum of this lifestyle through her friends and found herself somewhere in between. College was a theoretical world. The decisions and schoolwork you do seem to have no effect on anything else; it was practice for the real world. When you had a question, it was someone's job to answer it, or at least help you find an answer.

What was more important, she thought, *the grades she earned or the information she learned*? How could a sometimes disinterested professor make an objective judgment on what she had learned? She had seen people make good grades in classes without showing up or by cheating. The size of some classes made teaching and grading almost impossible. And what was it all for? So she could go out and try to get the highest paying job that she could? It seemed to be the obvious goal of most everyone there–get the highest grade, prepare the best resume, sell yourself the best, and begin your rise through the corporate ladder. Had education transformed into a sort of packaging, a mere marketing attempt to get the highest dollar per pound?

Maybe that was it. Maybe it was the abhorrence of what she felt was driving her now. How could she think about furthering her education when she needed to earn money to begin to pay back what her parents had over extended themselves for?

I really should've figured out exactly what I'm going to do by now, kept popping into her head. *I've got to know*. She knew she could probably work herself through nursing school, but not medical school. What if she got her nursing degree? Was she going to move back to Ardmore? There were too many questions there, so she retreated to another thought. "Maybe I should pray about it," she actually whispered the words. When she heard herself, she knew what the problem was.

College, for some reason, had changed her relationship with God. It wasn't an overnight collapse. She still prayed and occasionally read the Bible that her father had given her. Lately though, it seemed that she was just going through the motions. She felt like most of her time was spent sneaking around God, pretending that He was not watching. The word "compromise" kept coming into her mind. Had she compromised to get where she was right now? *Sure I have, but everyone does . . . everyone!* Then was it guilt that she felt? Guilt for not being the best person she could be. Guilt for not being the Christian she should be. "Guilty as charged," she said out loud as she looked into the mirror.

"Guilty of what?" asked Allison's roommate Rachel as she unexpectedly walked through the doorway.

Allison twitched in her seat with surprise, embarrassed at being caught talking to herself. She kept her eyes facing down at her desk. "Oh, I don't know, whatcha' got?"

Rachel laughed and said, "Girl, you got serious problems." She threw her backpack on her bed and said, "Come on, I'm getting out of here, and I'm taking you with me."

Rachel had been Allison's closest friend since she had come to college. She was from Dallas, raised in a well-to-do Catholic family. In a lot of ways things had reversed for them over the time they had known each other. Early on, Rachel had been the strong one that had taken Allison under her wing, showing her the ins and outs of sorority life. But lately Rachel had been depending on Allison more and more for the strength to face the finality of graduation. They were very open about their beliefs to each other and had talked through about every subject they could think of. Religion was always an acceptable topic. Allison loved to hear about the strange things that Rachel experienced growing up Catholic. Talk about strange, Rachel couldn't believe some of the things that Allison told her about her evangelist father and their traveling crusades.

"Where are we going?" asked Allison.

"Does it matter?" Rachel replied.

"Well, I have some things to do," Allison said without a whole lot of persuasive power.

"That's bull crap!" Rachel was not taking no for an answer. "This is the first day of class of our last semester together. I haven't seen you for any length of time in at least a month. We are going to hop in my car, pick up a six-pack and a pack of smokes, and drive out to the lake."

Allison knew it was useless to argue, so she said, "I guess that means we are going to miss the Chapter meeting."

"Were you going to give some kind of speech tonight, or what?" Rachel stopped herself and looked Allison straight in her eyes, her speech softened. "Look, I've missed you, and I need to talk to you."

Allison smiled and said, "I've missed you too, let's go."

Lake Austin, just minutes from campus, has some of the most beautiful scenery in Texas. It had been Texas' Colorado River years ago until dams had been constructed in several places to create the Highland Lakes. It still has all of the looks of a deep, wide river with huge cliffs and deep forests on either side. In places where they have cleared the native cedar trees, the lakefront is bordered by grass meadows, majestic live oaks, sycamores, and cypress trees that reduce the hot, humid summer temperatures and give you an unexplained sense of peace. Their sophomore year, Rachel and Allison had found their own private tree to park their car under and get away from the rest of the world.

Rachel and Allison quietly walked out of the sorority house as to not make their departure, and therefore their absence at the Chapter meeting obvious. They jumped into Rachel's BMW convertible and headed down the university drag. Every university has one; the University of Texas has Guadalupe.

Guadalupe bisects the university and the real world, and still yearns for the days of social justice. From 29th Street to Martin Luther King Jr. Boulevard, ten blocks in all, it houses all of your typical college stores, hangouts, and restaurants that feed off the tens of thousands of people that attend or work for this institution. This area also attracts a crowd that differs greatly from the students who can afford the tuition and who can meet the tough entrance requirements. It is a crowd that might be labeled by inadequate words such as hippies, generation Xers, new agers, and sometimes homeless. They are people who, for a variety of reasons unique to each one, have attempted to disassociate themselves with mainstream culture and the financial obligations that go along with it. Tattoos, body piercing, dyed hair, and black clothes are some of the marks and badges of this society. Art, peace, music, and sometimes drugs are their business. Markets are open in this area where their lifestyles are sold and sustained. Crystals, jewelry, tie-dye, and other things are made available to the public, especially the students who might be searching for an image or counter image. Ironically, it is next to this great university that this society exists in somewhat stark contrast to the principles and foundations that govern it.

As Rachel turned up the volume of the stereo to let the entire drag share in the music, Allison watched the odd mix of people that filtered through the street. Her eyes became newly aware of the diversity and strangeness of this cultural center. She wondered how each of the people, who she made eye contact with, really saw her. Did the skinny freshman, trying to "look cool" wish that he was in the car with them? Did the tired looking, dirty woman walking in rags with the knapsack over her shoulder wish that she was them? Did the large man in the black wool robe holding the sign that read "REPENT" see right through them? Luckily, at that moment, Rachel lit a cigarette and handed it to Allison. Somehow it allowed her to change her thoughts to the music that filled the air as they left this pulsating cauldron of activity and headed for the peace of the hill country.

As they pulled into City Park, they could see that they would have it virtually to themselves tonight. The chill was still in the air, and most lake people were still waiting for the trees to bloom and the grass to turn green. Lake Austin sat quietly and shimmered in the setting sun as they drove through their private sanctuary. They parked next to the old familiar sycamore tree, which seemed naked and lonely, but no less welcoming. They stopped and propped their seats back to fully take in the sky, which was preparing an audience of stars for their conversation. Rachel popped open two beers and handed one to Allison. As they got comfortable and listened to the music, they tuned in to their own thoughts and imagination. As simple as this method was for escaping, it went a long way to opening a person up for thought and communication. This was the silent time, the time to sift through thoughts; the time to gather your courage to reveal things. Tonight would be a night to reveal things, they knew it, and so they waited and enjoyed the quiet time.

Twenty minutes after the silence had begun, Rachel was the first to break it.

"Allison, do you think I'm a bad person?"

Allison awoke from her thoughts and said, "What? What do you mean?"

Rachel squinted her eyes as she looked into the rearview mirror. "I don't know, I just wonder what people think of me sometimes."

"Do I think you are a bad person?" Allison tried to answer her truthfully. "No, I don't think you are a bad person."

Rachel continued looking in the mirror silently and thought to herself how stupid that question sounded. She had been rolling things over in her mind along time and wondered why she couldn't think of a better way to express herself.

"I'm sorry," Rachel sighed, "I'm such a freak. I don't know, sometimes I think I've got things figured out, and then the next day I'm even more confused than before." She took a drag from her cigarette. " Sometimes I guess I have no clue what I'm supposed to do."

Allison could tell that Rachel had a lot that she wanted to get off her chest. "Well, how are things with John?" She figured it was a good place to start.

Rachel laughed sadly and shook her head. "Oh we're fine, I mean I guess we're fine. He's usually off doing something with his band or with his friends. I really don't ask a lot from him and, I guess, he doesn't ask a lot from me. Sometimes I feel like I'm his groupie, or his concubine, or something. It's definitely not like what I thought a relationship should be."

"Well, I'm sure he will grow up and realize what he's got in you," Allison assured her.

Rachel turned and looked at Allison. "You know, he doesn't believe like you and I believe." She slumped back in her chair and looked straight through the windshield. "And sometimes, I'm not even sure what I believe anymore."

"Do you guys talk about that stuff?" Allison asked.

"Yeah, sometimes, not very rationally," Rachel answered. "I don't know, he seems angry at religion, Christianity especially. It's those stupid TV evangelists; you know how they act."

Allison lifted up her brow. "Uh yeah, I know."

Rachel turned quickly to Allison as the realization of what she said hit her. "Oh Allison, I'm sorry, I didn't mean anything by that . . . but, you know what I mean though, don't you?"

"Yeah, I guess so," Allison started. "It's funny, I always thought of my dad as a hero. It wasn't until I came to college that I found out that a lot of people are immediately suspicious of what my father does."

"Anyway, it's not just religion. John seems to be mad at just about everybody, except when he's partying–then he's just out of hand." Rachel quickly skipped over Allison's comment.

Allison tried not to notice Rachel's selfishness anymore, but began to get a bit more sarcastic. "Well if he's causing you that many problems, dump him!

Rachel sighed and said, "Then what would I do? He's got me convinced we're soul mates. How do you dump your soul mate?"

"Soul mates, huh?" Allison shook her head. "I have a hard time believing that it is your destiny, to spend eternity with John Antonio Scagnelli."

Rachel laughed. "Maybe you're right, but then how are you supposed to know when you've found the right person?" Rachel asked, not really expecting an answer.

"I don't know, maybe nobody is the right person. Maybe you just make it the right person." Allison thought about what she said. "But then I guess there are always the signs."

"What signs? What do you mean?" Rachel asked.

"Oh, I don't know, like when you love someone so much it hurts inside." Allison looked up at the darkening sky. "Like when just kissing someone makes you want to cry."

Rachel thought about it. "Yeah, I guess I know what you mean, but that's never happened to me . . . how about you?"

"Not yet," Allison sighed.

"You know Allison, I envy you," Rachel said.

Allison slowly turned her head to Rachel. "Why would you want to do a stupid thing like that?"

"I just do," started Rachel. "You seem to have everything worked out in your head, and you seem comfortable with yourself."

"Why do you even say that stuff, Rachel?" Allison said, "Maybe I look like that on the outside. Inside, believe me, I'm as messed up as anybody."

"Well, you've hung on to your religion through college, that's something," observed Rachel.

Allison looked at Rachel with confusion, "What the heck does that mean? Everyone hangs on to one religion or another. Are you not a Christian anymore?"

"Not a very good one," Rachel said. "I haven't been to

confession in about a year, and when I was home for Christmas, I really didn't even feel like going to church. I don't know, it just seems that everything I do takes me farther away from where I was as a kid . . ."

Allison stared out the windshield as she listened. Rachel's words kept going, but they began to skim off the thoughts that they created in Allison's mind. She went back to her younger years as memories randomly popped into her head. She saw her mom and dad standing along the fence that surrounded their small farm. It was the fence that kept her from danger all the years of her childhood–the fence that she had long ago climbed over and left so far behind.

" . . . So I guess that's why I feel like I've turned into a bad person . . . Allison . . . Allison!" The second try by Rachel brought Allison out of her thoughts.

"Oh, I'm sorry, I was thinking about things . . . but yeah, I think I know what you mean." Allison tried to get back into the conversation. "I think you're right. I mean, I think I'm experiencing the same thing. It's easy to do."

"Well, what do you do about it?" Rachel asked.

Allison paused and thought about how she would answer such a question. As she tried to figure out how she would express in plain words this profound theological answer, the darkness finished pushing all of the sunlight to the other side of the world. The moon and the stars watched quietly as these two muses sang the mysteries of the universe. The trees quieted their rustling branches. The tall dying grass held still against the gentle breeze to discover if any secrets of life would be revealed. Unknown to the two girls, all of the immediate nature came to a halt in an attempt to hear this ultimate truth about life, death, and renewal.

Chapter 5

The first project that Ramana had assigned in his biology class was an exercise in evaluating an existing biological theory. Ramana thought it would be a simple exercise for his students to formulate their own ideas and spark some intuitive thought. He chose the endosymbiotic theory. This theory attempted to explain the origin of some of the essential elements contained within common animal cells. The theory had its champions and its detractors, so the paper forced the students to take a side, and through what they had learned so far, to defend it. The paper was only to be 350 words and had to use information only from the first six chapters of the text: *Life-The Science of Biology*. They could not go to outside sources to write this paper. They were limited to the facts that they had established in the classroom to this point. In addition, if a student were to take the position that the endosymbiotic theory was wrong, extra credit would be given if the student could propose an alternate theory.

Allison sat at the front row as Ramana explained the project. Two weeks into the semester and she actually enjoyed coming to this class, as opposed to many of the other classes she had endured. As she listened to the assignment, her practical nature told her that extra credit was something she would probably need. The first weeks of this class was basically review from the earlier science and biology classes she had taken. The area she feared most was genetics. She figured that a buffer zone of extra credit might make her journey through genetics a safer one. In the same vein of thought, she decided that she was going to take Mr. Punjabi up on his offer to be a lab assistant. As she thought about it, the fact that this would be her last chance to do it in her collegiate career sealed the deal in her mind. In fact, Allison's involuntary guilt muscle began to prod her on why she hadn't decided to work in the research labs earlier. Her attention was directed back to Mr. Punjabi as he began to close the hour down with some reminders and announcements. Allison smiled as she relived her first experience with Mr. Punjabi.

Allison stood up and moved behind a few students who wanted an audience with the professor. The majority of students quickly headed out of the classroom. Mr. Punjabi had gained the respect of his students, and Allison noticed the patience that he had in helping the students in front of her. Finally she stood alone before Mr. Punjabi.

"Well hello, Allison, how can I help you?" Ramana quickly thought to himself after the words. *No funny stuff this time, stud.*

"Hi Mr. Punjabi. I was thinking about what you had said a couple of weeks ago about helping out in the lab. I was wondering if you were still looking?" Allison rested her backpack on his desk.

The words were music to Ramana's ears, and he said, "Yes, we are always looking, and I happen to be in need of some specialized help on a research project that I am doing for my doctoral work also." Ramana twitched as he thought about the information he had just shared with a student, the discretion that David and he and agreed upon, and the fact that he could never be in the CIA or some sort of spy. "If you have some time, I could show you around the research lab and we could discuss some different options. How much time would you have available and what days could you be available?"

Allison thought about it and said, "I could be there on Tuesdays and Thursdays, probably for two or three hours."

"I think that could be useful to someone." Ramana looked

at the work on his desk and then his watch. "Do you have time to walk over to the lab with me right now?"

"Sure," Allison replied.

"Well, give me five minutes to get my things together and then we will go." Ramana began to organize his papers and clean up his desk as Allison wandered around the classroom.

The walk to the lab was about a quarter of a mile, and Allison began to ask Mr. Punjabi about himself.

"Do you still have family back in India?"

"Yes," replied Ramana, "my parents, two brothers, and one sister."

"Oh, so you came here alone," Allison started. "Wow, that must have been tough. America is kind of a crazy place."

Ramana smiled and said, "It has definitely been interesting. India is a crazy place as well." Ramana paused. "I guess it's just a different kind of crazy."

Allison nodded and said, "Your parents and family must be very proud of you and your accomplishments."

Ramana smiled at her truly American way of interrogation that he still had not yet grown accustomed to. "I guess so. I never have really thought about it that way. I'm not exactly sure they were so happy with me leaving."

Allison quickly decided that she was into the wrong area of discussion and said, "Oh yeah, I was thinking of trying for the extra credit on the paper you assigned today." She paused and thought about things. "Although some of my alternate theories might not be received too well."

Ramana, pleased with the change in topic, said, "Well let me be the judge of that. The great thing about science is that there is no limit on what you can propose. You just must be prepared to stand behind it."

Ramana walked up the remaining steps to the research lab and opened the door for Allison. She took a few steps and then stopped in her tracks as the smell of sulfur and formaldehyde entered her nostrils. The two went through the now standard security procedures before they were able to proceed.

After they were deemed clean, Ramana walked passed her and over to a desk near two large metal doors. He leaned over to sign a clipboard on the desk and picked up two plastic clip-on tags. He motioned for her to walk over and handed her a tag. "Here, put this on your shirt." She noticed that hers was a generic tag while Ramana's had his name and picture on it. Ramana spun around and opened one of the large metal doors and led Allison in.

The large room they had entered was wide open and had high ceilings like a warehouse. It was divided up into various roped off areas where metal tables and lab equipment were assembled together. About twenty people were in this room doing an assortment of tasks. Allison was in awe of the complexity of what appeared to be happening in this room as Ramana stopped to talk to a man in a lab coat.

Ramana walked back to Allison and said, "Welcome to the research lab. This room houses about thirty different experiments and research projects." Ramana led her along the pathway that was taped off to keep foot traffic away from the lab equipment. "The projects in this room are designated as 'low impact,' which means that they do not need isolation or special housing to keep them or us safe and controlled. This is where most first-time lab assistants work. Most of the work, as you can see, is taking chemical readings and charting them on the hour. In some cases, twenty-four hours a day." He finished off the sentence with a detectable sense of pride.

When they had reached the far side of the building, Ramana continued through a set of sealed double doors. "This is the entrance to the hot rooms, the clean rooms, the electron microscopes, and some other things." Ramana stopped and showed her his badge. "To get much farther, you must have a security clearance." Ramana turned and saw the snack room and looked back at Allison. "Can I interest you in a cup of coffee? We can discuss some different options for you." As Allison nodded her head and smiled, she wondered if this qualified in some strange scientific way as a date.

The snack room was small and had four round tables with padded chairs. Against the wall were assorted snack and drink machines, and in the corner were four rather large coffee urns.

Allison chuckled when she saw the coffee urns and said, "You guys go through a little bit of coffee around here?"

As Ramana poured their drinks he said, "Coffee is one of the most important substances that is brought into the laboratory." He paused. "That and Fig Newtons."

Allison laughed even louder and found a seat.

As Ramana sat down and began to talk, Allison noticed that something had changed about him. His facial features seemed stronger and not as foreign as they did when she had first seen him.

Ramana stopped his explanations and said, "Allison, if you don't mind, could you tell me about yourself?"

"Okay," Allison said. "There's really not a lot to tell. I was born and raised in Oklahoma, my parents and my little bother still live there . . . um, I should graduate after this semester . . . uh, what else do you want to know?" She giggled nervously.

"Oh, I don't know. What do your parents do?" asked Ramana.

"Well my father is a preacher, and my mom is . . . well, a homemaker, I guess," responded Allison.

"Did you come here on a scholarship?" asked Ramana.

"Nope."

"He must be a wealthy preacher to send you to this university," said Ramana. "This is an expensive school, especially if you are from out of state."

Allison laughed. "No, no, I really don't know how they can afford to send me here."

"So I assume that he is a Christian preacher?" Ramana saw Allison nod her head and continued, "And you, you are a Christian?"

Allison answered, "Absolutely, and I guess that you are a Muslim."

"Yes," replied Ramana, "although, I guess I would have to consider myself a somewhat less than perfect example of a Muslim."

"Well then, I guess that puts us in the same boat," replied Allison.

Ramana looked around the room and said, "Sorry, I don't think we came over to the research lab to discuss religion."

"I won't tell if you don't tell," laughed Allison. "Anyway, it's one of my favorite subjects. I don't know, not many people like to talk about it."

"I think it has something to do with the emotions that arise when talking about the subject," observed Ramana.

"Yeah I guess, but I see plenty of emotions arise when people talk about ordinary things like fashion, sports . . . and especially politics," Allison answered.

Ramana thought for a second. "I guess you're right, but you know, religion has caused more problems in this world that any other ideology. Look at all the wars fought and the people killed in the name of religion."

Allison frowned. "You don't really believe that, do you?"

Ramana smiled at the question she asked. "I believe that is one of the questions that people fear, Allison." Ramana paused as Allison looked puzzled. Ramana over emphasized his speech, "You don't really believe *that*, do you?"

Allison smiled as she nodded her head. "I guess you're right. I'm sorry, that is kind of an offensive question."

Both Allison and Ramana were startled as two lab assistants burst noisily into the snack room and headed for the coffee urns. They nodded their heads and Ramana and Allison continued their conversation.

"Well, back to the question at hand," Ramana started.

Allison shrugged her shoulders and looked at the two lab assistants.

"Where do you see yourself being most useful in the research lab?" asked Ramana.

Allison smiled and said, "Oh, *that* question."

They both laughed at her reply and took a sip of their coffee.

Allison started the conversation again. "You said that you might need help on your project. Do you think I could be useful to you?"

What a question, he thought to himself. "Well, it is a little too early to start on my project, and . . . well, it is kind of a confidential project at this point. I really shouldn't talk about it."

"Cool, a secret project," Allison said jokingly as she watched Ramana's face twitch. "Just kidding. Really, I trust you to place me in the proper place, though if there is space, I would like to work with you."

Ramana couldn't help but smile and hoped that he wasn't blushing. "Okay, I'll ask around and see what works out. I'll try to put you in a good situation if not with my project. When do you think you can start?"

Allison looked up at the ceiling and thought about it for a while. "I could probably start next week."

"Okay, good, I think we have settled that. Let me walk you out. I really should get back to work," Ramana said as he helped Allison with her chair. "Back to our class. What did you mean when you said that your alternate theory for extra credit might not be received too well?"

"Oh, I don't know, I have a lot of crazy ideas." Allison followed him out of the snack room and said, "I just have a hard time reconciling what I've learned in college and what I learned as a kid."

"I don't understand," replied Ramana.

Allison looked around and quietly said, "Well, maybe, I would like to propose that, maybe, God created everything." Allison finished her sentence with her eyes looking down as she waited for a response.

"Oh, I see . . . well that does create an interesting problem . . . if you'll pardon my choice of words." Ramana paused and walked with Allison into the noisier research room. "I guess the main problem lies in trying to prove that kind of thing . . . that and the abundance of evidence that seems to contradict it."

"Yeah, I know that it seems crazy," Allison started.

Ramana interrupted, "I didn't say it was crazy, I just said it would be very hard to prove. If it is something that you feel strongly about, don't let anybody make you feel stupid for believing it. I've found that everyone requires different levels of proof for their beliefs." Ramana chuckled, "Don't let anyone lie to you about it. I even know scientists who believe in things that are not even close to being proven."

Allison looked at Ramana in amazement. "Wow, that's definitely not the reaction that I was expecting."

"Like I said," he continued, "I believe that Allah has given me this mind and His word to better understand Him and this world more and more. I tell you the truth, there are plenty of mysteries about the origins of life that science has not explained yet. All I know is that we are getting closer every day. Even my project is . . . well, I shouldn't really talk about that." Ramana paused as they reached the front door. "Maybe sometime we can discuss it further, but please don't let my class be a hindrance to your beliefs." Ramana thought about it more and shook his head. "No, that is not what I want my class to be . . . no!"

Allison was trying to digest and understand everything that he had said and wasn't sure if he was finished yet, but she said, "Thank you Mr. Punjabi, that really means a lot to me. I look forward to talking more about this with you. Good bye."

After Allison had walked through the door, Ramana stood inside and watched her walk away through the window. The feeling in his chest was electric, and he could feel his heart pumping the blood to the rest of his body. *I am going to get in trouble with her, I can feel it*, he thought to himself. He knew he was falling in love with one of his students and he couldn't help it.

Who cares, he thought, *it's not like I am ever going to reveal it. It's not like she was ever going to have the same feeling for me.* He was content to keep this great feeling boiling within him and ride it out for as long as he could. All of these thoughts were soon accompanied by another–*I think it is time to go pay a visit to the beast.*

Chapter 6

David and Dr. Wallace Green walked out of the computer science building together and stopped on the sidewalk. "How about joining me for lunch? There's a place over here that's pretty good; I'll buy." David pointed to the drag.

Dr. Green looked at his watch. Nodding his head, he began to follow David toward the drag. He was nearing 70 years old and had lived through the pioneering days of modern biological research. The University of Texas had the privilege of having Dr. Green as a part of their faculty for going on 40 years, now dangling on the edge of retirement. The prominence and prestige that the university's biology department now received was in no small part due to his reputation and connections. David knew that his success in his current position was directly related to Dr. Green's opinion of him. David was hand picked for the job by this imposing figure, and thus far, Dr. Green was confident in that opinion.

The meeting with Jim Meyers went better than David expected, no doubt because he had persuaded Dr. Green to accompany him. David thought to himself, *the beast is mine*, and continued walking through campus with a confident stride.

The walk was a pleasant one. The winter chill was still lingering in the air, if you could call it a chill. The temperature had started that morning at around 45 degrees, and with the sun now reaching its zenith, it had climbed to just above 60. Most of the trees were barren, except the live oaks; the paths were still lined with crushed leaves and the remnants of a bountiful pecan and acorn season. As they reached the main student plaza, their eyes quickly examined each of the student organizations and protests that were assembled. The two professors walked through unaffected, desensitized to the flow of information and passion that played out before them.

"I thought the meeting went rather well. I'm surprised that Dr. Meyers gave me pretty much everything that I asked for." David paused. "I feel I have you to thank for that."

"Well, I don't know about that. Jim's a decent fellow," Dr. Green said. "Anyhow, I don't think he feels there is anywhere left to go with that computer. It's the reason he had it moved over to the natural sciences lab last year. I got the feeling that he was very intrigued about your idea, and wants to be a part of it. That's the only reason I can think of why he is letting you take control of the maintenance and programming team that's down there now, at least for the time being. That will save you a tremendous amount of preparation time."

David was amazed that Dr. Green had taken an interest in this project and quickly had summed up conclusions on the progress. He smiled and immediately thought of a hundred things that needed to be started tomorrow.

"It seems that this project really rounds out the projections and goals that the research council has talked about for the last year or so," started Dr. Green. "You have definitely come through for the department. I appreciate the organization that you have built, and I hope we can count on these projects getting us back to the forefront of the research game."

David smiled at the words coming out of Dr. Green's mouth. *He's thanking me*? David thought to himself. As they neared the restaurant, a man dressed in dirty clothes began to walk towards them with his hand outstretched. With a dazed look on his face, he continued his mumbled street mantra, " . . . Have any change? I . . ." David quickly reached for the door, which opened between them and the pitiful man, and swept Dr.

Green into the shop.

After they had ordered, David excused himself as Dr. Green found a table. He found a payphone and called Ramana's voice mail. "Ramana, this is David; we've got it! The meeting went great and we are okay to take over the beast on Monday. Get together at least five assistants for a preliminary meeting on Saturday, probably around eleven in the morning. Sorry for the short notice, but I know you can do it. I will be back in the office around one-thirty and we can discuss things further. See you then. Bye."

The next hour, David and Dr. Green discussed every experiment and research project currently housed in the research building. Even though David thoroughly enjoyed the conversation and the company, his mind was in a different place, and his pulse raced every time he thought of his new project.

Ramana got the message between classes and immediately had feelings ranging from panic to exhilaration. *He really expects me to get everything ready, all of the lab assistants, everything in a day*, Ramana thought to himself. His mind raced over the work he had done so far. *Was it a sufficient start for the project? How am I going to present it to everyone? Am I even on the right track?* He looked down at his watch and saw that he had one hour before his class. *I'll just skip lunch, I must get to work*, Ramana thought as he hung up the phone and headed toward his office.

As he entered the drab community office room, Ramana saw that most of his fellow grads were gone, probably at lunch. His eyes gazed upon the mess that he called his desk and it immediately brought a pain to his stomach. As he began to straighten things, his mind was racing over computer programs, papers that needed to be graded, and lesson plans. He began to pile stacks of papers upon each other in hopes of being able to later decipher the information strata that even a geologist would find intriguing. When he cleared a large space in front of his computer, Ramana sat down and said, "Allah, please help me get things organized in my mind. Help me to plan this project." He placed his hands upon the desk and closed his eyes, trying to relax. After about two minutes of silence, he opened his eyes, took a deep breath and grabbed a pad of paper.

In thirty minutes, Ramana mapped out his strategic plan for the next four days. His mind seemed to clear of all unnecessary information, and ideas and people came flowing to his mind. He thought of two graduate assistants who could very well be interested in this project, though he probably only needed one. He left them messages to talk to them later that afternoon to discuss the possibilities. He thought of Allison and a few other students who were lightly involved in other projects, and the possibilities of developing them into a team. He created an organizational structure with David and him at the top, and different departments with specific responsibilities all working together to process and develop the incredible amount of information needed. He began to think about the computer, the beast. Ramana smiled as he thought about the size and scope of the project they were about to embark on. He confidently leaned back in his chair and noticed a few grads were returning from lunch. His eyes looked down at his watch, and with an audible gasp he jumped up from his chair. His class had begun two minutes ago.

Allison was seated in the front row as usual and looked over the chalkboard from the earlier class. She could tell they were going to begin the section on genetics. As the clock ticked to five minutes past the hour, people started to mumble and look around to see if anyone was going to walk out. Allison took out her research paper and began to read it one more time. Most of the class was present today, and many people were doing the same thing. Allison's paper wasn't long. It was about three pages and neatly printed from Rachel's computer. She felt that it would get a good grade; she had used sound reasoning and, of course, the correct essay form that she had mastered during her freshman and sophomore year in English composition. There would be no attempt at extra credit though. In fact, Allison had chosen the position of defending the endosymbiotic theory. As she began to roll thoughts over in her head, Ramana appeared through the open door out of breath and made his way over to his desk.

When he had caught his breath enough to speak, he said, "Let me first apologize for my tardiness. It is a somewhat monumental day in my life and I got caught up in it. Secondly, I hope everyone has finished the research paper. Please leave them on my desk after class as you leave. Thirdly, I would like to introduce you to the second section in our text today on information and heredity." Ramana paused and looked to the chalkboard. He had taught the same lesson earlier and had left most of the information on it. To be very honest, the lesson was not the most organized or understandable among the few that Ramana had taught, but he got through it and could now turn his mind to other things.

As the students filed out and left their research papers on his desk, Ramana waited for Allison to drop hers and said, "Allison, could you stay after class for a minute or two? I need to talk to you."

Allison smiled and nodded her head. She thought to herself that Mr. Punjabi was still looked a little shaken from whatever happened to him. She took her seat in the front row as all of the students dropped off their papers and headed out of the classroom. As she watched the papers pile up on his desk, Allison thought about all the work that Mr. Punjabi, or any professor, had to accomplish to get through this job. The last of the students left the classroom and Ramana walked toward Allison's desk.

"Thank you for staying . . . I . . . uh . . . well, do you have any plans on Saturday morning?" Ramana managed to ask.

Allison shrugged her brow and said, "Um no, I don't think so, why?"

Ramana continued, "Let me see, how do I say this? I guess it's okay. We just got the go-ahead to start our project on Monday, a little ahead of what we planned, and we need to begin organizing the personnel structure tomorrow at around noon. It's very short notice–believe me I know–and I'm trying to get together about five lab assistants and others to meet tomorrow who I can count on for the rest of the semester."

Allison nodded her head slowly as she tried to understand what her teacher was proposing.

Ramana kept talking. "Now, we will be needing different types of assistance. We want researchers to gather data, computer programmers and operators, and well, you know, gophers and such. I will need some people to step up and provide some leadership and take a significant role in the project. I am projecting that the project would require about four to six hours per week from each of the part-time assistants and possibly more from the leaders. I can't promise that it will be exciting work, that is, until we are ready to unleash the final product. And the final product, well, let me . . . well, what do you think so far?"

Allison paused and said, "Well, Mr. Punjabi . . ."

Ramana interrupted her, "I'll tell you what, please call me Ramana."

Allison smiled. "Okay, Ramana. I'm pretty sure I can make the meeting tomorrow, and I would love to help out on the project. I mean I guess I would. I don't really know what you guys are trying to do. Um, I'm not really what you would consider a computer programmer, but I'm a pretty good researcher. And if my schedule and everything works out, I could take on some responsibility."

"Wonderful," said Ramana, "I was hoping you would be interested; in fact, I was counting on it. We can figure everything else out tomorrow."

"Can you tell me about the project yet, or is it secret until tomorrow?" Allison asked.

Ramana paused and said, "You know, I'm not sure where to start. I've kept it secret for so long, I've really never told anybody about it. To tell you the truth, you are really the first person that I am going to tell." Ramana looked up in the air and grabbed his chin in a classic thinking position. He began his explanation, "Let's see . . . although this will be a biological experiment, we will not be using organic material. We will be attempting to create the basis for computer generated life."

As Ramana continued to tell his story, Allison's enthusiasm was piqued with the combination of the fascinating project and the idea of being one of the first to be told. Ramana could read it from her reaction and knew that she would be an integral part of the team. When he finished, they said their good-byes and confirmed the times and duties for the next day.

Chapter 7

Ramana woke up early and walked out into the frosty yet humid Texas morning. He didn't sleep much during the night; the fact was, he hadn't been sleeping very well for at least a week since the project began. He could not turn his mind off and stop thinking about the endless tasks that lie before him. As Ramana walked out of his apartment, something about this quiet, dark morning allowed his perception to extend beyond just the present moment. He stood on his small concrete porch feeling the cold wind on his exposed hands and feet as his mind floated over his work of the past days. With so much work to be done and so many people to supervise, Ramana's own thought processes had become scattered and reactionary. He could see it so plainly in the solitude of this winter morning.

I have to relax, he thought, *find some peace and quiet*. Fortunately, this day had every indication of being a perfectly peaceful day. It was Sunday after all, and Ramana truly had nothing to accomplish. Right then and there he decided that today would be his day to allow his mind to regain its clarity.

Despite Ramana's anxiety, the progress of the project was beyond what anyone had expected over its inaugural two weeks. They were ready to begin experimenting with some simple compounds and amino acids early the next week. The programming team that Ramana and David had inherited was top notch. Even with Ramana's knowledge of computers, he was amazed at the complexity that had gone into the environmental program and the realism with which the theater-like monitors displayed the results.

The team had created everything in a brand new computer language using a trinary format that worked perfectly with the three-dimensional structure of the silicon gel memory core of the beast. As he walked down the almost empty drag, he tried to get his mind off the project and onto the God that had been neglected for too long.

Ramana walked into the *Quackenbush*, an Austin coffeehouse and bakery always inhabited with locals. He got his coffee, a muffin, and a newspaper and sat at the open window facing the university and the majestic UT Tower. Opening the paper, his attention was immediately grabbed by an article that chronicled the long conflict between India and Pakistan. The conflict that took on an even greater significance since the terrible events that brought another war to neighboring Afghanistan. Even in this now targeted country of America, he felt more secure than if he were at home.

His thoughts traveled farther back in time to his family and his country. Ramana thought about the people who made up his ancestry–an ancestry of more than a hundred generations that made up the substance of who he was today. They were a people that, in some ways, still lived tribally despite the West's technological and cultural advances. He'd abandoned his home land, leaving his family to walk the ancient ground of India never to experience what the rest of the world was like. He wondered if this more primitive existence left something to be desired. Civilization had started in these fertile lands of his ancestors. Was the New World of the West truly new? Did this new enlightenment really offer anything new under the sun? Had he left his homeland to discover this new knowledge and bring it back to his ancient roots? Or, was he to be a citizen of the New World now for the rest of his life? Strangely enough, these thoughts served to relax Ramana as they took his mind far away from his work . . . at least for a short time.

Ramana sat motionless in the plastic patio chair that engulfed his body. His mind began to flutter into the vastness of communal human existence. The lack of sleep, the fast food, and the excess of coffee were taking its toll. His eyes slowly lost their focus as he stared out of the window, and the thoughts in his head began to scatter and dissolve. The vision in his eyes soon turned to darkness and his eyelids closed. Ramana had started to dream with all of the force of a regular dream, yet he was not asleep. Thoughts had no apparent beginning or end as they swirled around in his mind. His stomach cramped and his body sweat as the vortex of thoughts transported him to another place.

He was taken to a realm that was dark, cold, and void of anything he could see. The air was heavy and moist and smelled of rust and dirt. Ramana waited and rested in the thick darkness as his mind became still and clear. He noticed that he felt no clothes on his body. He seemed to float naked in the blackness; his eyes were unaware of anything that was around him A familiar sound could be heard in the distance, and as soon as he thought about it, he began to feel himself move toward the sound. The cold wind made his body shiver with anticipation and fear. As the sound became louder, a faint pulsating light emerged from the distance. The light allowed him to see more of the environment around him. The darkness was replaced by a thick, dense fog that felt heavy against his skin. He moved through the mist without the use of his feet, the untouched fog swirling around him. The sound became more familiar as he approached, and his mind strained to identify it. *The beast*, his mind whispered as the fog parted around him and left him face to face with the large computer. The beast was different though; it seemed chrome and translucent. Ramana could see everything that was happening within the computer

Both Ramana and the beast stared at each other, trying to discover why they were there. Ramana made the first move. As he lifted his hand, the beast came to life with lights and sounds.

Ramana's eyes gazed down upon the window of the large memory storage area. He could see within the silvery gel core. The sweep of the flat red lasers through the core seemed erratic and confused. He lifted his hand and began to move it slowly back and forth in front of the window. The computer responded by mirroring his movement, and the two started to move in a smooth balanced rhythm. At that moment, he realized he controlled the beast with his thoughts, his words, and his hand motions. The computer seemed eager to please its new master and ready to do anything.

Ramana straightened up, moved back from the beast, and hovered over the computer. He circled the computer with his new knowledge and wondered what he would do with it. He thought of the project, the work with the elemental compounds of life. As he began to contemplate these ideas, the substance within the computer's memory core moved and slightly bubbled. Ramana noticed the movement and moved closer to identify what the cause was. It began as a small ripple, and as Ramana's thoughts became more complex, the immovable gel within the beast transformed before his eyes. Ramana could see the thick silicon gel slowly changing into a soup of elements and compounds. The liquid core started to swirl around in its secure compartment as his eyes grew large in wonder. Ramana thrust his hand forward and a bolt of electricity ran through the storage compartment. The primordial audience of elements came to attention.

Ramana spoke and the electrical bolt lined up an assortment of amino acids. As his mind developed recipes for simple proteins, Ramana wove these primary building blocks into chains of intricate design. He stared into the window of the beast as it turned into a factory of organic material swirling around in anticipation of its master's work. Ramana continued to fire bolts of electricity with a thrust of his hands, and the proteins wound up in long chains of beautifully complex structures. Membranes and organelle structures began to bubble together in the fringes of the active mix of chemicals. These structures flowed around in the chaotic waves of activity and found themselves captured in differing combinations within the bubbling membranes. Ramana's eyes widened as he recognized the organized structures that were created, and he placed them within various membrane bubbles. They resembled varying life forms that he had studied for years.

Ramana took a deep breath and with both hands sent a huge clap of electrical energy through the core. Before his eyes, the cells leapt into a fully independent existence. At the same moment, the surge of energy blew the metal top off of the memory core of the computer, and the mix of primitive life came overflowing like a waterfall into this virgin dreamland.

Ramana gasped and struggled to keep up with this amazing performance. The complexity of the creatures continued to grow as his knowledge skyrocketed. He began to see how to form multi-cellular organisms giving rise to a simple form of algae. Algae quickly grew and formed on the edges of the pool that rose around the beast. He saw how to give these cellular structures a working metabolic system and a cooperative existence that, in effect, gave them life. The various single cells were again woven into microscopic bug and shrimp-like creatures, then right into small eels and fish. A firmness began to grow out of the overflowing water under Ramana and raised up under his feet as he slowly came down from his lofty, floating position, though still naked as the realm he inhabited. He found himself standing on what felt like cool sand, and the once foggy darkness began to clear with the appearance of a warm light radiating from an unseen source. As he continued, Ramana noticed out of the water and onto the dry land crawled newly formed snakes, frogs, and lizards over his bare feet.

Ramana's emotions were as extreme as the creative process that he was directing. Ideas and elemental difficulties were almost instantaneously replaced by insight and implementation. The corresponding emotions of frustration and exhilaration were climbing as the complexity of this symphony of life continued to grow. A warm wind brought the smells of the plants that grew on the ever-increasing land surface to his nostrils, and his senses were alive as they had ever been. The beast glowed and pulsated with the same fervor as its master. A symmetry of thought and actions now existed between master and servant; the two were becoming one.

Ramana now approached this process with an enhanced awareness. He realized that the newest creatures had a mental capacity that contained thoughts approaching consciousness. The organization of this complex mental capacity allowed for the insertion of ideas and patterns. Instincts, emotions, and intuition were mixing with the chemical reactions and genetic information. A parade of ancient species began to invade the realm that the two had created. Creatures were growing bigger and more diverse as the dream labored on. Ramana saw how the basis of communication was formed as land and sea mammals came forth. With a tremendous effort and strain, Ramana and the beast formed the wolf, the dolphin, and lastly, a walking pygmy ape that resembled pictures he had seen of australopithecines. At this triumph, he stopped and tried to take in what he had done. Ramana stood among all of these creatures, breathing heavily, in what had transformed into a lush tropical forest. The beast knew that this was the finish and slowed to a normal pace of activity. The computer's lights and noises quieted to allow the beauty of their work to dominate the realm.

Ramana's emotions were not quieted because he realized what lay ahead of him. He would need every ounce of strength and power he had to take this last step. His mind raced as he tried to grasp what that final element was to endow to his creation humanity. As he searched in his thoughts for this last piece of the primal puzzle, he sat on a boulder that had appeared and gazed into the pool of water that lay beneath him. The water was dark and had calmed to appearance of mirrored glass. In the black water, he saw himself. He stared and pondered for what seemed an eternity, trying to unlock within his very being what made him what he was. The questions seemed to be without answer, and his mind swirled with abstract thoughts of consciousness and existence. Ramana became distraught and angry at the seemingly impossible question. His emotions took him to the point of tears, and a single tear left his eye and headed for the still water beneath him.

The water exploded with sound as it was pierced. The waves spread out from this point and shot light and color in all directions. "That's the answer," Ramana said to himself. He stood up as the light and prismatic colors flashed around him. He walked toward the beast where it sat in the middle of the tropical forest, humming and clicking. Ramana stopped himself and gazed upon the creatures throughout this shadowy realm. He smiled through the tears that came down his face as he now understood the balance between their creations and the millions of cells and compounds of which they consisted.

His attention went back to the beast, and he slowly walked towards it. The computer seemed to recognize what was happening and began to increase its activity as Ramana approached. His hands were outstretched and made their way to the outside of the computer. He felt the warm metal and slid his hands around as he closed his eyes, taking in the moment. Ramana opened his eyes, moved his hands down to the side panel, and tried to find a place to get a good grip. Once his fingers found their way into some narrow ventilation slots, he braced himself and jerked back using all the weight of his body. The whole side panel was dislodged from its frame and flew off to the side as Ramana fell back into the soft dirt.

The beast was opened to the new world that the two had created. It seemed to sense this and worked even harder to decrease its vulnerability. Ramana got to his knees and gazed into the beast. He saw that the wires and components shined like fiber optic cables as the electrons raced through them. The many processors and transistors pulsated and moved like they were breathing and pumping electrons to the different components.

The two felt each others' presence, feeling the mutual basic elements they shared, the raw silicon and refined metal. Ramana crawled near the machine to look closer inside, moving as though he was frightened he might upset the beast. The main central processing unit sat in plain sight surrounded by four metal posts that locked it into the power grid. Ramana knew what he had to do and moved with determination. He slowly moved close enough to reach inside and confirm the polarity of each of the posts around the CPU. As his body entered the pulsating cavity of the unit, the rhythmic vibrations of the processing unit shook the muscles of his body. Ramana took a deep breath, spit into his hands, and rubbed them together. Deliberately, he extended his shaky hands into the beast and grabbed one negative post and one positive post.

Ramana and the beast screamed in harmony as white sparks flew in all directions through the once quiet environment. The sparsely populated coffee shop was startled as Ramana awoke in the middle of this mad scream. The waitress closest to him dropped her tray in surprise; cups and plates crashing to the floor accompanied the echoing scream. Everyone in the shop, and even a few people on the street, turned to look to see what was causing this blood-curdling scream. As the customers realized what had happened, most laughed when they realized that it was just this poor Eastern Indian who had fallen asleep over his coffee and muffin. The angered waitress bent down to the floor to begin the clean up, muttering obscenities under her breath. Ramana took a few seconds to take in what had happened and to regain some composure. His limbs shook and felt hollow as though electricity had just run through them. His stomach was empty and sore. He felt the tracks of tears on his face. Ramana closed his eyes as he felt a wave of relief waiting beyond some neurological gate. As the seconds ticked away, the pain and nerves slowly eased and Ramana regained some of his balance.

"Whew, what was that?" he said to himself as he opened his eyes. His thoughts went to the dream he just had. This was unlike any dream he had ever experienced; it was so real it had taken him to a point of fear unknown to him. He quickly attributed the dream to the fact that he had deprived himself of so much sleep over the last two weeks. Ramana looked down at his muffin and took a bite of it while automatically grabbing for his coffee. As he lifted the coffee to his lips, his stomach wrenched with an almost accusatory reflex. He slowly pushed his chair back and tried to stand and immediately fell to his knees. Helped to his feet by strangers, Ramana could only make out mumbling voices and fuzzy faces.

    Ramana stumbled through the coffee shop, keenly aware of the stares from the people who had seen his outburst. As he walked home, his mind relived what he could remember about the dream. His thoughts were swirling around in his head, and thoughts about the project and biological concepts were mixing with his dream and ideas about Allah and his religion. Avenues of thoughts were speeding along in one direction until they ran into a wall of some steadfast principle, which stopped it in its tracks. Then his mind would take off in another direction, looking for its supporting facts. Ramana sweated as he tried to keep up with the race in his mind. When he finally made it home, he stripped off his jacket and pants and lay down on his couch, still trembling. The last thought that popped into his head before he fell into a deep sleep was, *I understand, now, how to proceed.*

Chapter 8

Allison awoke quickly and immediately sat up in bed. Her covers were pushed off her and lying on the floor along with her pillows. She looked around in an attempt to get her bearings; Rachel was gone and the room was empty and silent. When she looked at her alarm clock that read 11:23 a.m., she gasped with the realization that she had slept through her morning class. Trying to figure out whether to jump up or lay back down, Allison began to roll over in her mind a dream that she had. It was difficult to remember exactly what happened, but she knew it took place at one of her father's revival meetings years ago. She closed her eyes, and in her mind she could see their large white tent rippling in the dusty Oklahoma wind. Small crowds of people stood in different areas of the tent, listening to her father preach. A few of the crowd were in wheelchairs with family members attending to them and pushing them close to see the young, dark headed preacher.

Allison swung her legs over the edge of the bed and began to recall the constantly changing life that she lived as a small child. She remembered her job to greet and comfort the people who showed up that needed extra help. She was never officially given this job by her parents; it was a game that she had made up to make the time pass quicker. She would sneak communion crackers and juice to those who looked like they needed it and pass out the fans that seemed to wave in beat with her father's sermon. She would stand behind certain people, usually those in wheelchairs or noticeably crippled, and say prayers for their healing, trying not to be noticed. Allison's stare began to rise from the floor as the dream began to come back to her. Though her eyes were open, they were focused hazily on the opposite wall and she could imagine clearly the scene that played out before her.

She could see herself as a little girl standing with her head bowed behind a small group of people that surrounded an old man in a high-backed wooden wheelchair near the back of the tent. She heard the poem that she had made up as a prayer and her lips began to move along in synch with it.

" . . . *Truly, truly be with me as I try to be like thee. Take this sickness far way, make your children well today . . .*"

As the poem continued, she could see the wheelchair begin to jostle as its occupant shifted his position. She could see a head with tufts of white hair slowly attempt to turn and move to the side of the wooden back of the chair. This got the attention of the younger man whose hands were placed on the handles and he looked back at the young girl who continued to pray with her head bowed down. With a grunt and move of the head, the young man began to slowly turn the wheelchair to the side to reveal the old man to Allison. His face seemed to have a look of pain carved into it; his sunken eyes straining to see what was behind him. Quietly, the small group that attended this old man were turned around and staring at the little girl who was finishing her prayer. The group's stare shifted to the old man wondering what they should do.

Slowly, the little girl's head rose to see the stares of the small group and her eyes began to grow in size with fear. With a shaky move, the old man's hand slowly raised to try to calm the frightened girl. His shoulders shrugged and his head lowered as the look of pain on his face was turned into a tearful smile. The small crowd around him sighed in relief as they looked at each other with approving faces. The old man reached out his trembling hand towards Allison who was still frozen from the surprise of the situation. She reluctantly walked toward the old man and took two of his long, wrinkled fingers in her tiny soft hand. She could see him mouthing some words, but she could not understand what he was saying. When he finished, he let go of Allison's hand and nodded his head. Immediately, the little girl began to run away towards the opposite side of the tent to hide. Sitting on her bead, Allison smiled as the memory of the event ended. Slowly, she stood up and began to get ready for the day as she tried to determine what the dream meant.

Ramana hit the research lab early Monday morning still reeling from the vision he experienced the day before. Thoughts were racing through his mind, but they flowed with an organization and purpose that drew him out of his bed and into the lab at this early hour. Ramana had at least three hours of privacy before the first assistants were expected, and he knew that some changes were necessary for today's experiment to work. As he walked into the computer lab, Ramana flipped on the wall switch, replacing the dim green glow of the room with a bright fluorescence that made him shade his eyes.

He lowered his hand and gazed at the familiar shape of the beast's outer skeleton. The computer was unlike any conventional design, resembling a turbine generator at an electric plant more than anything. Spherical housings of the intricate mechanical workings gave the beast a futuristic appearance and diffused the soft grinding and clicking sounds through the large basement space. The main structure of the beast stood in the middle of the room. It was made mostly of a gray metal, though the cubic memory core glowed red through Pyrex windows on three of its sides. Inside was a silicon gel that had a translucent appearance. Dozens of flat, red lasers visibly swept through the gel from the beast's unseen machinery as it read and managed the information that was held in its three-dimensional mass. The lasers moved in an unending rhythm, horizontally and vertically as they constantly updated and checked the integrity of the informational structure within.

Ramana started over to the input station on the immediate left as he walked in the large room. He stared at the large monitor screen that was mounted above the various input devices. The background color on the screen was a blueish-green, the color that the team had picked for the environmental program, or the E.P. as they began to call it. It was the only program in the main partition of the memory core, a virtual environment for the virtual organisms that they would eventually place in it. The E.P. also acted as the operating system for that section of the computer. It was better constructed than Ramana could have ever imagined. Hundreds of theoretically natural variables could be relayed by the E.P. to any compound or organism that they created and placed within its strange new environment. It would be manipulated to offer an extremely nourishing environment that would be able to nurse or rebuild any ailing organism within its perimeters. Conversely, it could be set at a challenging and harsh environment to test an organism's ability to survive. A small section of the memory core housed the work area, partitioned off from the E.P. This is where the programmers would create the compounds and organisms, and through a specially secured tunnel, send them into the E.P.

Ramana sat down at the keyboard and accessed the work area. He quickly got to work on the membrane programs with which they would be experimenting. The membrane programs were the easiest to create so far. The makeup of the membrane was hundreds of amino sugar programs that replicated a layer of peptodoglycan and formed into a simple spherical ball. The team was successful in knitting it together and keeping it together in the work area, but no one knew what would happen when it was exposed to the "elements" in the E.P.

The project for this week was to successfully release a membrane and create an isolated environment within itself to house the contents of the eventual test cell. These membrane programs would be the primary contact between the E.P. and any organism that lived within. Once the membrane reacted with their environment, they created data for the researchers to analyze. The eventual DNA within the nucleus of the cell would rely on this data to make its own decisions. Ramana worked and reviewed his changes until the maintenance team showed up and his first class of the day was about to start.

At around 2:20 PM, Allison saw Ramana on the way back to the research lab.

"Hey, Ramana, wait up," Allison called out.

"Oh, hi Allison." Ramana turned and let Allison catch up to him.

"Today's the big day, isn't it? You're going to release a membrane into the E.P., aren't you?" Allison asked.

Ramana smiled, "Yes we are. You're coming, aren't you? This will be a big milestone for us."

"Sure I'm coming," Allison responded, "I wouldn't miss it. What do you think are the chances?"

"I'm actually pretty confident we should be able to get some satisfactory results." Ramana paused. "How have you liked working on the project so far?"

"Oh, I love it. It's really quite interesting," Allison answered. "Everyone seems to be working together pretty well, and I think it is even helping me in your class."

Ramana nodded his head and looked at Allison. "Speaking of that, I've finished grading the research papers, and I must say, I was a little disappointed when I read yours."

Allison's eyes widened. "Really? Oh no . . . What was wrong with it?"

"Well you did get a decent grade. It was a well written paper, at least as a grammatical composition." Ramana continued, "That was not the point of the assignment though. I was under the impression that you were going to write a paper that tried to disprove the theory and attempt to propose another one."

Allison smiled and looked down as she spoke. "Yeah, I guess you're right. Well, I did think about it, but I guess I didn't want to . . . I don't know . . . look like a whacko or something."

"Do you believe in the endosymbiotic theory?" asked Ramana.

"Not really," answered Allison.

Ramana shook his head. "Then why would you write a paper defending it?"

Allison was getting uncomfortable with this line of questioning. "I guess it was easier to defend it than defend what I believe."

Ramana heard the crack in Allison's voice and realized that this was a sensitive issue for her. He stopped walking right outside of the research building and tried to say the next sentence gently. "Let me give you some advice, and I say this because I respect you very much. The last thing that science needs, any science, is more people who don't want to cause a stir, or who find it easier to defend someone else's beliefs rather than their own. Science is bigger than that; it can handle it. Scientists don't have to agree. Most scientists can handle that, although, I must admit, some can't. I guess my point is that you are much more valuable to science and to me when you think for yourself and stand on your own two feet."

Allison had a feeling in her stomach like she had just been scolded by her father. She didn't know what to say. She was speechless; she didn't even know if she fully took in what Ramana had said. In the uncomfortable silence, she thought she had to say something, so she opened her mouth. "You really know how to charm a girl, don't you?"

Ramana's mouth opened in confusion. It was the last thing that he expected out of her mouth.

She smiled in response to her set up, then turned serious. "I guess I know what you mean, but sometimes, you know, you don't want to draw attention to yourself. Sometimes it's a question of choosing your battles."

Ramana blinked and swallowed at her response; he quickly wondered if he would be having this discussion with any of his other students. Was it fair to be pushing this student differently? Was it fair that his emotions for her could be affecting the way he treated her?

Ramana spoke. "Allison, I'm sorry. I guess I have a lot of expectations for you. Like I said, your paper was great. I just don't want to be responsible for creating unscientific scientists. There are enough out there already." He lifted his finger to try to change the subject. "I'll tell you what; we'll discuss this later. We have a membrane to bring into the world, and we're gonna need everyone's help, including yours."

Allison smiled and nodded her head as they turned and started to walk into the lab. As the large gray metal doors swung open and they entered, Allison asked, "By the way Ramana, how many students in our class attempted to propose another theory for extra credit?"

Ramana hesitated and squinted up in the air. Performing an imaginary count, he said, "Ah, let's see, well all total . . . none." He continued looking up in the air.

Allison stopped in her tracks as her temper began to rise with the revelation. Ramana noticed her stop and did the same.

"What?" he asked.

"Let me get this straight," she gasped. "You're giving me grief when nobody else did it either?"

Ramana felt her anger and began to walk out of her immediate area. She quickly raised her hand and clenched it in a fist. She thrust her hand and hit Ramana playfully on his shoulder as she began whispering and mumbling her version of alternate expletives. Ramana was knocked out of stride and tried to regain his balance as he couldn't help but laugh. Ramana picked up his pace trying to avoid the next round of assault from Allison. He stayed one step ahead of her as Allison eventually began to laugh with Ramana all of the way to the computer room.

In the computer room, David stood near the entrance door while talking to one of the programmers. Two other programmers were in the room along with two other student assistants.

The room was mostly quiet except for the sounds of the beast when Ramana burst through the door. Allison leapt in behind him, smiling and giggling as she entered. Every head turned at the noise, and the two quickly tried to change their playfulness into seriousness. David lifted his brow as he looked at Ramana, who had a nervous grin on his face.

"I see you are both very eager for the release of the membrane," said David.

"Ah, yes," Ramana responded in an exaggerated seriousness. "I made some changes early this morning. I think we are ready to make it happen." Ramana looked at his head programmer. "Did you notice anything different Mark?"

Mark Stephenson had years of experience in electrical engineering and computer sciences, and was primarily responsible for the quick and thorough work performed over the last two weeks. He looked up from his terminal and said, "Yeah, I was wondering what had happened. The whole membrane structure looks considerably more stable. What did you do?"

"I'll tell you about it later; it came to me in a dream." Ramana walked to his terminal and said, "David, Mark and I have put together a routine that will make it a little easier on the membrane. It will make the E.P. conditions similar to the work area and slowly dial it up to whatever environment we choose. For this experiment, we have chosen a lukewarm aqueous environment."

David nodded his head and said, "Good, we should be able to detect any problems, hopefully before they manifest themselves or damage the membrane."

Ramana headed for his terminal and began to set up the E.P. and the dial-up routine. As he did this, Mark began duplicating the original membrane structure to be used in the experiment. After another fifteen minutes of testing, Ramana stood up and said, "Okay everyone, please go to your stations and get ready to monitor the experiment. Release of the membrane will commence in five minutes."

Allison had no monitoring responsibilities, so she positioned herself in a chair with a good view of the video screen. As the countdown was ending and everyone got in their place, Allison looked over at Ramana. As he looked up to the screen, she caught his eye and he paused to look at her. Allison winked at him and mouthed the words, "Good luck." Ramana took a deep breath and fixed his eyes onto the screen.

"Okay, here we go, releasing the membrane." Ramana pressed a button, and suddenly the round membrane appeared on the right side of the video screen. The membrane was a tiny sphere on the large video monitor and had a grayish tint. It was somewhat translucent, but was clearly visible on the blue-gray screen. "Okay Mark, let's isolate on the general area and magnify it." He paused until he saw the membrane enlarged. "Initiating dial-up routine." Ramana pressed another button, which began the process of slowly creating a viable environment within the memory of the computer.

About twenty seconds into the routine, the spherical structure of the membrane started to compromise. It began to slowly move, and Mark had to scroll the viewable area to keep it in the middle of the screen. It appeared misshapen and discolored as it reacted with the compounds and variables that the E.P. created.

"What do you have, Mark? Anything?" barked Ramana. All sorts of data were being produced by this reaction, and Mark attempted to review and analyze it in real time.

"It seems to be holding together, no problem signs yet," responded Mark.

Ramana looked at his small terminal screen and said, "We are at 50 percent of E.P. settings and everything looks good. Proceeding to 100 percent."

Allison felt like she was at NASA watching a space shuttle launch.

The E.P. continued its climb toward reality. At about 75 percent of normal settings, the membrane began to shudder until it folded into half a sphere. As the structure collapsed, an alarm began to sound followed by sighs and mumblings from the crowd. Ramana looked at Mark and said, "Crap, what's the problem? I'm going to start to scale the E.P. back. Do we have a tear in the membrane?"

Mark responded, "The membrane seems to still be holding; I don't see a tear. Uh, it possibly has collapsed from the pressure it is experiencing." Mark looked back at Ramana. "Is there some way we can increase the pressure inside the membrane, Ramana?"

"Possibly, let's see what happens as the pressure decreases," Ramana responded.

Just about when the E.P. was reduced to 50 percent, the membrane popped back into its original shape and lunged to the opposite direction. As soon as the structure was regained, the alarm stopped sounding. Mark was busy reading the data and didn't see it move off of the screen.

"Mark . . . Mark, we've lost it on the screen," noticed Ramana.

"Oh, I'm sorry," answered Mark as he began to look for it. "Uhm, did you see which way it?. .oh, there it is. It seems to have regained its shape."

Ramana stood up from his terminal and walked toward the screen. "Let's keep it at 50 percent and switch to 3-D mode. Allison, will you pass out the glasses?"

Allison sprang up and moved to the other side of the room. She picked up a box and began to distribute black-framed, polarized glasses. Once the computer screen was put into three-dimensional mode, it could only be seen properly with these filtered sunglasses. Ramana looked around and saw that everyone present had the glasses on, so he hit a key that brought the screen to life.

Allison had yet to look at the screen in 3-D mode, so she let out a whispered "Wow!" as the screen went from its normal appearance to a large square box that extended six feet into the room. Everyone moved toward the center of the room, as the effect was more pronounced from directly in front of the screen.

The box still had a blueish-green tint and the membrane was even more distinct than before. It had a shiny, metallic look as it hung in space.

Ramana walked closer to the edge of the imaginary environment and said, "As you can see, the membrane seems to have maintained integrity to somewhere just above 50 percent of a normal environment. I think we can be sure that once we insert the contents of the cell, it will hold up better under that pressure."

David looked at the screen with a smile, nodding his head. "Ramana, it's beautiful. Now let me get this straight. What we are seeing on this screen is basically what is happening in the memory core of the computer."

"Yes," replied Ramana. "You can faintly see the corresponding sweeps of the lasers on the screen. You must take into account that we have enlarged a small portion of the E.P., and also the partitioned work area of the computer will not be visible."

Ramana walked over to Mark's terminal and looked at the huge amount of information that was being produce by the membrane's reaction to its environment. He looked over to Mark, who had left his terminal to see the screen better, and said, "Okay Mark, let's begin printing this output to see what happened at the point of collapse and at the point it regained its shape. Hopefully we can learn something more before we try to fill this membrane with some cytoplasm and a nucleoid."

David turned from the screen and said, "Good work guys, Ramana. So when do you think we will be ready to test a full cell?"

"Well," said Ramana, "I am very optimistic based on these results. Of course, we will have to examine the data further, but we may be able to experiment with a bacterial cell by the end of next week."

Chapter 9

The majority of the contents within most cells are referred to as cytoplasm. Within the cytoplasm, the cell houses various machines, or organelles, whose main function is to create energy or synthesize proteins. In bacteria, the cytoplasm is made up of ribosomes, various enzymes, and catalysts that carry out these functions. The ribosomes are one type of cellular machine that take instructions from the "brains" of the cell, located in the nucleus.

Nucleic acids within the nucleus function as the operations and management of the cell. Deoxyribonucleic acid, DNA, and ribonucleic acid, RNA, are the famous compounds that make life possible. The DNA communicates instructions to the RNA, which then manages the creation of the compounds and proteins necessary to sustain the cell.

When Ramana and David first began discussing the process of duplicating nucleic acids two years ago, both were certain that creating the DNA would be the most difficult task. It is the massively complex code structure containing the genetic instructions for life. As the work began, they soon realized that duplicating the intricate cooperation between the DNA, the RNA, and the ribosomes to create proteins would be the most difficult task. The ribosomes that exist within the cytoplasmic soup, outside of the nucleus, had to get the information from the DNA, inside the nucleus, and act upon it. Once the information is received from the DNA, the RNA and the ribosomes in the cytoplasm are charged with the responsibility of creating the proteins necessary for a cell to carry out its specific function.

Hundreds of ribosomes are contained in the cytoplasm along with many different compounds. Within the nucleus of a cell, strands of DNA contain the script for the events that take place in the cell. The seemingly insurmountable task for the project team was to manually construct the cytoplasm to perform in an organized and efficient manner. One option for the team was to reduce the number of ribosomes and compounds within the cytoplasm in order to simplify the process. Neither David or Ramana wanted to choose this option, for it would have made the eventual test cells less than realistic. They had to uncover, in their research, a way to carry out this fundamental process that molecular biology has named the Central Dogma.

The Central Dogma of molecular biology concerns how proteins or polypeptides are created within a cell. A cell's purpose is carried out by the creation of specific proteins that perform a necessary function. The DNA transcribes, or writes a recipe, for the necessary protein and uses a messenger RNA to carry the information from the nucleus to the cytoplasm. Once the messenger RNA has delivered and begins to translate the recipe to the ribosome, or the protein machine, a transfer RNA helps the ribosome to find the necessary amino acids to create the particular protein.

The DNA, in effect, is a huge recipe for every protein needed for a cell to survive, reproduce, and carry out its function. DNA along with its accompanying RNA is an intelligent machine that can reproduce itself, or small parts of itself, and also determine which parts need to be reproduced.

To simplify this complex undertaking, David and Ramana decided the first organism they would attempt to bring into existence would be a simple bacterium of their own design; one with very little function and few needs. The bacteria would be cocci, which refers to its spherical shape. Despite the bacteria's simplicity, the DNA program would take up huge amounts of memory space. The work on the intricate relationship between all of these various chemical and compounds was almost complete when they had their successful membrane testing.

Ramana sat in his small living room of the university provided apartment, thinking about these relationships and the week that lay ahead of him. Saturday night, 9:00 p.m., and Ramana was alone on his couch with nothing to do. As he thought of that fact, his mind raced over fantasies of things he could be doing: Dining with a beautiful woman, hanging out at a local joint with friends, even dancing like he had seen the local cowboys in their big white shirts and tall hats. He lifted the soggy piece of delivery pizza to his mouth as a glob of tomato sauce fell and joined with the communal mosaic stains on the avocado colored couch. Just at that moment his TV, which still had knobs to change channels, played the familiar opening tune to the only show that Ramana really cared about. Thirty years after its time, Ramana had fallen under the dizzying spell of *Star Trek*. Not the new ones, though they were more rational and up-to-date. No, Ramana loved the grit and passion of the original.

The show was still way ahead of its time. Nations, races, and planets cooperated together in the Federation of Planets, the universe's version of the United Nations. Even the crew of the Enterprise was a thorough mix of all peoples, though Ramana rarely saw an Indian. To lead such a noble endeavor, the Federation chose their best man, Captain James T. Kirk. Kirk was a hero for the ages. He could hold his own with any of literature's best. Though he occasionally lost an Ensign or a Yeoman to the ravages of space, he fought and tangled his way out of certain death many times for himself, his ship, and his crew of 430. Not only could Kirk outwit most humans or aliens, if he couldn't, he would resort to a flying body slam that could knock as many as three alien evildoers unconscious in the blink of an eye. Kirk had devoted his life to the Federation and had remained a bachelor throughout his service, and his power to charm and conquer women seemed to be as limitless as the universe that he explored. The appeal of the show to Ramana had as much to do with this enigmatic character as with any of its creative story lines and innovations.

About half way through the show, a knock on the door startled Ramana. He sat in his clutter with an open cardboard box almost emptied of pizza, a plastic bottle of Pepsi, and various papers and articles of clothing scattered across the small room. As he rushed to gain some small semblance of order he yelled, "Who is it?"

His greatest fears were realized when he heard, "It's me, Allison."

He stopped in his tracks when he heard those words. A dozen thoughts zipped through his head, none of which made much sense. He managed to speak the words, "Give me one minute, please, Allison," as he wondered how one minute could really change the appearance of his apartment. His mind tried to prioritize which things needed to be removed to provide the least embarrassing environment.

Allison stood outside the door listening to Ramana scurrying around his apartment and wondered what she was doing there. She found herself laughing at the comedy that was playing out, and slowly began to walk back down the stairs from his door. She turned back around as she heard the door open.

"Allison, hello. What are you doing here?" Ramana stammered.

"I'm sorry," Allison started, "I don't mean to bother you. I really just came by to see you and, you know, talk."

Ramana looked puzzled. "Talk about what?"

Allison shrugged her shoulders. "I don't know: class, the project, life, whatever... I'm sorry... I should've called. You're probably busy... I should go."

As Allison turned and started to walk away, Ramana opened the door and said, "Wait, no... I mean, I'm glad to see you. You just took me by surprise. I am really embarrassed. My apartment is a mess, and I don't usually have company, but please come in."

Allison turned back around with a nervous smile on her face as she again wondered why she had come to his apartment. She walked into Ramana's apartment and tried not to be too judgmental. After all, Ramana was a male, and she had determined that most males could live in their own excrement. She noticed the large amount of texts scattered around his desk and computer. She gazed at the pictures on his desk as she walked by them and figured they must be his family. Ramana guided her to a chair next to the couch and walked over to the TV. As he began to reach for the knob, Allison said, "Oh cool, Star Trek."

Ramana stopped, turned his head back to her and asked, "You like Star Trek?"

Allison shrugged her shoulders. "Oh yeah, it's a great show. I don't watch it much anymore."

"That's interesting," said Ramana. "I really don't have much time to watch television, but I love Star Trek."

Ramana walked over to the couch and sat down. He immediately stood back up and said, "I'm sorry, may I get you something to drink or anything?"

Allison smiled. "Well, I don't know. Don't go to any trouble."

Ramana walked over to his kitchenette. "Let's see, I have Pepsi, water, apple juice . . . um, wine." Ramana peered over his shoulder as he mentioned the last item.

Allison thought about the choices and said, "Hmmmmm, how about a little wine?"

"Great," he said as he tried to find an appropriate way to serve it. "Now I don't have any wine glasses, so will these be okay?" Ramana held up two different sized glasses.

"That would be just fine," Allison responded. She turned her attention back to the TV, quickly identifying the episode.

Ramana grabbed a bottle of white wine out of his groaning refrigerator and poured the drinks. He set them down on his black laquer coffee table. "Okay, so what do you want to talk about?"

Allison took a sip of her wine. "I don't know. Nothing about school right now, that's for sure." She took a look back at the TV and said, "Maybe Star Trek's a good start."

"There you go," said Ramana as he sat down across from Allison. "Let me ask you, do you believe that there is life out in the universe?"

Allison laughed. "You mean like Klingons and Vulcans?"

Ramana smiled. "Yes, or any life, like what they found on that meteorite from Mars."

Allison stopped herself. "I'm not sure I'm ready to tell you what I believe about extraterrestrials. Tell me what you think."

Ramana paused as he thought about the question. "I would say with the enormous size and age of the universe and the unlimited possibilities of nature, the chances are very high that life exists on other planets. Now if we will ever discover this life, that is an entirely different question."

"What, you don't believe the thousands of people who have seen UFOs or have been abducted?" Allison asked with a faked sincerity in her voice.

Ramana was unsure how to answer. "Well it is very interesting, the psychology of abductions and UFO sightings. But, I really find it hard to believe that little aliens are flying hundreds of thousands of light years to probe some . . . hillbilly's body cavities. But, I may be wrong."

Allison laughed and took a sip of her wine.

Ramana began again. "Another thing, the chances that life forms from another galaxy would evolve to have the same basic body structure: two eyes, two arms, two legs, head on the shoulders." Ramana paused as he remembered who he was talking to. "Well, I guess that opens a whole new discussion. Let me ask you, do you believe that God created beings other than what has been on this Earth?"

"Well yes, of course," Allison answered with a smile. "God created the angels and all of the heavenly hosts. You know

. . . the cherubim, the seraphim . . ."

Ramana looked at her, trying to figure out if she was serious. "Ah yes . . . the cherubim and seraphim." He thought about them for a second, as his attention went to the TV. "Now let's see, are they a part of the Federation of Planets or not?"

Allison couldn't help but laugh. "I'm serious. I believe in angels. A lot of people do, even non-Christians. Don't you believe in angels?"

"Well yes," answered Ramana. "The Koran says that Allah sent the Angel Gabriel to Mohammed. So yes, I guess I believe in angels." Ramana paused and wondered about his answer.

"Then let me ask you another question," Allison said and waited for a nod from Ramana. "Do you believe in heaven?"

Ramana continued in his thoughts. He found himself in an area he was beginning to make him feel uncomfortable. "Heaven, huh? Well yes, the Koran speaks of heaven. I believe that heaven exists on some level."

"What does the Koran say about heaven?" asked Allison.

Ramana woke up from his deep thoughts and looked around the room, somewhat stunned at his company and the direction of the conversation. He looked at his glass of wine and grabbed it. "I'm not sure I can sit here and quote from the Koran or interpret what it says about heaven."

"Fair enough," replied Allison. "You know, I've never read any of the Koran. There aren't any things that stick out in your memory about it?"

"Well . . . let's see," Ramana started with a smile. "I seem to remember the Koran speaking of gardens and rivers of wine . . . and I guess there's the part about being served by numerous virgins . . ."

"WHAT?" screamed Allison. "You're kidding me!"

Ramana tried to keep his embarrassment to himself as he wondered why he said the last statement.

"What exactly is being served?" Allison asked, as it seemed that she had the floor in his wake of silence. "Wow! I know a bunch of guys that would convert to Islam today if they knew about that."

Ramana tried to understand how this girl had gotten the upper hand in this discussion of beliefs when obviously she had the stranger of the two. "Hold on Allison, I thought that you, especially you, would not make fun of things like that."

Allison stopped and said, "I'm sorry, I don't mean to joke about such things. I guess it took me by surprise. I've never heard of that before."

Ramana nodded his head in acceptance of the apology, and their attention went back to wine and Star Trek.

After a few minutes of silence watching a particular scene, Allison couldn't resist taking one more jab. "Whew, if this were Star Trek, you guys would definitely be the Klingons."

Ramana dropped his head in disgust, then stood up and grabbed their empty wine glasses and headed for the kitchenette. Allison leaned back in her chair and kept giggling. "I'm sorry, I'm just kidding."

Ramana refilled their glasses and returned to the couch. He had caught himself from getting too upset about her jokes by realizing how happy he was that she was sitting in his apartment on a Saturday night, and she was obviously having a good time.

After Star Trek was over, the TV offered nothing comparable, so Ramana turned it off and asked Allison if she would pick out some music to play on his portable stereo.

She hopped up from her chair and headed toward the small stack of CDs. "Cool, I'm good at this."

"Maybe it's time we talked about the project," Ramana said as he sat down. "You know, I think we're going to be ready to test a complete bacterium this week."

Allison picked a CD and started it on his portable stereo. "I figured that we were close. Have you been able to incorporate the Central Dogma? We've gathered enough information about it."

"I think so," replied Ramana. "We have set up a communication routine within each ribosome that allows the nucleic acids to keep aware of any protein synthesis and its progress."

"Do you think that is the way it's done in nature?" asked Allison.

Ramana thought about the question. "There are some questions that microbiology still has not answered. We have to fill in some of the gaps, until . . . there are no more gaps. I think it is a strong possibility that we are duplicating a large part of the Central Dogma correctly."

Allison looked up at the ceiling and repeated the words. "The Central Dogma . . . sounds Catholic. Who came up with the name for that? The Pope?"

"The pope of microbiology, Dr. Francis Crick," answered Ramana. "Well, let me clarify that. He along with many other scientists developed this theory. I'm not sure who named it."

"Will the bacteria be able to reproduce itself?" asked Allison.

"Yes, I sure hope so," replied Ramana. "It will be able to reproduce itself if everything works, but we must enable the reproductive system for it to do so."

"Do you have a name for the first bacteria?" she continued her inquiry.

Ramana laughed. "I guess *cocci experimentus* could be its name."

Allison shook her head. "No, that won't do. You have to give it a common name. You know, like that first sheep that they cloned . . . uh . . . Dolly."

"Well maybe you can help us with a name then."

"Let me ask you another question," Allison started. Ramana nodded his head in approval.

"Once the bacterium, or any other cell, is functioning in the environment program, who is in charge?" Allison stopped. She thought her question was going to be longer, but for some reason she stopped.

Ramana looked puzzled at her question. "What do you

mean?"

"Well," Allison thought out loud, "I guess you would say that once it is functioning, the cell is making decisions, right or wrong, for itself, right?"

"I would agree with that," Ramana replied.

Allison continued. "Then, who makes the decisions that are not up to the cell? Like, when you turn it off or how long it lives; that kind of thing?"

Ramana thought about her inquiry, wondering if it was a trick question. "David and I will be setting the general policy of what will happen to each cell for each experiment. I'm not sure what you're asking."

"I'm not sure what I'm asking either," said Allison. "Never mind. Hey listen, it's getting late, I probably should think about getting back to the house. I really appreciate you letting me come over and gab all night. I had a great time."

Ramana nodded and stood up with her. His mind was unsure how to proceed in this situation. "Thank you Allison, for thinking of me and coming over. It is always interesting."

Allison smiled as she moved toward the door and opened it. "Sorry about showing up without warning. I'll try to call next time."

Ramana smiled at the thought of a next time.

Allison walked out the door and down the three steps before she turned around. "Thanks for the wine, and the conversation. I'll see you tomorrow at the lab. Bye, Ramana."

Ramana waved, then stood in his doorway and watched her walk away as the music that she picked, which immediately became his favorite song, quietly played in the background.

Chapter 10

The project lab was full by the time that Allison arrived. All of the lab assistants were there along with about ten other spectators. Both Dr. Green and Dr. Meyers were seated in the front row surrounded with their respective entourages. The day had come for the project team to animate a fully functioning, independent cell, the first living organism to be created by this collaboration of science departments. Although David and Ramana were a little uneasy about the presence of a gallery that included their boss, they were determined to not let it affect them. Once Dr. Green found out about the timing of the event, he decided to invite the present crowd. Allison smiled and waved to Ramana and others present as she found a seat in the back row of the chairs set up in front of the monitor.

As twenty minutes passed by the scheduled launch time, the gallery gradually grew louder with conversations. Ramana was becoming frustrated at the apparent disregard for their work. These people made it harder to concentrate. David could see the tension and anxiety growing in the project team and decided to go into action.

As he cleared his throat loudly, the crowd became silent and gave him their attention. "Thank you, and welcome . . . I must first say that we are very unaccustomed to having a crowd watch while our team is working, so we would appreciate your restraint." David looked up at the ceiling and thought of what he would say. "The experiment that you will be watching today is the culmination of about two years of work. With this fantastic research team and the help of Dr. Meyers and the computer science department, we have made incredible leaps in just weeks and are ready to begin the first true test of this project. Today, we will be attempting to bring to life the first man-made living organism . . . the first living organism to exist outside of what we call nature. This first organism will be a simple spherical shaped bacterium. Although it is one of the simplest forms of life, I can assure you that within this bacterium millions, if not trillions, of processes will be happening before your eyes. You may not be able to see all of these; in fact there is no way that you could. But believe me, the cell will be in constant motion. The test bacterium is one of our own designs, and its main function is to process food-type compounds in the environment, and once enabled, reproduce."

David seemed to hesitate and smile. "The first test cell has been given the name 'Kirk' by its creators."

A smile finally came to Ramana's face. He glanced over to Allison, who had to look down in order to stop her urge to giggle.

David continued, "As you can probably tell, the name is taken from the TV series *Star Trek*, whose Captain Kirk fittingly described what this experiment is attempting to do in boldly going where no man has gone before and seeking out new worlds and new life."

The gathered crowd smiled, chuckled, or nodded their head as their varying degrees of approval and recognition dictated.

"Speaking of the world that this cell shall inhabit," David explained, "the Environmental Program, which we are calling the E.P., is as much of an accomplishment as the cell itself, if not more. The E.P. has hundreds of variables that attempt to duplicate the many different natural environments. It contains many elemental compounds and conditions found in nature, such as temperature, pressure, and the like. Once the E.P. is fully operational, the cell must interact and interpret its environment, and take the appropriate action to ensure its survival."

"Once we feel that the test cell, Kirk, has proven that it can survive in a normal environment, only then will we enable it to reproduce, or duplicate itself. The form of reproduction, of course, is mitosis, where the DNA is duplicated, separates, and then directs the cell to split and re-form as two separate cells. For me, this is the most exciting part of the experiment. Once the cell has successfully completed this phase, we will be able to speed up this process to the point of sending it thousands, possibly millions of years into the future in just days, maybe weeks. The insights and discoveries from this type of experimentation may hold the key to discovering the hidden mechanisms of evolution. No doubt, the ability to experiment on inorganic tissues and organisms holds great importance as our society continues its evolution. As this type of research continues, and the ability of computers continues to skyrocket, the complexity and realism of these trinary organisms could rival any carbon-based organism."

David had said much more than he planned and looked back to Ramana as he began to run out of words. Ramana, appreciative of his introduction, gave him a thumbs-up. The room was full of excitement. During the pause of words, the noise level began to grow again.

"Okay," David said with relief. "I believe that we are ready to begin the experiment. Now, please, once the experiment has begun, I must ask you to remain patient and most of all, silent. Ramana and his team must communicate to direct the E.P. if they feel that the cell may suffer irreversible damage. Once the experiment has begun and the cell has entered the E.P., please put on your polarized glasses to view the experiment in three dimensions. Okay Ramana, Mark, please proceed."

Mark and Ramana's relationship had really developed during the few weeks they had worked together. Though their areas of science differed, their commitment and work ethics were almost identical. A mutual respect and interest made the long hours and tremendous workload bearable. They were the true brains behind the project–the only two who truly understood the project fully. Even David did not possess the intricate knowledge that came from developing every phase of the project.

Ramana turned to Mark as David took a seat next to Dr. Green and said, "Okay Mark, looks like it's show time."

Mark lifted his head from his terminal screen. He looked at Ramana with a smile on his face and nodded his head.

Ramana began calling out to each station and got an affirmative response from each. He said, "All right, introduction of the first test cell, Kirk, into the E.P. will commence in three minutes. Prepare E.P. for the dial-up routine." Ramana paused as he waited for the E.P. station to acknowledge his command. "Mark, is Kirk ready for transport?"

Mark smiled. He was tempted to respond with a "beam me up, Scotty" or a reference to Mr. Spock, but prudently chose instead to just say, "Yes."

As Ramana kept the countdown to himself on his watch, he saw that the E.P. was dialed down to zero effect for the introduction of the cell. The test cell would be introduced in a dormant condition. All of the cellular functions of the cell would be at rest until the team enabled it to operate. Once the cell was enabled to operate and the E.P. was dialed up to a normal environment, thousands of reactions and microscopic processes would begin.

"Thirty seconds to transport," Ramana said as he looked down at his watch. "If anyone sees a problem or is not ready, please let me know right now." Everyone looked around the room at each other, but no one said a word. "Switch into 3-D mode and let's initiate a ten second countdown." The audience responded by placing their glasses on as the monitor screen leapt out into the dark room. "Okay, release in ten . . . nine . . . eight." Allison closed her eyes and silently prayed until, "two . . . one . . . release."

Mark initiated the computer to transport the test cell from the work area through the secure tunnel into the E.P. The process was instantaneous. Kirk appeared before the amazed gallery that sighed and whispered in response. The cell moved from the back of the E.P. screen to the middle and slowly came to a stop. The cell was tiny in comparison to the six-foot cube it inhabited. Ramana called to the E.P. station, "Okay, let's isolate on the immediate area of the cell and magnify."

The programmer at the station tapped out a set of coordinates, and the screen flickered as the cell suddenly grew about ten times. Through the transparent, blueish-green tint of the E.P., the cell was fully distinguishable. The membrane had a silvery appearance that bordered on transparency. The diameter of the cell was now about twelve inches on screen as it hung in the air. Inside the cell, the most obvious structure was the nucleiod. It was the darkest and largest of all the parts and set just off center inside of the cell. Around the nucleiod, many smaller dark structures hovered in a yellowish fluid. These structures were the ribosomes, which would be responsible for manufacturing needed proteins from the available materials within the cytoplasm and the E.P.

After Ramana had made a visual inspection of the cell, he spoke to Mark. "If everything checks out on your end, Mark, let's go ahead and enable the operations."

Mark's eyes went back to his monitor to evaluate the cell's condition. "Everything looks good, Ramana . . . I'm enabling operations."

Moments after Kirk was enabled, the cell seemed to bulge as it probed the environment it now occupied. Every eye soaked in each motion as the cell came to life. As the computer tried to sustain this huge set of new instructions, the surge in power and vibration could be felt by everyone in the room. The contents of the nucleiod shuttered as an RNA program accessed and read a portion of the huge library of information contained within the DNA. Ribosomes seemed to wiggle in the pool of cytoplasm as they attempted to identify the different compounds that surrounded them. Everything that was happening at this point was a diagnostic of sorts, as no environmental pressures or challenges had been introduced.

Ramana had seen this reaction within the work area of the computer and concluded that everything was working properly so far. After a few minutes of tense waiting in silence, Ramana gave the order to proceed. "Okay, let's initiate the E.P. dial-up routine on my mark."

The programmer sitting at the E.P. station turned to look at Ramana and nodded his head in response. Ramana looked at Mark and got a nod from him, then said, "Initiate E.P. routine; let's see what happens."

The E.P. took about five minutes to fully dial up to the specified environment. As with the membrane testing, the chosen environment would be a very safe one that replicated a simple, aqueous environment that would not offer any blatantly harmful challenges to the cell. The E.P. surrounding the cell began to come alive visually on the screen with a growing activity as it approached its final destination. Different compounds and environmental factors were introduced as the E.P. approached the 10 percent mark. Mark noted on his monitor that this was the mark that the cell came alive with operational activity.

"We've got some initial signs of activity, Ramana. Kirk is waking up," commented Mark. "Looks like it is starting some polypeptide production . . . I can't yet tell what it is producing . . . um . . . give me a moment."

"Where are we on dial up?" barked Ramana.

The E.P. station responded, "We are at 13 percent . . . 14, and still proceeding."

Ramana walked out from his station where he could get a better view of the screen. He scanned the nucleiod to see if he could see the RNA programs carrying out the transcription process. Ramana strained his eyes. He thought he saw a small transfer RNA program attaching itself to a portion of a strand of DNA. "Do you see it there?" Ramana pointed into the three-dimensional area to identify what he saw. "Do you see the transcription process here, David?"

David nodded his head. He wasn't really sure that he saw the exact process that Ramana pointed to, but looked to the general area. The other eyes in the room scanned the specific area but were unable to detect the minute movements of the RNA programs.

"Mark, have you detected what the protein production is for?" Ramana asked.

Mark was deep into the data being produced. "Not yet, Ramana. I can't determine the exact structure of these polypeptides, but Kirk seems to be at just about full production. It seems that all of the production, well at least the majority of it, is focused on the same thing. I can tell you that the production seems to be very organized. No problems yet."

The beast hummed and clicked as it provided the stage for this initial performance. The red lasers sweeping back and forth through the silicon gel provided an eerie backdrop for the drama. Allison sat with her back to the large computer just a few feet away. Her eyes shifted from station to station then back to the monitor as she tried to keep up with everything that transpired.

Unknown to the team, Kirk had detected a weakness in the membrane construction as soon as the E.P. was initiated. It was working feverishly as the increasing pressures of the E.P. began to eat away at its outer layer.

Ramana's eyes were glued to the nucleiod. The transfer RNA had finished transcribing the information and now made its way through the membrane of the nucleiod into the cytoplasm. As the dial-up program reached the 25 percent mark, Ramana tried to grasp what the cell was trying to accomplish.

Mark had focused his concentration back on the tremendous amount of data that was being produced. "Ramana . . . let's see . . . there seems to be something happening here."

The crowd's attention was grabbed by Mark's words and the room became silent.

"I recommend that we slow down the dial up until I can

figure out what is happening. Something doesn't seem right," Mark said.

"Where are we, E.P. station?" Ramana asked.

"We are approaching 40 percent, 38 . . . 39," responded the anxious assistant.

"Okay, let's slow it down by half," instructed Ramana. "Mark, where does the problem seem to be coming from?"

Mark was shaking his head as he answered. "I can't tell. The cell definitely seems stressed. I'm not sure if this would be a normal reaction or if there is a problem somewhere."

Dr. Green, Dr. Meyers, and David were silent, their attention truly captured as this molecular drama played out before their eyes.

As Ramana stared deeper into this new world, his vision began to tunnel around the 3-D screen. In an odd instant, he began to lose all recognition of the room and people around him. The coffee shop dream began to have its way with Ramana again.

"There it is!" screamed Mark. "The data is similar to the initial moments of the membrane release. I think it is in stress due to the pressures being exerted on it from the E.P. I'm not sure that the cell will be able to handle 100 percent of the final pressure."

There was no response from Ramana, so Mark took it as an indication to proceed. His attention went back to the data.

Ramana was aware of nothing but himself, Kirk, and the beast, and he began to realize what was happening. Kirk had diagnosed the problem before anyone else had and was busily trying to correct it. As the dial up routine was approaching the 60 percent mark, the ribosomes, aided by the messenger RNA programs, were constructing new membrane proteins to repair the weakening structure. There was a minute flaw in a small area membrane, and now it was beginning to tear. The flaw must have occurred when the cell was duplicated for the experiment. None of the programmers, not even Ramana, had caught it, but the cell did and began fixing it shortly after it had encountered the increasing pressures of the E.P.

Mark, who was now aware of a problem, began calculating the time that was left before the membrane would compromise again and the cell would burst or tear. The room remained quiet except for the sounds of the beast and Mark's hands busily typing on his keyboard.

Ramana was deep inside the cell. He silently watched the ribosomes piece together long chains of amino acids and sugars. He was amazed at the beauty and precision with which his intricate creation worked.

Mark became anxious as the seconds passed. He knew that a breach or collapse of the membrane was drawing nearer. "Ramana, something strange is going on here. The cell seems to be going into a high stress routine. The structure of the cell seems to be compromised and I can't tell why. If this continues, we could lose the whole cell. We are at 75 percent of E.P. I recommend that we stop or reverse the dial-up routine."

Ramana again did not respond. The production of the new membrane proteins was now complete. He gazed in awe of the magnificent structures that Kirk had built on its own. Although he was not directing the process as in his earlier dream, he was just as much a part of it. Ramana gazed around the cell and with the membrane programs, began to move towards the problem area.

"Ramana, we don't have long before the cell membrane ruptures. What do you want me to do?" Mark pleaded. "Ramana . . . Ramana!" Mark's voice grew louder and the gallery's attention turned to a dazed Ramana, who still did not respond.

At that moment, everyone was startled by the alarm that sounded as the E.P. detected the imminent breach. The cell was poised on the brink of collapse. Mark quickly stood up and began to head over to the E.P. station, certain that the experiment was finished and the first test cell had been ruined.

The crowd sighed as a tiny hole on the side of the cell

seemed to tear open. The yellowish cytoplasm could be seen oozing out of the small opening. The cell reacted like a balloon that had just been untied and started to move as the change in pressure pushed it.

Ramana and hundreds of membrane proteins were speeding to the tear. He began to sweat as he realized that they would have one chance to fix it. The appropriate enzymes moved in ahead of them and attached to the torn areas. Organelles and compounds went spilling into the E.P. with the cytoplasm in the general area. Kirk pulsed with a hurried pace as it fought to survive. The new membrane proteins hurled toward the tear, placing themselves in the frenzied danger zone to pile on each other and try to mend the breach.

The crowd pointed and spoke as the cell moved off the screen. Mark looked up from his personal monitor. A look of disgust came over his face, seeing the yellowish trail that the cell left. His hand moved toward the abort button as Ramana yelled, "Yes! That's it, you've done it," and grasped his hands together in front of his glazed eyes.

Mark was surprised and the reaction and stopped his hand just above the button. The alarm silenced and the crowd waited in confusion. Ramana, breathing heavily, came back to reality as the sounds and sights of the lab came back into focus.

"Ramana, what happened to you? It's finished, the cell ruptured, it's gone." Though whispered, Mark's voice had an angry tone.

Ramana stood there speechless as he tried to recover from his dream. He became aware of the stares that now were focused upon him.

David stood up, embarrassed at the apparent confusion that was taking place on his watch. "Where is the cell? What has happened to the cell?"

Mark began walking over to his station as the E.P. reached the 100 percent mark. "Let me find it. I'm sure it's guts are spilled out all over the place."

Ramana looked back at the crowd and saw the accusing stares of the front row. His eyes finally met up the sympathetic eyes of Allison, who slowly shook her head and shrugged her shoulders. He found his voice. "Didn't you see it? It was beautiful. Didn't any of you see what just happened?" The crowd tried to understand as they glared at Ramana's almost child-like reaction.

Mark took the E.P. out of its magnification and the small cell was visible once again. "Okay, let's magnify it and see what shape it's in." As the area was magnified, Mark stared in amazement. Kirk appeared to be fully intact and had regained its spherical shape. "Oh my God–what just happened?"

No one said a word. Their eyes went back and forth from the cell to the apparent mad scientist who stood next to it.

Finally David spoke up. "Ramana, I'm somewhat confused. Would you mind telling us what we just saw?"

Ramana looked at David with wide eyes and moved over to his terminal before he answered him. "The cell seems to be stable and fully functional." Ramana stared into his monitor screen and then turned around to the crowd. "We have just witnessed this first inorganic cell perform a very natural, yet incredible function to ensure its survival. Kirk went into polypeptide production to replace a flawed membrane construction to stop its own certain demise."

"What?" David said in disbelief. "How do you know that?"

"Flawed membrane construction?" added Mark. "How do you know that the membrane programs were flawed?"

Ramana squinted his eyes as he whispered, "I saw it happen." His voice quieted as he heard himself say those words.

The room stood in silence from Ramana's answer until Dr. Green broke it. "Well something remarkable happened, didn't it? The cell was bursting open, but there it is, as good as new." Dr. Meyers, sitting next to him, nodded in agreement.

"Well, you're right, the cell is stabilized and functioning at a hundred percent of the environmental settings," David remarked. "We should be able to determine exactly what happened once we analyze the data."

Ramana stood in confusion as his face gleamed in sweat. He was the only one who saw what had happened and everyone, it seemed, was looking at him as if he were crazy.

Allison, sensing Ramana's embarrassment, slowly stood up on the back row and quietly began to clap. Everyone immediately turned around to look at her, just as two of her fellow assistants decided to join in. Dr. Meyers and Dr. Green looked at each other and smiled at this idealistic gesture. They turned around and looked at Ramana and began to clap loudly. Their respective staff in attendance knee-jerked into action, and the whole room erupted into a standing ovation for this miraculous creation and triumph in scientific history. Both David and Mark immediately lost their accusatory mind frame as they focused their attention back to Kirk. It was true; the cell was fully functional in a real environment. This was a major triumph for the research team, for the two science departments, for the school, for all mankind. As they realized this, they turned toward Kirk and joined in with the applause.

Kirk was unimpressed with all of the accolades that it was presently receiving. Its work was nonstop now, and the stress level was high. The breach and hurried work to repair its membrane had depleted many of the compounds that it needed for survival. The membrane programs were alerted and began to search outside of the cell to replenish the supply. As appropriate compounds were found near the cell wall, the membrane proteins attracted them and allowed them to pass through the secure boundary. The nuclear chemicals worked together to interpret its environment and busily followed the DNA's instructions as it attempted to stabilize its own functions.

Dr. Green took off his glasses as the applause died down. He looked down at his watch and decided that this would be an appropriate time to lead the gallery out of the lab and let the research team plow through the mountain of data that was before them. He started the process of hand shaking and complimenting with instructions to David to keep him informed of the progress; progress not only about the research, but also of the time frame of the papers and articles that needed to be released. As the room emptied, Allison saw a chance to speak with Ramana.

"That was incredible, Ramana," Allison said as she turned to look at the cell again. "You guys really put on a show."

Ramana turned from his computer screen, somewhat annoyed until he saw it was Allison. "Oh yes . . . I guess we did. Somewhat of a freak show."

Allison laughed. "Yeah, what happened to you?"

Ramana paused. "I'm not sure what is happening to me. Anyway, do you think you can help me for an hour or two? I'm sorry to ask, but I really need to identify some things, quickly."

Allison thought about all of the things that she had to do, but nodded her head anyway.

"Thank you Allison," Ramana breathed. "Actually, if you could come back in about 20 or 30 minutes, I need to meet with David and Mark for a few minutes. Then we can get to work."

"Okay, Ramana," Allison said. "I guess I'll see you then."

"Thank you Allison," Ramana repeated as she turned to walk out of the project room. This time he thanked her for the applause that saved him in his time of need.

Chapter 11

The fight for survival did not stop inside the memory core of the computer. Hundreds of factors had to blend just right for the test cell to maintain its integrity. The environment inside the memory core was constantly monitored and refreshed by filtering routines much like an ocean aquarium, trying to provide optimal living conditions. Huge amounts of electricity flowed through these components as the beast was running constantly at its highest performance levels.

The work on developing the more complex eurokaryotic, or animal cells, had continued while Kirk was being evaluated. The work area of the computer contained dozens of individual programs in various stages of completion, which attempted to replicate these more complicated processes. The research team now worked even harder on this goal, motivated by the overwhelming success of Kirk. The original cell had now survived for five days in its present environment and showed no further signs of degradation or malfunction. The next major decision was to determine when to enable the test cell to reproduce.

Although no one could understand how Ramana could have been aware of what was happening during the original test, his assertion regarding the membrane's flaws were fully proven. The data showed, as Mark had originally detected, that the cell's polypeptide production was for preserving the membrane. In addition, damaged membrane programs were found in the E.P., and after examination, the flaws that Kirk had detected were revealed. Though the facts of what had happened were agreed upon, the fact that Ramana had seen the process happen was something that David refused to accept. He had explained the strange episode as coincidence mixed with the long hours that Ramana continued to work.

Although undetectable within the research team, Ramana felt his relationship with David had begun to change after the incident. It was now a business, and he began to feel more like an employee than a partner. Not only did Ramana sense that David's trust in him was questionable, he now began to feel the pressure to publish a paper on the apparent success of the first bacterium experiment. The amount of resources that the research project used was immense. The technical staff, the huge amount of electricity, and the personal hours of the Director of Research made the project one of the most costly operations on the campus. He knew that Dr. Green was pressuring David, but to make any type of conclusions on such a complex project so early made Ramana very uncomfortable.

Kirk was oblivious to the politics that swirled around in the world outside it. Its concentration was focused on survival. Even though its biggest test lay ahead when it would attempt mitosis, Kirk was in constant motion. Almost every type of program within its structure had been evaluated, and many had already been replaced with a duplicate that it had produced. All of this was done by replicating portions of the huge DNA program. The upcoming experiment with mitosis would require Kirk to reproduce the entire DNA sequence, while attempting to split itself in two. If Kirk could perform mitosis successfully, it would truly demonstrate that it was as much a living organism as any in the world outside. Kirk lay in the exact position that it ended up in the first test five days ago. It had no means of motion and the E.P., although able to produce forces that would move the cell, had not been programmed to do so. So far, the game was survival. Every program that the research team wrote and became a part of Kirk consisted of this simple instinct. Just like any form of life, the ultimate directive was survival.

The area where most of the action was taking place was the membrane. The interaction of the E.P. and the membrane programs was constant and varied as each nanosecond passed. The membrane would gauge the temperature, the pH, the pressure, hundreds of factors instantaneously, and relay the information to the necessary areas. As the membrane interpreted the data from the E.P., small bits of its programming would be captured and stored. Just like any amino acid programs found in the E.P., Kirk would attempt to identify and store the pieces of the E.P. in the cytoplasm for future use. Most of the pieces were only small parts of the huge E.P. and were eventually discarded when no use could be found for them. This process of capturing part of the E.P. was not unexpected by the research team. Each day the E.P. would access its backup program in the work area and replace the missing or damaged parts. Amino acids and other compounds were replenished to the E.P. in the same way. The latter was valuable information to the team. Identifying the amino acids and compounds that the cell "ate" provided crucial information to the researchers.

When the research team created the E.P., the main focus was to enable it to relay the hundreds of variables to any test cell as quickly as possible. Since this computer would not be interacting with any other computers, little attention was paid to creating a secure firewall isolating or protecting the E.P. Because this was an isolated computer with restricted access, David and Ramana were not concerned about someone hacking into the system. In fact, in its present condition, the beast would be extremely vulnerable if exposed to other computing environments. This would not be the case however, since this was a safe and sanitary area that would not be contaminated by the outside computing world. They did not realize that the life they had created would pose the biggest threat to contaminating the E.P.

On the evening of the seventh day, Kirk reached out and consumed a huge piece of the actual E.P. operating system that contained the controls for a major portion of the environmental variables. It was packed away in the cytoplasm until Kirk could figure out whether or not to discard it. The next morning, the E.P. accessed the backup program and automatically repaired itself. As Ramana entered the research lab and turned on the lights, the programs had regained their normal function.

"Hello Kirk, how did you sleep last night?" Ramana playfully asked. He accessed his terminal to run a diagnostic on Kirk and the E.P. The beast went into action and shortly displayed the results to its master.

"Interesting, look's like you were very hungry last night." Ramana quickly reviewed the data. "You are going to need all of the strength you can get, my friend. Today, you are going to be a father." Ramana paused. "Or a mother . . . well anyway, you are going to be a parent."

The rest of the team arrived shortly after Ramana as the reproduction test was to start a 9:00 a.m. that morning. The reproduction today would be slowed down to make sure each step went properly. From beginning to end the mitosis experiment could take as long as 30 minutes, assuming everything went as planned. By 8:30 a.m., all of the tests and diagnostics were completed, and David and Ramana agreed to proceed. Today, Allison would be operating the E.P. station. She had earned the trust of everyone involved and was an integral part of the team. She would be the first from the purely research side of the team to make the move to the programming side. Although she felt that she was prepared, her stomach was queasy with the thought of all the things that she could screw up.

As David examined the room, he nudged Ramana and whispered, "Do you think it's smart to have a rookie in the mix today?" His head motioned over to the E.P. station. Ramana looked over at Allison and then back to David. With his bottom lip pursed with confidence, he nodded his head. Ramana's attention went to the clock on the wall. "Okay people, we will enable reproduction in 10 minutes." As people got themselves into position, Ramana slowly walked over to Allison. Her complete attention was on the monitor, reading the variables and checking with the spiral-bound manual mounted next to the controls. She was surprised by two hands that came to rest on her shoulders.

"Are you ready to go, Allison?" Ramana asked calmly.

Allison's head turned to the side quickly. "Oh yes, um, the E.P. seems to be functioning normally."

"Hmm, are you functioning normally? You seem nervous," Ramana noted.

Allison's shoulders deflated as she lowered her voice. "Well, to tell you the truth, I'm nervous as hell. Are you sure you want me at this station for this?"

"Allison, you are as competent as anyone for this job. I have complete trust and confidence in you. You will do just fine . . . anyway, I think Kirk needs you here." Ramana massaged her shoulders as he spoke his words. "Just listen for my directions and give me the information that I ask for. In all likelihood, most of the action will be at the nucleus station."

Allison closed her eyes and stretched as he spoke his words. She sat straight up in her chair and moved her hand to touch Ramana's as it slipped off her shoulder. "Thanks, Ramana."

David watched the conversation from across the room and made a mental note of it.

Ramana walked back to his station and put on his 3-D glasses. "Switch into 3-D mode and let's take Kirk into S-phase."

Once the cell was enabled, it would immediately duplicate its DNA program. This is called the S-phase, or synthesis phase.

Only Dr. Green sat in the gallery today with his 3-D glasses and a front row seat. He was very familiar with cellular mitosis, and was there to see how closely this trinary life form would duplicate it.

Mark initiated the process, and the test cell began to replicate the huge strands of DNA.

"N-station, C-station, tell me what's going on," Ramana barked to the nucleus and cytoplasm stations.

"We have DNA synthesis under way," replied one programmer.

"The ribosomes have initiated histone production," responded the other.

"Good, let me know of any changes. This should take a while on these settings. I would guess about ten minutes." Ramana took a seat in the gallery a few seats down from Dr Green and looked at the cell to see if he could tell what was happening. Within the nucleus, he could see the activity beginning to escalate. He glanced at David and Dr. Green, who were busy doing the same thing.

Allison began to calm down as she realized what Ramana said was true. The E.P. had very little to do with this process. She just had to keep the E.P. stable. From her spot, without her 3-D glasses on, the monitor was indistinguishable and fuzzy, so she concentrated on the data that was coming across her station screen.

After about 15 minutes, the N-station operator broke the silence. "The chromosomes are beginning to coil."

Everyone's eyes strained to see the apparent confusion within the nucleus begin to form curled strands.

"Looks like we are entering the prophase," commented Ramana. "Where are the centrosomes?"

The C-station operator's eyes scanned the data. "Centrosomes are moving apart, away from each other. I do not see any spindle production yet."

"Okay, Kirk, take your time. Let's do this right," Ramana said to the screen.

The numerous strands of genetic material were well into the process of coiling around different forms of proteins, called histones, produced by the ribosomes. They continued to coil until they had formed about a dozen strands. The two centrosomes would travel to opposite ends of the cell and eventually form a grid of tubes, called microtubules, that would divide the genetic information in half and pull it into each new cell.

"Looks like we are well into the prophase," commented Ramana. He looked over to Allison's station. "How does the E.P. check out?"

Allison was deep in concentration. "E.P. is stable, replenishing numerous amino acids."

"Nuclear envelope beginning to disappear," called a voice from the N-station.

Ramana's attention was back to the screen. "Entering prometaphase. Where is kinetichore production?"

"Microtubule and kinetichore production very high . . . the equatorial plate is being constructed," the C-station leader replied.

Dr. Green was riveted to the monitor. The very drama of molecular procreation was playing out right before his eyes. David's palms were wet, like an expectant father full of anxiety about giving birth to his creation. The visual interpretation of mitosis, a process that few people understood let alone observed, was being performed like a ballet on the big screen for their private audience.

They were 20 minutes into the experiment when the apparent organization of the cell turned into chaos. The membrane around the nucleus vanished and the cytoplasm took on a stringy composition. The cell had fully entered the prometaphase, where the microtubules had formed an envelope around its genetic material. These structures began to attach themselves to parts of the coiled chromosomes in order to pull the respective duplicated pairs apart to form two nuclei for the two new cells.

"How is the outer membrane holding?" asked Ramana.

"The membrane is expanded and stretched but holding," a voice answered.

"What's the progress of the equatorial plane? Is it finished yet?" Ramana asked.

The C-station operator studied his console. "No, not yet. It is still forming the microtubule grid . . . It seems that many tubes are forming but not attaching to anything, then disappearing. It may take some time to get through the prometaphase."

David, alerted to that observation, said, "That's not unusual for a cell to experience that in this phase." He stopped as he realized the similarity to nature. "My God, Ramana, the cell is reacting just like a natural cell."

Ramana smiled with pride. "So far, it is going better than I hoped. If we can get through this phase, the rest should be incredible."

Chapter 12

"Oh, things are great, Dad. The weather is beautiful, not too cold, but I'm glad I brought down some of my winter clothes," Allison said into the phone. "How are you and Mom?"

"It doesn't look like I'm going to make it up there until Easter. I'm involved in a pretty important project here, and I promised that I would be available until then." Allison sat on her single bed neatly made in her grandmother's sheets and quilt. Her eyes gazed across four years of memories neatly arranged on the walls and shelves. "Well, it has to do with trying to replicate biological functions on a computer. You should see this computer we are using; I have never seen anything like it. I'll tell you more about it over Easter.

"My classes? Actually, I think I'm doing pretty well in all . . . well, most of my classes to this point. I met with my counselor the other day to do a graduation check, and it looks like they are actually gonna give me a diploma." Allison laughed. "Not that I've figured out what happens after that, or anything.

"Yes I remember," Allison said. "You've told me for years that there is something important that you are supposed to tell me when I graduate. I just wish you would go ahead and tell me, I hate surprises." Allison listened. "I know, I know. Well, maybe you can tell me when I'm home for Easter. I mean, like I told you, they said I'm going to graduate. It's done."

"No, I'm not really dating anybody. Anyway, I don't want to talk about that," she quipped at her father playing the relationship card to change the subject

"Dad," Allison started, "do you know anything about Islam?

"Oh, it's no big deal. I just met someone and was talking to him about stuff . . . and we started talking about things . . . and well, he's a Muslim.

"No, don't worry; I'm not going to convert or anything.

"Like, I guess they don't believe in Jesus, or that he is anything more than a prophet. Yeah. So, I guess they really wouldn't accept what the New Testament has to say.

"What about the Old Testament?

"Yeah, I don't know either. It sure doesn't seem likely. The Jews and the Muslims are not exactly allies.

"What about that Mohammed guy?

"Yeah, he said something about the Angel Gabriel.

"Kinda sounds like what happened to that Joseph Smith guy, doesn't it?

"Uh huh.

"That's probably a good idea. He seems open enough to talk about it. It's kind of a weird situation though.

"Okay, well thanks, I will too.

"Okay, Daddy, bye. I love you too . . . Hi Mom . . ."

The original test cell, Kirk, hung suspended in its virtual reality, split in two by the successful mitosis that had occurred days ago. This feat was a huge triumph, and all of the project team felt they were making unanticipated progress. The beast hummed and clicked as it wove its lasers through the silicon gel that held its two occupants. The two cells were almost exactly alike. They floated in the computer, side-by-side, unaware of each other's presence. Both were busy trying to survive, completing countless routines and processes to ensure their existence.

The two were not alike, however. The process of mitosis had changed one of the cells. Their outward appearances were identical. The membranes, the ribosomes, the RNA all came out of the process unscathed. The DNA, however, had gone through a change, an unexpected synthesis. As the DNA was being replicated, the captured piece of the environmental program controls had been carried from the cytoplasm and mistakenly woven into the new chain of DNA. A mutation had occurred on their first attempt of mitosis and would forever change the rules of the experiment.

The three primaries sat below the screen and gazed upon the two dimensional cells charting their next course.

"So, what is the word on high? What is Dr. Green saying?" asked Ramana.

David looked down from the screen. "You saw him. After that amazing show we put on for him the other day, he's behind us all the way."

"And Dr. Meyers?" asked Mark.

"You probably need to find out about that one. You know him better than I do," David answered. "Although I have no reason to think he is anything but pleased." He paused. "I think we can safely assume that we have this lab for as long as we need it . . . that is, for as long as we are producing results."

David started, "To that end, I am of the opinion that since we have successfully performed mitosis, we should go ahead and start the evolutionary routine, at least in part of the memory area."

Mark nodded his head. "We've got plenty of room."

Ramana was in thought. "Well, there are some other concerns, but I agree."

David looked at Ramana. "What concerns do you have, Ramana?"

Ramana looked back at David with puzzlement. "There are plenty. Space concerns, control factors, processing space– where would you like me to start?"

"Space? We've got plenty of space," answered Mark as he looked at David.

"Not really. Think about it," started Ramana. "Once we start an evolutionary routine, the cell will eventually duplicate thousands, rather millions of times. Where will we put all of those cells? Eventually, it would take up all of the memory space."

Mark lifted his head in realization. "Oh yeah, I see what you mean."

"Well," David said, "what do you propose?"

"I don't know," answered Ramana. "I will need to think about it. Maybe they can be transferred to external drives. Maybe they can be sent to other hard disks. I don't know."

"Well let's come back to that one," answered David. "What are your other concerns?"

"Well, we will need a control cell to compare to the eventual products of the experiment," Ramana said.

David's eyes looked up to the screen. "That's an easy one; we've got your Kirk cell. Let's keep him right where he is and not touch him. He'll be the alpha cell."

"The alpha and the omega," laughed Mark as he pointed to the two cells.

"Which one is Kirk, anyway?" asked David.

Ramana looked to the screen. "Both of them are Kirk, I guess."

David sat up. "Well then, we shall have two control cells, Kirk and . . . Uh . . . Picard."

The other two had no response.

"Well, at least we will have two control cells," David stated. "What do you think about that?"

"Works for me. We can give them an identifying marker of some sort," Mark said.

Ramana nodded his head.

"What else?" asked David.

"Well, I'm sure we would like to continue to try to develop new and more complex cells. We have all sorts of different programs getting ready to construct into eukaryotic cells."

"Sure," said David. "What's the problem?"

Ramana looked at Mark and wondered why he felt like he was on trial. "Well, the processing speed would be reduced if an endless evolution routine was constantly running."

"That's true," David started. "We will just have to prioritize functions then, schedule time for each."

Ramana lowered his head as he realized who would be in charge of prioritizing functions.

"Hey, I got it," Mark said.

"What?" David asked as he and Ramana turned their attention to him.

"A way we can accomplish the evolutionary routine," he finished.

"Let's hear it."

"Well, once the routine has duplicated a number of cells, say 10 or 20, we can program the E.P. to erase some of them . . ."

David interrupted, "Ah yes, there you go Mark. And we can save examples from each of the number of years that we are replicating. I suppose we could program it to save a cell at 10 or 20 or even a hundred year intervals. Then we would have sample cells that we could compare to the control and to each other."

Mark regained the floor. "It could be done. We would have to change the E.P. somewhat, but I'm sure it could be done."

Ramana stayed silent as the two began to rewrite the project he had worked so hard on. He was saddened as they began to work each other into a frenzy that was traveling farther away from his hopes and desires for the project.

David began calculating as he spoke. "We should start the erasing at around 30 or 40 produced cells. That would be, uh . . . five rounds of mitosis. It would give us 32 cells, of which we only need to save one."

"How do you propose we determine which cell to keep?" asked Mark.

David flashed with insight. "To make this true to nature, maybe we should introduce a harsh environment and see which one survives the longest, then use that one to begin the process again."

"On the other hand," David continued brainstorming, "we

could erase one cell every time mitosis was performed. Split one cell in two, then erase the original cell . . ." David finished his sentence and looked at Ramana.

"Ramana, what's the matter?" David asked. "Do you have a problem with this?"

Ramana paused and slowly blinked his eyes. "Well, again, I have concerns about this kind of path."

"What now?" sighed Mark.

Ramana sat motionless, wondering if he was being too protective of the project. "Where should I start? There is the safety loop that is built into the E.P."

"Safety loop?" asked David.

Mark caught on. "Yes, there is a safety loop that Ramana wanted incorporated into the E.P. controls that helps any cell to rebuild itself in the event of an emergency."

David lifted his head. "Why wasn't I informed of the safety routine?" Neither Mark nor Ramana answered the question. "Was it on in the first experiments?"

Ramana spoke up. "No, I did not think it would be necessary."

"Then what is the problem?" asked David.

"Well, David," Ramana said, "we may need it when we introduce more complex cells into the E.P."

"Yeah?" prompted David.

"To destroy cells in the E.P., the safety loop would have to be turned off during the evolution routine," Ramana explained. "The safety loop would not allow cells to be destroyed; it would try to take over control of the E.P. It could not be used while the evolution routine was running."

"Destroy? Is *that* what you have a problem with, Ramana? You think we want to destroy the cells?" David asked with a sarcastic smile on his face.

Ramana shuddered as his feelings for David began to change in an instant.

David began again, "I still don't see a problem with what

you're saying, Ramana. Do you have any other concerns?"

Ramana, feeling ripped away from the control of the project, looked David in his eyes and said, "Well."

"Go ahead," said David.

"Well, these cells are extremely delicate," started Ramana. "Any small error in any of the thousands of programs that make up a cell can result in its destruction–that is, if the cell does not catch it in time and fix the problem, if it even can. The chances are high that during mitosis, some problems are going to occur, especially if we are running it at a speed that is not even normal in nature."

David and Mark stared silently at Ramana.

He continued, "I just find it hard to believe that a process like the one you are suggesting would result in something coherent. It may even do damage to the E.P."

Mark turned his head to David, letting him field this question.

David smiled and shook his head. "Let me ask you a question. We have duplicated everything that goes on in nature here, haven't we?"

Ramana paused. "To a certain degree."

"I would say by my observation, to a large degree," David returned. "So, nature has found a way to deal with the problems that concern you, hasn't it?"

Ramana nodded his head and said, "Well, yes, but . . ."

David interrupted, "That is the heart of the experiment, Ramana, to discover these secrets of life. Sure, we will run into some problems. I'm sure of it. But in the end, I think we have the strong possibility of discovering some incredible evolutionary truths."

Ramana conceded his point in silence.

"Okay," said David, "do you have any other concerns?"

Ramana shook his head in defeat.

"Fine then, let's get to work," David said, now empowered. "All efforts will be put to setting up an agreeable evolutionary routine. Mark, I want you to start devising a couple of options for the evolution routine, and we as a group will decide which one is best. The work area will still be used to work on more advanced cells. Ramana, I want you to continue to develop things in this area. Once a eukaryotic cell is developed, we will talk about scheduling the E.P. for processor time."

Chapter 13

"Okay, Mark, before we get it rolling at top speed, let's see what the process looks like in real-time motion," David suggested.

Mark nodded his head and adjusted some controls at his terminal. He had made the final changes to the E.P. and was ready to begin experimenting with the evolutionary routine the team had chosen.

Ramana sat in the row of chairs away from his terminal, subconsciously not wanting to be a part of this exercise. He struggled to define what he was feeling. It was understood that the whole of the research project was David's. The work and the responsibility of creating the framework, though, had been his. These were his creatures, his design. He stopped himself as he could feel his anger building. The feeling was horrible, and the worst part was that he really could not understand why he felt this way. Was he immature to the extent that if he didn't get his way, he was going to act like a child? At that question, Ramana decided that he would not be a part of this project in anger. As soon as the realization passed through his mind, the tension in his body started to fade.

Mark finished his adjustments and looked back at David and Ramana. "I am ready to start this. Just give me the word."

David looked at his silent partner and then back to Mark. "Initiate evolutionary routine at real-time."

As Mark started the new experiment, Allison adjusted her

glasses and looked upon the three cells that hung in the three-dimensional space. The two Kirk cells were off to the side and now had an alpha and omega symbol floating in front of them to identify each as the control cells. One bacterium was at the center of the screen as the performance began. The process they had watched a week ago was happening at a speed that was similar to nature's speed, but much harder to see and decipher.

As the process began, the Kirk cells were taken out of sight and the E.P. zoomed in on the test cell. The bacterium went into action and quickly turned into two bacteria, then into four. The organisms clung next to each other as the process continued. Within the span of three minutes, the one cell had now become a cluster of cells while the project team looked on in excitement. Just as suddenly as the process had started, it stopped with what looked like a family of bacteria huddled around itself. Mark hit his keyboard, and the screen panned back to keep the large mass visible.

"Here comes the sorting routine," Mark spoke up.

The E.P. produced what looked like a current that flowed between the mass of bacteria. The cluster was pulled apart and began to form two rows as the E.P. separated them and quickly checked them for any visible mutations. The current began to swirl around the organized cells until it formed an isolated field that enclosed the participants. The environment within the enclosure started to change according to a random selection by the E.P. The pH began to lower and the environment became more acidic. One by one, the membrane of the cells slowly melted away. Though the harsh changes in environment would be varied, the winner of this first test was a matter of position rather than strength.

Allison's eyes were at the top of the screen until she saw what looked like the two bottom cells disappearing. Her attention went back to the two rows of cells in the middle of the screen. She looked on in amazement as the cells were slowly being eliminated. She quickly looked over to Ramana who was watching intently. When the E.P. decided a specific cell was past the point of recovering, it was erased until only a single cell remained at the top of the row. Without stopping, the single cell was moved back to the center of attention and started up the process of mitosis again.

"Is everything working according to the plan?" David asked.

Mark looked at his terminal. "Everything's working beautifully; no problems yet."

"Okay then," started David, "let's go ahead and start speeding up the process, see what happens."

As Mark made the appropriate adjustments, the crowd watched the cells begin performing the routine in a faster and faster tempo. As the minutes passed on and the speed continued increasing, the process was becoming indistinguishable.

"How fast do you want to take it to?" asked Mark.

David turned his head. "Um, let's keep it at around 50 to 75 percent of top speed, and then check it in about a hour or so. If everything checks out, then let's crank it up and leave it alone for a while."

David paused then turned back to Mark. "Tell me again the time scale acceleration when the routine is running at a hundred percent."

Mark looked down at his notes. "Let's see, and Ramana help me with this. We calculated that running the beast at top speed, the evolutionary routine could accelerate the process of mitosis to where every hour the cells would experience the equivalent of about 500 years."

All heads turned to Ramana to confirm Mark's explanation. Everyone remained silent until Ramana nodded his head.

"Great," said David. "Now who wants some lunch?"

As David led a group of hungry researchers out of the lab, the remaining people in the audience squinted their eyes and cocked their heads to try to see what was happening within the blur of activity on the monitor screen. The beast was running at a constant frenzy to facilitate this experiment. Unbeknownst to all of the participants, the real action was being performed by the alpha and omega cells.

The Kirk cell they had labeled as the omega cell was continuing its metamorphosis. The transfer RNA began to look for the membrane recipe on the long DNA chain. It found it nestled among the mutated environmental controls containing the safety loop and began to transcribe the code for the replacement of its own membrane. The RNA transfered the codes to the cytoplasm, and the ribosomes, with the help of the messenger RNA, attempted to synthesize the new proteins. The raw materials to build the programs could not be found in the cytoplasm, so the search went outward to the membrane. Outside the cell, the membrane found a vast storehouse of the materials and began to cut and pry the needed building blocks from the E.P. and deliver them to the cytoplasm.

These events were unnoticed by everyone as the beast feverishly worked to send the evolutionary test cells far off into the future. Changes occurred in this part of the computer as well. Just as Ramana had warned, as the cells duplicated themselves at the increased rate of speed, small mistakes were made in various places. The mitosis process would not successfully be completed or the outcome would produce two cells that immediately fell apart. The hour ticked away with no one aware of what was happening.

David returned with the group of lunchers. They took their assigned places in various parts of the lab.

"Alright Mark, let's see what we have created so far," said David as he took a sip of his Diet Coke.

Mark acknowledged him and sat down at his terminal. He began to bring the routine to a close. The blur on the screen slowed down to reveal a collection of parts that looked somewhat like chicken noodle soup. Parts of cells floated in the isolated environment, stirred up and falling apart from the whirling action within the E.P.

"Um, Mark," David started, "what are we looking at? Where have the test cells gone?"

"Well . . . they should be right there," he pointed to the screen. "I don't know what happened." Immediately he started to scan the data that was on his monitor.

"Obviously something has gone terribly wrong," observed David. "How does the E.P. check out?"

"The E.P. seems fine, it is . . . well, wait, something's funny here."

Ramana's attention was grabbed by the observation and finally spoke up. "What is wrong with the E.P.?"

Both David and Mark looked back at their now vocal partner.

Mark finished his quick diagnostic and said, "Nothing's wrong with the E.P., Ramana. It just seems that a portion of its programming has disappeared. I've just told it to back itself up to replace the missing parts. I don't know why that would've happened."

"That's one of the problems I was worried about," Ramana again spoke. He walked over to his terminal and began to run his own diagnostic.

David's eyes followed him over to the computer. "Like I said, we are going to run into some problems. This is not unexpected. Maybe we made the selection process too harsh. Maybe there was already a flaw with the cell that we chose to start with. It happened with the first experiment."

At the same time, Kirk had begun replacing its membrane with a new type of program. As the first new programs were snapped into place, the omega cell suddenly became aware of the environment around him. It became aware of another presence similar to itself in the area. More and more membrane programs were replaced with the mutated duplicates until the omega cell needed more building blocks. Content with its progress, the cell shut down membrane production and attempted to flex its new muscles.

A warning light came on at Mark's terminal and an alert signal started to sound. Heads turned as the surprising situation caught everyone off guard.

"What is it?" asked Ramana.

Mark frantically scanned his terminal. "I don't know. It looks like something is happening with the E.P. The environmental controls spiked up and then returned to normal. Did you mess with any of the controls? Did anyone mess with the E.P. controls?"

The room echoed with the strange alarm sound while the team struggled to decipher the riddle.

David looked anxiously over Mark's shoulder as he waited for an answer. "Turn that thing off!" After Mark hit the alarm, he continued, "Is the E.P. still fluctuating?"

Ramana studied his monitor. "No, the E.P. is stable, back to its original settings . . . I don't understand. The E.P. cannot adjust itself."

"Maybe it was an unfinished loop from the evolutionary routine," suggested Mark. "It could've been shut down before all of its instructions were completed."

David nodded his head. "That's it; that's gotta be it. No big deal. Let's go ahead and set it up for another run."

"Wait, David," started Ramana, "I think we should run a complete systems check before we attempt that kind of routine again. There is no telling what damage occurred during the first run."

David started to respond then turned to Mark. "Okay, Mark, what do you think?"

Mark paused as he realized the positions that were being staked out. "Well David, I can see Ramana's point. It doesn't seem like a big deal, but I think I would feel better if we checked the system before we start another routine."

David nodded his head. "How long will a complete system check take?"

Mark looked up in the air as he calculated. "About an hour

and a half, I suppose."

David looked at his watch and said, "Tell you what, let's spend the rest of the day checking out the computer until everybody is satisfied with the results. Mark, you set up an evolutionary routine to work through the night and we'll see what we have in the morning." He looked around the room, soaking up all of the nodding heads. "I've got to go, Ramana. Are you okay with all of this?"

Ramana nodded his head. "Yes I am. We'll get it all set up, don't worry." Ramana turned around to find Allison. Without saying anything, she knew he wanted her to stay and help him check out the computer. She smiled as she thought about the big list of things in her mind that she needed to do, then nodded her head. Ramana smiled back and said, "Mark, why don't you take a break too. Allison and I will check out the computer and get it ready for you. Let's say by four o'clock."

Mark looked relieved at the words and started to gather his things. "Thanks, Ramana."

When the room was emptied, Ramana directed Allison to Mark's terminal to begin a certain diagnostic while he started another. After the initial set-up, the beast displayed the estimated time of completion and began its task.

Allison pushed her chair away from the terminal into a more comfortable position and pulled out a bottle of water. "Is it just me, or has the atmosphere around here changed a little?"

Ramana could feel another friendly interrogation coming. "Oh, would you like me to adjust the thermostat?"

She shook her head. "You know what I mean. It seems like their teaming up on you."

"Wait just a second, Allison," Ramana started. "I am not going to start getting into that kind of thing. Let's just say that we are having professional differences." Ramana spoke as the thoughts came to him. "I am lucky to be working with these two. These are two of the brightest minds I may ever know. No, personal differences will not get in the way of this project. It is too important."

Allison was impressed as he turned an opportunity to bad-mouth his colleagues into praise for them.

Finished with that area, Ramana hesitated as he tried to approach another. He looked around the lab to make sure no one else was with them. "Allison, maybe you can help me with some questions I have."

Allison spun her chair to face him. "Yes?"

"Well, it's about David. You know he's Jewish, don't you?" asked Ramana.

She nodded her head. "I figured he was. You know, his name and all. Is he a practicing Jew?"

Ramana tried to keep his voice down. "I don't think so. I really haven't asked him about it. I probably won't either; it might get a little uncomfortable. But I wanted to know your thoughts on it."

"My thoughts on what? David?" Allison asked.

"Not exactly." Ramana looked up at the monitor and saw there was 20 minutes left on the diagnostic routine. "I'm more interested in your perspective on the Jewish faith."

"Oh, I see." Allison looked up as she gathered her thoughts. "Well, I would say I have a tremendous amount of respect for the Jewish faith, although I've really never sat down a talked to a . . . uh . . . Jew about it."

Ramana suddenly felt subconscious and guilty about the discussion he was having. "Tell me if you don't want to talk about this stuff, okay?"

"Okay, but really, I don't mind at all. What do you want to know?" she asked.

"I don't know, um, they say that the Jews are the "chosen people." Do you think they are the chosen people?" he asked.

"The chosen people," Allison said in a deep voice and laughed. She paused then said, "Yes. Yes I do."

Ramana waited for the rest of the answer.

"Okay," he said slowly. "Do you wish to elaborate on that,

Miss Wilson?"

Allison smiled. "Well, I guess you have to ask better questions."

Ramana paused. "Let's see, do you believe that they are the only chosen people?"

Allison quietly said, "I believe that they are the only chosen people of God. The only people that God has chosen to come down from heaven and reveal himself to."

Ramana was amazed with her answer and his eyes widened as he listened.

She continued, "And, I believe that God will not be finished with us until He is finished with His chosen people."

Ramana tried, "Why?"

"Why?" Allison frowned. "I don't know why."

Ramana composed himself. "No. Why, then, aren't you a Jew?"

"Oh," answered Allison, "I guess I am in a sense. Well, I don't know. I mean, this is where it kinda gets tricky."

Ramana stopped her. "Then let me ask you this. Do you believe that everything that they say happened back then really happened?"

Allison said, "Do you mean what happened in the Old Testament?"

Ramana nodded his head.

"Yes, I believe the Old Testament," she answered.

"You mean everything?" he asked again.

"Yes, everything."

"Do you think most Christians believe that?" Ramana asked.

"Probably not. I don't know," she answered.

"Interesting, I guess I didn't really know all of that. I appreciate your honesty," he summed up.

Allison started the questions. "Let me ask you. Do you believe what they say happened back then?"

Ramana paused and said, "Well, I believe something happened."

Allison laughed. "Okay, would you like to elaborate on that, Mr. Punjabi?"

Ramana smiled. "Well, first of all, if you were to ask even the Jewish people, I bet only a small minority of them would say that they believe that everything really happened."

Allison nodded her head. "I'll give you that one."

"Second of all," Ramana started, "just like many of the cultures back then, they probably exaggerated, or rather, created a belief system that they could use for their own purposes. I find it highly improbable that everything that they wrote down is true. Sorry, that's just how I feel."

"No, don't be sorry," Allison said. "I can understand how you feel. I take a lot of it on faith that I can't necessarily explain, you know, like the Jonah thing and Noah's Ark."

"See that's what I mean," Ramana observed. "Why is it so important that you believe stuff like that? Does it have anything to do with what we are experiencing today?"

"Yes, I think so," she answered.

Ramana paused. "Okay, maybe we're getting too deep, but let me pull out my theory buster." He waited for Allison to respond. "For a step of faith like that, even for some kind of scientific theory, there has to be something more than just a desire for it to be true. There must be more–some kind of special circumstance, a piece of evidence, even an unexplainable coincidence. Do you see where I'm going?"

"I'm not sure," she said.

"Can you give me any scientific or observable evidence for your belief in the history of the Jews?" he asked.

"Hmmm, let me see," she started scanning her brain as she looked at the three minutes left on the diagnostic routine. "Let me try this. Okay, you said that you believed that the Old Testament could just be another mythological story that they dreamed up to control or rule their people with, right?"

"Yes," he said.

"Have you ever read the Old Testament?" asked Allison.

"Well, no, not all of it," he answered.

"Okay, I have, and for the most part, it does not have a lot of good things to say about the Jewish people. It talks about how every step of the way they grumbled, or built altars to other gods, or stuff like that. They were really jerks most of the time; not that any other people would have acted differently."

Ramana nodded his head.

She continued, "And their kings, well first of all, *they* wanted a king. This God of theirs advised them against it. And their kings, well most of them were idiots. The Old Testament has awful things to say about them. Even their greatest king, David, well it goes into as much detail about the things he did wrong than anything else."

"Yes," replied Ramana.

"And look at the prophets," she said. "They were outcasts for the most part. They kept reminding the Jewish people about the commitments that they had made to this God of theirs and how they were not living up to their promises. And most of them were killed for the stances that they took."

"What is your point?" asked Ramana.

Allison quieted herself. "Well, they must have known it was true. The Jewish people, I mean. They kept these scrolls around not because they had great things to say about them, but because they saw from first hand that it was the truth. These scrolls were not tools for the kings to rule their people. If anything they were obstacles. The words of the prophets were kept after the prophets themselves were killed because what they said came true. It was not a book of myth to them; it was a book of truth."

"Hmmmm," started Ramana, "that is very interesting, Allison." The computer sounded as its first diagnostic routine finished its work. "Well, round one is over. Looks like everything is okay with the hardware. Let's see how the E.P. checks out."

Chapter 14

"Dr. Green . . . is that you? What are you doing here so early?" David asked as he was finally able to distinguish the person in the hazy, dark morning.

"Good morning, David. I was hoping to find somebody here this morning. I heard that the team had started the evolutionary testing and I wanted to drop by and see the progress you are making."

David laughed. "Well, to be completely honest, I'm not sure progress is a word I would use to characterize it. We were able to make a nice batch of bacteria soup yesterday in our first attempt."

"Ah, really. I wouldn't be too discouraged," Dr. Green started as he made his way up the stairs. "Your team has made incredible progress so far."

David nodded his head. "You know, you're right. I would never have guessed that things would come together so quickly. I wish all the projects were running so smoothly."

The two men chuckled as they reached the main door to the research lab. David opened the door and followed his boss in. As they walked in, the two were met by an armed security guard sitting behind a portable table.

The nightshift guard raised his head and began his modified script. "Okay guys, you know the drill. Everything out of your pockets and on the desk, and let's see some I.D."

The lab staff behind the main desk gasped as they realized

what was happening. A senior staff member ran to the security desk and began stammering. "I'm sorry gentlemen. Please forgive him, he's new here. These gentlemen are okay . . . I . . ."

Dr. Green smiled as he offered his pocket possessions. "No, no, that's quite alright. We don't want to be treated any different than anyone else.

The red-faced security officer quickly scanned the contents and motioned for them to pass. The two doctors signed in, attached their I.D. badges, and made their way into the main laboratory.

They methodically strolled through the maze of experiments that were scattered across the vast space. The two tried to categorize each of their projects and their ultimate potential as they passed them. David pointed out a few projects that had been producing good results, and Dr. Green made mental notes of them.

"So, what's the status on articles about the new life that you have created? We really should get some simple results out in the public arena." Dr. Green continued, "I would hate to see some other school steal our wind on this one."

David's thoughts went to Ramana. "Yeah, I think you're right. I'm counting on Ramana to put it together. I think he is in the best position to publish something. He . . . uh . . . well, he's been told, and hopefully he's working on it. I'll confirm a deadline with him today."

When they reached the stairs that led down to the realm of the beast, Dr. Green said, "Let me ask you this. Has Ramana had any more episodes?"

David smiled. "No, no more episodes. I don't think that was anything but the lack of sleep and excitement taking its toll on him. That's not to say that I'm exactly sure what's going on in his brain, though. He has shown some . . . let's say, concerns, for the current path that we are taking."

"I see. My only point is," Dr. Green explained, "I wonder if we should rely solely on him to publish an opinion."

"What do you have in mind?" David asked.

The two doctors made it to the basement and headed for the project lab.

"Well, I don't usually like to take this approach," Dr. Green started, "but I've talked to the science editor at CNN. He's an old friend. I've asked him if we could get a reporter to cover the story for a week or so . . . and . . ."

"Oh, I don't know about that, Wallace," David interrupted.

"I know, I know. It's not the first approach that I would like to take, but every day that goes by is an opportunity for another research team to stake out this type of work." Dr. Green stopped at the bottom of the stairs. "I don't think I have to tell you how important it is that we are the first on this."

They entered the computer room and turned on the lights. Dr Green could tell that the screen was still operating in 3-D mode, so he went straight for the glasses. David headed over to the conference table and set his things down without even looking at the undistinguishable screen. Dr. Green put on the glasses and turned to the screen.

"See David, how can I trust even you when you don't keep me up to date with the new milestones that you achieve?"

David turned around to see Dr. Green staring intently at the screen. "What are you talking about?"

"You didn't tell me about these," Dr. Green pointed to the screen.

David squinted his eyes as he tried to see what was on the screen. When he perceived movement, he quickly walked over to the box of glasses and put a pair on. He lifted his eyes and his jaw immediately dropped. "Oh my God!"

The screen packed full of bacteria, but not like the bacteria that they started with. These bacteria were swimming around the three-dimensional screen, darting back and forth, bumping into each other. Most of the bacteria had little tiny hairs on the outside of their membranes that were twitching back and forth.

David scanned the screen to try to take in all that was happening. He looked at the beast to try to gain some understanding, but it was not revealing anything.

"What's the matter, David?" Dr. Green asked. "Is something wrong?"

"Um . . . I don't know what's happened. Mark and Ramana were supposed to set up an evolutionary routine to run through the night. I don't remember Ramana saying anything about creating a new bacteria, but . . . I'm not sure."

Dr. Green looked back at the screen. "You mean this is the result of the evolutionary routine?"

"I'm not sure, Dr. Green. It's not how the results should be displayed. I mean, it should still be running, it shouldn't be stopped, but I don't know. I'll have to talk to Ramana and Mark."

Allison sat in her chair, tugging at some loose threads on her backpack when Ramana walked in to class. His face had an expression that she had not seen before. His shoulders were back in confidence and duty. His movements were slow and methodical. It was like he had seen the burning bush on Mount Horeb and had come down to fulfill a great mission. He set his materials on his desk and turned to Allison. The classroom was still noisy from students talking and finding their seats. When their eyes met, Allison was puzzled at the ever-widening smile that Ramana wore. He began walking over to her desk in what seemed like slow motion. Allison shifted in her seat to conceal the unpleasantness of the moment. When Ramana stood in front of her, he placed his hands on her desk and said nothing.

"What is it?" asked Allison.

Ramana hesitated, as he didn't know where to start. "The project . . . the beast . . . it changed. You must come with me over to the lab after class and see for yourself."

"What? It changed? What changed?" responded Allison.

"Just come with me, after class," Ramana said as he turned

back around and strutted back to the blackboard.

Ramana checked the clock. It now stood at the start of the hour. He cleared his throat and the noise in the classroom slowly disappeared.

"Good afternoon class. We will be finishing our study of the evolutionary process and the diversity of evolution today, and getting prepared to begin reviewing for the test on this section, which will be on Friday. Be sure that you have read chapters 29 through 34 by the beginning of next week. We will start a new section discussing the biology of plants and then quickly progress into the biology of animals."

"But before I go any further, I want to address a concern that a few students have brought to my attention. Some of you have mentioned that this course is tougher than you expected and are sitting at a lower grade than you think you deserve." Ramana looked around the classroom as students nodded their heads in assent.

"I will agree with you. This field of biology requires more thought and more studying than some of you are willing to give it. Beyond the formulae, the structures, beyond the memorization of data, there is the necessity of understanding the big picture of the amazing phenomenon called life. True knowledge requires knowing what is possible, what nature allows, and how natural laws govern life. It requires the ability to not only learn more and more about them, but to be able to formulate your own ideas and theories about life. This is where, I believe, the problem lies. Equally, this is where the solution lies.

"You must show me that you are willing and able to comprehend the big picture of life while using the established laws that govern life." The faces in the crowd were changing from agreement to confusion as Ramana continued speaking. "The last time that I gave you students a chance at extra credit . . . well, let's just say that it was not all I had hoped for. I am willing to give you another chance though.

"You have the rest of the semester to write another paper."

Ramana scowled as he heard the room deflate with a collective sigh. "What is wrong with you people?" Ramana asked rhetorically as his speech became more forceful. "If you want to improve your grade, you will write a paper. This paper is to be written from *your* thoughts, from *your* mind," he said as he pointed to his own head. "Push yourselves a little. Go sit out in a meadow or by a creek and ponder life for a while. Try to figure out a concept that no one else knows or sees and write about it. Develop a theory, an idea, or even propose a contrary idea to what science teaches. Go out on a limb for once!"

The crowd of students laughed at Ramana's fervor. But it was working. Each student began to think and wonder if they could discover some new concept. Heads began to move up and down in understanding and acceptance of their professor's words.

Ramana began to feel it too. He could see that maybe he was getting through to his students. "You will receive an unlimited amount of extra credit based on the paper that you write and the ideas that you generate. Most importantly, get out of your comfort zone and create something great, something beautiful."

Allison felt proud of Ramana as he finished. She brushed her arms as she felt the start of goose bumps. She decided that there was no way that she would sit this one out.

"Okay," Ramana said as he tried to change gears. "Let's review the section on evolution."

Mark sat at his console, trying to discover exactly what happened the night before. The day started abruptly for him; yanked out of bed by the early morning call from David, a two-hour meeting over this unexpected event, and the inability of any of the three to explain what had happened. It was not surprising to Mark, however, that he was given the task of trying to sort through the mountain of data and organize it in a way that maybe could make some sense. He shook his head as the odor of his unshowered body greeted his nostrils, and wondered about the dim prospects of resolving either matter.

He was the one who had set up the evolutionary routine after Ramana and Allison completed the diagnostics on the whole system. After all, Mark was the one who adjusted the E.P. to make the evolutionary routine even possible. After rechecking the system, he tried to decipher the output data that was generated from the routine in question. It made no sense to him. How could he tell if the results were valid? He had nothing to compare it to. As he scanned over the results, Ramana's concerns about damaging the E.P. were shooting through his mind. The data had to be wrong; the E.P. appeared to be out of control. Maybe they didn't find the problem that had caused the control spike the previous day.

Mark heard David re-enter the lab with their lunch and pushed his chair back from his terminal. He grabbed for his 3-D glasses and continued moving his chair until he had a good view of the busy creatures.

"Any luck?" asked David as he began dividing up the contents of the plastic bag.

Mark sat shaking his head. "Not really . . . too bad no one was here to watch it last night."

David frowned. "You mean we can't just rewind and replay it, like a tape recorder?"

Mark chuckled. "This is a little more complicated than a tape recorder. It's kinda like asking to go back in time."

"Well, have you been able to decipher any of the output data?" David lifted a sandwich to his mouth.

Mark unwrapped his lunch, unsure of how to answer the question. "A little . . . it doesn't really make sense. It seems that the E.P. was directing a lot of the changes."

David nodded his head while he was chewing. "That's what it's supposed to do, isn't it? I mean that's what you programmed it to do, right?"

"Well, yeah, I guess," Mark paused. "You know, this whole experiment is getting so complicated that it is hard to get my mind around it anymore. I'm not sure what I am looking for.

I mean the changes I made to the E.P.; I couldn't really tell you how they would affect all of the different programs. It's so big now, so fluid, that it really has a life of its own."

David smiled at his confession. "I love it. That's what I want to hear. We're never gonna get anywhere until we allow this experiment, this computer to live . . . to grow on its own."

"I guess you're right," Mark said. "Where do you think we go from here? Do you want to send these new creatures into the evolutionary routine?"

"Yes, eventually. Have you analyzed the new creatures DNA yet?" asked David.

Mark shook his head. "No, I think I will leave that up to Ramana. He'll know where to look and what to look for."

Chapter 15

"How can I write about it, David?" Ramana asked. "I don't even understand what happened."

"You don't have to make any conclusions. We just need to get something out there to mark our territory," said David. "I'm getting a lot of pressure from Green, and if we don't get something published soon, he's got his own ideas of publicity." David felt his message still wasn't getting through. "Okay Ramana, how do I make this clear? I'm ordering you to write an article documenting the set-up process and early results, and I'm giving you until the end of this week."

Ramana laughed guardedly. "Yes, General Levin . . . sir."

David gave a disapproving stare.

"Let me ask you then: how would you classify these early results?" asked Ramana.

David paused. "Well, I think we've found a process that may have isolated the vital factors that dictate life. It is very possible that we have keyed in to the very essence of life in this experiment."

"Which factors are those?" asked Ramana.

"It has to be in the environmental program. Somehow we must have boiled it down to the variables that really matter." David continued talking as he was thinking. "Were there any significant changes that Mark made when he configured it to run the evolutionary routine?"

"Well yes, in my opinion, quite significant," Ramana

answered. "But I think that its effect is nominal to what we've seen happen. I'm still not convinced that the whole evolution programming didn't corrupt the system–that the results are corrupted . . . or manufactured."

"What? Manufactured? You think somebody is playing around with the experiment?" David asked.

"It's just that I still find it hard to believe, with the intricacy and the . . . delicate nature of these programs, that these results are valid." Ramana finished his sentence and waited for David's anger.

"Okay," David started, "let me get this straight. You think that somebody is tampering with our results. You don't believe that these new creatures sitting in our computer are results of the evolutionary routine." David didn't get an answer. "Where did they come from? Who do you think created these things and stuck them in our computer?"

"Listen, David," Ramana said. He tried to remain calm and express his thoughts. "I've been working with these programs for going on three years now. It just doesn't make sense. The cilia programs that are on these new creatures are incredibly complex structures. They have numerous parts that need to be set in place all at once, with new instructions, new proteins. I would just like to examine the results more, give it more time before I reach a conclusion on what has happened. We need more trial runs attempting the same thing before I can be certain this was a completely natural process."

"Ramana, you are treading in deep water if you want to start accusing people of tampering with the results." David continued, "In my mind, there are only two options. Either the results are as you put it, a natural process, or one of our research assistants is trying to fix this experiment. But tell me, why would somebody want to mess with these results? How would it help them?"

Ramana scanned over all of the participants in his mind. "You really can't tell what people will do, for whatever reason.

But you're right; I don't want to start accusing anybody on this team."

"On the other hand," David started, "it probably is a good idea to take inventory of who we have working with us and our security procedures. We could eliminate some people from even suspicion . . . like Mark . . . don't you think?"

"Absolutely. I have complete confidence in Mark's integrity," answered Ramana.

"That only leaves the programmers and the maintenance team–well, and Allison. She's now working on the computer, isn't she?" David observed.

Ramana smiled. "I don't think we have anything to worry about her."

"Why do you say that?"

"Well, just between you and me, she doesn't necessarily believe in that part of the experiment," said Ramana.

"What do you mean, Ramana?"

"Again, this is between you and me. She is a, well, somewhat of a religious person, and believes in . . . um, the creation story, you know, in the Bible." Ramana felt his voice crack as he said the sentence.

"What!" yelled David.

Ramana was surprised with his reaction.

"Then what the hell is she doing on my research team? You have got to be kidding me! You are worried about the integrity of this experiment and you put some . . . some . . . nut in a position of leadership. What were you thinking? Oh man, that's just great," David said as he angrily ran his fingers through his hair.

"Hold on David, that's not fair," Ramana shot back. "She is the best research assistant I've ever worked with. She is dedicated. She is a great student . . ."

David interrupted, "And one good-looking co-ed, but I'm sure that had nothing to do with it either." He looked back at Ramana. "What else is she good at?"

Ramana stood motionless and speechless. He glared at David for the suggestion.

"I can't believe this. I just can't trust your judgment anymore. Maybe Dr. Green is right. Maybe we need an outside source to cover this story." David held his hands up in the air and began to walk out of the research lab. "I'm not sure that a paper from you would help this situation."

As David approached the door, he was startled when it began to open. Allison peeked around the door and walked into the room. "Hi Dr. Levin," she said.

"Oh, hi sunshine," David said coldly. "How's everything in your world?"

Allison got out of David's way and he walked out of the room. "I'll leave you two alone." David looked back and gave Ramana a cold wink.

Ramana looked down in disgust and embarrassment, and then slowly raised his eyes to meet Allison's.

"What was that all about?" she asked.

He couldn't think of anything to say as he headed for the conference table. He pulled out a chair and dropped into it.

Allison followed him, wondering why there was no answer until she saw that the screen was in 3-D mode. She grabbed for a set of glasses on the table and put them on.

"Oh my," she started, "what are these guys? Look at all of them." She smiled as the new bacteria darted around the E.P. "So this is what you were talking about. When did you put these together?"

"That's just it. No one put these together. They were just here this morning when we got here."

"You're kidding," she started. "How did they. .?"

Ramana interrupted, "That's what we are trying to figure out."

Allison tilted her head as she tried to understand. "They were just *here* this morning?"

"Yes," replied Ramana.

"Somebody had to put them in there, unless your evolutionary routine actually worked. Do you think the evolutionary routine worked?" asked Allison.

Ramana frowned. "It isn't my evolutionary routine, and anyway, it is very possible that they are the result of the routine."

"What do you mean, very possible," Allison smiled. "You don't think that's what happened, do you?"

Ramana tried to understand what she meant. "I am not sure what to believe yet. I haven't processed all of the data yet, but I believe that it is possible, yes."

Allison's attention went back to the swirling action on the screen. She followed the bacteria around the E.P., trying to see what they were doing.

"They're so cute!" she giggled. "Where are the Kirk cells?"

Ramana's head popped up as he grabbed for a pair of glasses. He walked towards the screen, staring intently. "There's one, the alpha cell."

Allison moved to the side that Ramana was on. "Okay, there's one. Where's the omega cell?"

They tilted their heads and moved to different spots in the room trying to locate the omega cell, but could not.

"I guess we didn't even think of that earlier. We were so concerned with the new cells. Let me check my terminal." Ramana took his glasses off and made his way to the keyboard.

As Ramana worked to locate the omega cell, Allison continued staring at the screen. "This is amazing. These cells look alive. They look real."

Ramana didn't hear her. He was concentrating on what his terminal was showing. "How did it get there?"

Allison faintly heard the question and moved closer to Ramana. "What?"

"Kirk . . . the omega cell is in the work area," Ramana said louder. "What is it doing there?"

"He's in the work area? That can't happen, can it?" she asked.

"Well, no, it couldn't happen," answered Ramana. "The work area is partitioned off . . . securely partitioned off. It could not just move into the work area. In fact, the Kirk cell can't move. Maybe Mark put Kirk in the work area, but I can't think of any reason why he would."

Allison walked over to Ramana's terminal and looked over his shoulder. "Is the omega cell still functioning normally?"

Ramana was busy hitting some buttons. "I can't tell. I'm gonna go ahead and move him back to the E.P. and see what happens. By the way, you haven't been doing anything to the computers, or seen anybody do anything out of the ordinary?"

Allison began to walk back to view the 3-D screen. "I haven't touched the computers since the first mitosis. And no, I haven't seen anybody doing anything weird with it. Why? What's going on?"

Ramana hesitated. "Well, we just want to make sure that everything that has happened is . . . real, you know, that no one is tampering with things."

"Oh, no, I haven't seen anybody tampering with anything, not that I would be able to tell." She continued looking at the screen. "There he is. He's back in the E.P. How does he check out?"

Ramana stared at his monitor. "He looks all right. Something is different with him, though. He looks different than the alpha cell, doesn't he?"

Allison studied the two cells. "Yeah, I guess . . . kind of. Maybe a little bit bigger and some discoloration there. What do you think that means?"

Ramana shook his head. "I don't know. It could mean anything."

Allison stepped back from the screen. "Man, the screen is full. That's gotta take up a lot of memory. What are you gonna do with all of these new cells?"

"That's a good question," Ramana answered. "We haven't got that far yet. We are still trying to figure out how they got here, but I'm sure David's gonna want to send these guys through the evolutionary routine."

"Have you looked at their DNA yet?" Allison asked.

"Not yet," he replied, "but that's the next step. Have you got some time? We could check it out now."

"Sure, let's do it," she said.

"Okay then, pick one out for me." Ramana sat down in his terminal chair.

Allison began looking around the screen. "That one, on the left."

Ramana couldn't distinguish which one she was talking about and began moving a cursor on the 3-D screen. "This one?"

"Yeah, that'll do," she replied.

"Okay, first let's grab him, and then we'll move him to the work area." Ramana reached behind his monitor. He pulled out a multi-levered joystick device and began to use it to manipulate the cell.

"What's that?" she asked.

"Mark just set it up to better manipulate the individual cells. I haven't used it much yet, so I'm not exactly sure how everything works," Ramana admitted. The cell was isolated and began to move towards the back of the screen. When it reached the back, Ramana hit a function button on his keyboard and a small hole opened up, which he directed the chosen cell through.

"Where did it go? I can't see," Allison complained. "Can you put the work area on the 3-D screen?"

"Sure," Ramana replied and hit a few buttons on his keyboard.

"Okay, welcome to the operating room."

"Alright," she said as she took a seat. "Is this where you put together Kirk?"

"Yes." Ramana stared intently into his monitor. "Okay, are

you ready Allison? This could get messy."

"I'm ready," she replied.

In front of Allison was a huge three-dimensional bacterium. Its hairy cilia on the outside of its membrane flickered and twitched as it tried to get away from the vice-like grip of its captor. "I guess this one's going to have to be sacrificed in the name of science," Ramana said jokingly.

The cursor on the screen now changed from a grabbing hand to what looked like a scalpel. Allison's eyes widened as she realized what was about to happen. The scalpel moved toward the top of the cell. Ramana pushed the joystick forward until it appeared to be resting on the surface of the membrane. He depressed the trigger and moved the joystick back slightly, and the membrane began to open. The yellowish contents of the cell began to spill out into the room.

"Yuk!" gagged Allison.

Ramana didn't stop to respond. He continued to slice the cell open more than half way around the sphere. The cilia at first moved wildly, began to twitch, then slowly came to a halt. The scalpel then changed into what looked like tweezers as Ramana hit another button.

"Okay, we're going in to remove the nucleiod," Ramana announced as he entered the dying cell. The screen followed the tweezers into the cell through the cytoplasm until the nucleus was in view. Once he grabbed the nucleus, Ramana began to move it forward until they exited through the initial incision. The nucleus was spherical and held what looked like a bundle of dark material.

"Now let's clean up some of this mess," Ramana said. He pressed a button that turned his tweezers into what looked like a round cylinder. He moved the cylinder around the screen, and anything in its path was immediately sucked into it. He worked until all that remained was the nucleus.

"You are quite a surgeon," Allison observed, smiling at the realism of the operation.

Ramana smiled. "This works very well. Mark did a great job as usual."

Again, Ramana used the scalpel to open up the nucleus. He peeled the nuclear membrane from around the genetic material and discarded it to the side. With his tweezers, he started to unravel the blob of material and laid the chromosomes side by side. Allison sat speechlessly as she watched this operation that few had ever been witness to. Twenty minutes passed before Ramana had all of the chromosomes neatly arranged on the screen. As he started to clean up the mess again, Allison got up to stretch her legs and said, "Hey, I'm going to get something to drink. Can I get you something?"

Ramana paused and bent his neck back to stretch his muscles. "Yes, please, a Dr. Pepper."

Allison walked down the hall and headed for the stairs. Her head was light and slightly spinning from the intense surgery that she had witnessed. She felt queasy and wondered how she was going to make it as a doctor if she couldn't even handle a virtual operation. As she walked into the snack room, she was startled to see David finishing a sandwich and organizing paperwork. "Hi again, Dr. Levin," she said.

David turned toward Allison and nodded his head.

Allison looked at him and said, "We've been dissecting one of the new cells and examining the DNA." There was no response. "It's incredible . . . the controls that Mark put together seem to work great . . . I was just getting a drink for us."

David said nothing and watched Allison. His face seemed to be set in stone.

Allison turned to the Coke machine, happy to turn away from the uncomfortable situation. She tried to look involved and over exaggerated her motions in choosing a soft drink. She then was self-conscious of her movements and felt David's eyes all over her. She hit one of the buttons just to get through it, then bent over to grab the drinks and was able to steal a look behind her. Her body shuddered as she saw David's eyes still staring at her, his eyes shifting from her frame to directly into her eyes. She jerked upward to hide the surprise and paused for a moment. As she turned around, she felt that her face was blushing and said, "Well Dr. Levin, I guess I'll see you later."

Her head quickly turned as she began to walk out, but the unchanging expression on David's face was stuck in her mind. Her steps were uneven as she walked back to the computer lab. She shook her head as she tried to figure out what his problem was and why it had affected her so much. She tried to relax and regain her composure with each step. She was back to normal as she opened the door to the lab.

Ramana was finished arranging the chromosomes and was walking around the lab when Allison returned. He took the drink from Allison and they sat down at the conference table for a good view of the genetic material.

"It doesn't look like a double-helix," Allison said.

Ramana laughed. "We would have to magnify it to the atomic level to see that."

"Can you do that?" she asked.

"Sure," answered Ramana as he got up and walked back over to his terminal. He moved his mouse and hit his keyboard and the screen began to change. The screen isolated one chromosome strand and magnified it. It revealed a mass of the famous double helix form, which looked like a twisted ladder, wrapped around itself like a spool of yarn.

Allison shook her head. "Look at all that information. How did you put together all of that?"

"Well, most of it was put together by a construction routine that built it to our specifications. We didn't attach every protein together. That would take a lifetime . . . a hundred lifetimes," Ramana explained.

Allison took a drink and wondered if she should go this direction. "See, that's what I have a problem with. How did all of that information get organized in nature if somebody wasn't there to build it?"

Ramana smiled. "I guess everybody has their opinion on that question."

Allison again wondered if she should keep going. "I don't know, Ramana. That's just it. Most people don't have an opinion about it. Most people don't even think they can understand it; they just wait for somebody to explain it to them."

"It is a very complicated matter," said Ramana.

Allison nodded her head. "Some of it is . . . not this. The question whether information . . . this DNA code could just build itself . . . it's a simple question."

"A simple question, huh?" Ramana chuckled. "Then why don't you try to answer it for extra credit?"

"I will . . . I mean I'm gonna try . . . something," answered Allison. "I haven't figured out what yet. But I need something to bring up my average to an A. I'm gonna do something great . . . something beautiful." She laughed.

"Do you think I went a little overboard when I assigned that?" asked Ramana.

"No way. You were great. I was totally inspired," she said.

"By the way," she continued, "I saw Dr Levin in the snack room and he was acting weird. He didn't say a word to me. I felt like . . . I don't know . . . it was just weird."

Ramana looked down to try to hide his embarrassment. "Um, there is something I probably should tell you."

"What?" she asked.

"I'm sorry," Ramana started, "I probably shouldn't have said anything, but we were discussing the research team and I told him about you and your beliefs . . . you know, that creation thing."

"Oh." Allison lifted her head as she reacted. "I guess that explains it. What did he say?"

Ramana paused as he thought about how much information he wanted to divulge. "Well, he was sort of mad at me. He didn't understand why I would put someone like you on a project that is experimenting with evolution."

"What did you tell him?" she asked.

"I didn't really tell him anything . . . Allison, I'm sorry. I shouldn't have told anybody about it. It's nobody's business."

"Don't worry about it." Allison squinted her eyes in frustration. "I'm a big girl. I'm sure I can handle it. What gets me is him being mad at you. That makes me mad . . . I mean, does he want me to leave the project, or what?" She began to build up steam. "Whatever! He just stared at me with that patronizing look . . . geez . . . I . . . I should . . ."

Ramana panicked and tried to figure out how to put out the fire that slowly began to build. "Allison . . . Allison, please. Forgive me. I don't think it should cause any problems . . . don't worry about David, he's not going to do anything. He doesn't want you off of the project." He reached out his hands and grabbed hers. "I don't want you off the project."

Allison looked down at their clasped hands as thoughts were streaking through her mind. Ramana was unsure about the move, but it seemed to calm her down. He now tried to figure out how long he should hold them. They sat silently together until they heard the door of the lab close, and the two automatically jerked away from each other. They turned to face the door and the stranger that now stood in the computer lab, unsure if he had noticed their previous position.

Ramana wore a pinched look on his face as he stood up and walked toward the man. "Can I help you, sir? This area is restricted you know."

The man looked around the room, back at Ramana, then down at a note in his hand. "Uh, yes, I am looking for David Levin or um . . . Rrraammaaani Puuunjabba."

Allison couldn't help but chuckle at the man's pronunciation.

"That's Ramana Punjabi," he corrected. "I am he. Dr. Levin is not here at the moment. What is it that you need?"

The man walked towards Ramana with his hand outstretched. "My name is Arthur Lewis," he started, reading off the note in his hand. "I was sent her by request of Dr. Wallace Green. I am a science and technology writer."

"Uh-huh," responded Ramana, slightly nodding his head.

"I was sent to gather some information for publication on the project that you have going on here," he added.

"Publication? Where?" Ramana asked.

"Freelance really," said Arthur, using his hands. "But I mainly write for USA Today and CNN."

"I was unaware that those were science publications," observed Ramana.

"Touché," the sly reporter answered. "And who may I ask is your young lady friend?" He began walking toward Allison.

"Just a minute," Ramana tried to stop the man to no avail. "Sir?"

"Arthur Lewis, pleased to meet you," he said as he reached for Allison's hand.

"Allison Wilson, likewise," she said as her smile gleamed.

"Mr. Lewis," Ramana said louder.

The reporter swung back around with a smile, already writing on a notepad that he pulled out of his pocket. "Please, call me Arthur."

Ramana looked down at the notepad, watching him scribble. "Now tell me again exactly what Dr. Green wants you to do, Arthur?"

Arthur finished his scribbling and said, "Well, I just got the assignment from my editor. I didn't actually talk to Dr. Green, but my understanding is that you guys have some pretty significant work going on in here and the department wants people to know about it."

"I see." Ramana brought his hand to his chin. "Let me tell you, first of all, I am very uncomfortable with a reporter having access to this facility. I will need to talk to Dr. Levin and Dr. Green before you . . . by the way, how did you get past the security desk?" Ramana stared at the "all access" badge that he wore. "Where did you get that?"

"Oh, I picked it up at the front desk; it was waiting for me," he answered. "And Mr. Punjaba, I understand your concern. Believe me, I know that there are a lot of bad reporters out there. I am here to get the facts and report them in a non-biased, even-handed fashion. That's why I left the political desk. I wanted to get away from that Enquirer type stuff, and get to the stuff that really matters–you know science, medicine, and technology."

Ramana was unimpressed by his defense, and he immediately was sorry that he didn't have anything to publish. He knew that he would now be in a race with this hired gun.

The reporter's attention was now turned to the lab. "Take a look at this place. This is really incredible. Why's that screen look all fuzzy? Something wrong?"

Allison held out a pair of glasses. "You gotta use these."

Ramana gave her a disapproving stare for helping him.

"Oh wow!" Arthur said as he tried to get the best view. "A 3-D show. What is that stuff? It looks like a bunch of wires bundled up."

The room stayed silent.

"Is it some sort of new fiber, or one of those Ebola or Anthrax viruses or something?" he asked.

Ramana closed his eyes in disgust. "It's genetic material, highly magnified."

"You mean like DNA and genes? Wow, that's great. What are you doing with it?" he continued the interrogation.

Ramana crossed his arms. "Listen Arthur, I don't have time to sit here and answer all of your questions. I would appreciate it if you would leave us alone for the moment. We have work to do. Once I have talked to David, then we can talk about giving access to this room. For now, however, I must ask you to leave."

"What?" Arthur turned to look at Ramana with his glasses

still hanging from his face and mouth open. "No . . . No, I won't bother you. I'll just sit over here and . . . and you won't even know I'm here. I . . . I . . ."

"You . . . you will be leaving now," Ramana trumped as he pointed to the door.

Arthur looked down at his badge then quickly decided that he had better play along. "Okay, okay, I am here to play by your rules. Here is my card . . . that's my cell number. Let me know what you decide. I guess I'll go and gather up some historical information on the university." He gave the glasses back to Allison. "Very nice to have met you, Miss Wilson."

Allison nodded her head.

"Thank you for your time Mr. Punjaba . . . sir," he offered as he began to walk toward the door.

Chapter 16

Allison sat at Rachel's computer, staring at the blank document in front of her. Her mind was thinking about everything except the paper that she wanted to write. She leaned back in her chair and turned her attention to the pictures on her dresser: the family picture, the picture of her on her horse, her grandmother. All of them comforted Allison as she gazed at them. Her eyes went back to the books and papers scattered over her desk. She began to organize the clutter until everything had its place, another activity to keep from the project at hand. When she finished, her eyes noticed the two books on either side of the computer. On the right was her Bible; on the left was her open biology text. She shook her head and smiled as she pondered their relationship, if there was one.

She opened her Bible, and the pages opened to the letter that Paul wrote to the Romans. Her eyes started to scan the greetings and introduction of the missionary in the first chapter. She began to read closely at verse 16:

> "I am not ashamed of the Good News, for it is the power of God for the salvation of everyone who believes: first for the Jew, then for the Gentile."

Her head nodded as she gained strength from Paul's declaration. She read on:

> "The wrath of God is being revealed from heaven against all the godlessness and wickedness of

men who suppress the truth by their wickedness,
since what may be known about God is plain to
them, because God made it plain to them."

Allison's attention was grabbed as she felt the power of the scriptures closing in on her:
"For since the creation of the world, God's
invisible qualities-his eternal power and divine
nature-have been clearly seen, being understood
from what has been made, so that men are without
excuse."

She looked at the computer screen in amazement. She felt that God was speaking to her at that very moment. She felt the hair on her neck rise as the chill of the experience affected her physically:
"For although they knew God, they neither
glorified him as God nor gave thanks to him,
but their thinking became futile and their
foolish hearts were darkened. Although they
claimed to be wise, they became fools and
exchanged the glory of the immortal God for
images made to look like mortal man and birds
and reptiles."

Was this confirmation of the task before her, or was it just coincidence that these words were speaking to her soul?
"They exchanged the truth of God for a lie,
and worshiped and served created things rather
than the Creator . . ."

Allison closed her eyes and silently mouthed, "Oh my God." Her pulse raced as if she had just worked out. "The answer has to be here somewhere. I just have to find it."

"Where should I start?" she wondered. Her thoughts went

back to Ramana's explanation of the assignment. Her lips moved as she mouthed the words, "Something great, something beautiful . . . go sit and ponder nature." She smiled as she began to figure out a strategy. "He's right, I've gotta get out of here."

She heard someone walking towards her room and recognized Rachel's voice as she got closer. Allison turned back to the computer and began to close the blank document on the computer as Rachel walked in.

"Hey Rache," said Allison as she heard the slightly open door move.

"Hi," she replied in a somber tone.

Allison turned around to see Rachel still in her sunglasses. "What's wrong?"

"Oh nothing," Rachel answered with a sob.

"What is it? What happened?" Allison pursued further.

Rachel sat on her bed and slowly took off her sunglasses and rubbed her eyes.

"You've been crying." Allison sprung into action and moved to Rachel's bed.

Rachel's stare went to the floor as Allison's arm went around her back.

Allison's mind raced as she tried to imagine what happened to her friend. "Rachel, it's okay. Tell me what happened."

Rachel's sobbing became more evident. "Why are people so mean?"

"Who was mean to you?" Allison asked as she grabbed a box of tissue.

Rachel took a tissue and brought it to her face. "Oh, just my soul mate."

Allison shook her head. "What did he do? Did you guys break up?"

"I don't care if I never see him again," Rachel sobbed.

Allison tried again. "What happened?"

Rachel lifted her head and looked at Allison. "I caught him, with another girl . . . at his house . . . in his bed! After everything he told me, everything I've done for him, he . . . he . . . oh Allison, why would he do something like that?"

Allison was not surprised but didn't think that was a good direction to go. "Who knows? Rachel, I'm so sorry." Allison brought her other arm in front of Rachel and hugged her. Rachel's head moved toward Allison's shoulder and found rest there. Allison's hand moved up to Rachel's head as she stroked her hair. Rachel continued to cry as Allison kept her position of comfort around her.

After about five minutes of sobbing, Rachel straightened up and let Allison go back to her own bed.

"I'm a mess," Rachel decided.

"No you're not, Rachel. You're gonna be just fine," Allison told her. "It's just awful what you've gone through, but I promise you're gonna be fine."

Rachel fell back on her bed. "I don't know. I feel like doing something drastic. I feel like screaming . . . I feel like killing him!"

Allison got an idea. "Hey, how about getting out of here? Let's go out to the lake or maybe the greenbelt. It's a beautiful day. The leaves are just starting to come out . . ."

Rachel groaned, "I don't know about that. This is major, Allison. I just feel like lying right here and crying."

"I know, but it'll get your mind off him," she tried. "Anyway, I've got to get out there–or somewhere–and contemplate creation."

Rachel lifted her head slightly from her pillow. "What?"

Allison smiled. "Oh, I've kinda got myself into a jam and have got to figure a way out."

Rachel sniffed, "What did *you* do?"

"I'm kind of embarrassed about it," she started, "but I guess I can tell you. I told my biology teacher that I was going to write an extra credit paper that tries to disprove the theory of evolution."

Rachel chuckled through her tears. "Oh, that's all?"

Allison smiled as her dilemma seemed to lift Rachel's spirits. "Yeah, can you believe it?"

Rachel's head hit the pillow again. "Why would you want to expose yourself to the embarrassment?"

"Well, hopefully I don't have to read it in class or anything," said Allison. "I guess I'm just tired of people telling me that God didn't create this world."

Rachel thought about the offer. "I'm sorry, Allison. I can't go. I feel like part of me was just ripped out. I need to sulk."

Allison knew it was a long shot. "I'll stay here with you if you need me."

"No seriously, go ahead. I'm gonna stay here and try to figure out what to do. I think I need to be alone anyway."

Both girls were startled as the phone rang. Rachel sat up in bed and yelled, "Don't answer it!"

Allison replied, "What if it's for me? If it's John, I'll tell him that you're not here."

Rachel reluctantly nodded her head and Allison picked up the phone.

"Hello," she said looking at Rachel. "Hi Dad."

Rachel lied back on her bed.

"Well, I'm trying to write a paper for my biology class and I was just about to drive out to the lake. How are you guys?

"Yes, I'm still coming home for Easter. We've got a party on Friday, though. I'm driving back early Saturday morning.

"No, it's definitely not an Easter party."

"Sure, I've got some time. David told me that a reporter would be arriving. Come on in," Mark said as he showed Arthur into the deserted project room. "We're kind of at a stand-still at the moment. We're not too sure how to proceed yet with these new bacteria that appeared."

Arthur nodded his head like he understood and followed the scientist in the room. "I see."

"Okay, this is the computer over here." They walked

toward the computer. "You see in that window there, that's a silicon gel core used for the memory, instead of a hard drive. It's a technology developed right here. In fact, it's the only one of its kind–very experimental."

"Really?" said the reporter.

"We have turned that silicon core into a working environment with virtually all of the variables that you would find in a real environment."

"Interesting. An environment for what?" Arthur asked.

"Anything, I guess. I guess it kind of like a Petri dish that you grow bacteria in. And that's what we've gotten so far, bacteria," Mark explained.

"So where are they? The bacteria," asked Arthur.

"Well, you have to put these on," Mark said as he handed a pair of glasses to him. "And let me switch the screen to the E.P."

Arthur stepped back and put his glasses on as the screen revealed its many teeming inhabitants.

"Wow, that's pretty impressive. So you've made virtual bacteria," observed Arthur. "Why?"

Mark chuckled. "Well, we made a form of bacteria, so we could probably make any single-cell or even multi-cellular organism."

"So it's a bacteria program, like computer code?" asked Arthur.

"Actually, each of those cells that you see is actually thousands of programs, each one mimicking a real protein or compound that exists in nature," Mark started. "Already, this experiment has allowed us to witness and analyze some processes that are seldom seen. It really has unlimited possibilities."

"So you made all of these bacterium?" said Arthur incorrectly.

"Not all of the bacteria. We have created the two cells marked with the alpha and the omega. See there and . . . there. And actually, we only created one of those. All of the rest were formed by mitosis." Mark began to realize that the reporter didn't fully comprehend everything that was being said. "That's when one cell splits to make two cells. Notice that these original cells do not have the capability of movement. All of the others are a product of what we call the evolutionary routine."

"The evolutionary routine?" Arthur repeated. "So what does that do?"

Mark paused as he thought. "Well, you've heard of evolution, right?"

Arthur nodded his head. "Of course."

"We are experimenting with a macro-routine that recreates the process of evolution." Mark's attention went back to the screen. "We can take an organism and send it into the future . . . thousands of generations. Then analyze the changes . . . how the changes came about . . . and hopefully get some idea of how we've changed."

Arthur's eyes finally sparked with insight. "Oh, I get it." His head started nodding. "That's really something . . . so you got it to work . . . the first bacteria changed into these that are swimming around."

"That's what we are trying to determine," said Mark.

David and Ramana got to the bottom of the stairs of the lab and headed for the project room.

"You seriously don't think that it is a problem to have a reporter hanging over our shoulder?" asked Ramana.

David tried to hide an accusatory tone. "Ramana, what do you want me to do? Green wants something released now. Do you have anything to release now?"

David pushed the door open and they walked into the project room. Ramana's eyes widened and his body became tense when he saw Mark standing in front of the screen, obviously explaining the project to Arthur.

"What are you doing, Mark?" blurted out of his mouth.

The two twirled around in surprise, and Ramana retreated to a less threatening posture.

"What is your problem?" David whispered as he left Ramana and walked toward the two men.

"Arthur Lewis, I presume," David greeted the reporter.

"Dr Levin?" Arthur extended his hand.

"I see Mark is giving you a tour of the place." David looked around the room.

"Yes, he's been extremely helpful." Arthur's eyes turned to Ramana and then back to David. "I am very impressed with what you have going on here. From what Mark has told me so far, I think you have quite a significant experiment assembled."

"Thank you." David couldn't help but smile. "I assume that you have met the man most responsible for its success." David turned his attention back to Ramana.

David's words caught Ramana off-guard. The three Anglos looked back at the strange look on the Indian's face.

They all stared back at Ramana in silence until the reporter spoke up. "Uh yes, we've met." Arthur paused as he practiced Ramana's name in his head. "Hello, Dr. Punjabi."

Mark started to raise his hand in response.

Ramana chuckled. "Yes we . . . I mean hello . . . I'm not a . . . uh."

David quickly turned to Arthur as the situation grew more uncomfortable.

The reporter wondered if he butchered the man's name again and interrupted Ramana's explanation. "I'm sorry, I have to apologize . . . I . . . we got off on the wrong foot yesterday."

Ramana stood wondering why he felt like he now had to apologize also. "That's okay," came out of his mouth as he approached the three. "By the way, you can call me Ramana."

Arthur's lips moved as he tried to memorize the pronunciation by repeating it in his mind.

"Anyway," David shook his head in confusion.

"Anyway," Arthur interrupted, "Mark was just explaining things to me. I'm a little lost with some of the biology . . . it's been a little while since I studied it. But I think I understand now what you guys are doing, at least in part."

"Great," said David as he looked at Ramana. "I hope you can understand that having a reporter around in this type of environment is unusual and will make it harder to accomplish our work."

Ramana slightly smiled at David's direction.

"Therefore," David continued, "we will need to restrict your access to this facility to only a couple hours a day."

"But . . ." Arthur tried to interrupt.

David started again as he raised a finger. "I have worked with many reporters, and truthfully, most have not done their work accurately or in a courteous fashion. I am hoping that you will be an exception to that rule."

Arthur gathered himself. "Dr. Levin, let me say that I completely respect your opinion. I will do my best to communicate your work accurately and stay out of your way. But I must say that *my* work will be much harder with those kinds of restrictions."

The three scientists nodded their head in agreement with the reporter. David added, "Well then, I hope you're not afraid of a little hard work."

Mark and Ramana smiled at David's remark as Arthur began to rethink his assignment.

"By the way, Arthur," David said, "we are having a party on Friday. The biology department is trying to show its appreciation to all of its contributors, and faculty, assistants, and so on. Why don't you come along? It should be quite a time. You might even get some of us to open up a little."

Arthur's face lit up to the offer. "Sure, that sounds great. What, is it formal?"

"Uh, I'd wear a jacket," David explained. "But it's not black tie or anything. There'll be food, live music, and a cash bar–that kind of stuff. Ramana, remind me to put Arthur on the guest list."

Ramana nodded his head.

"Now, however," David started, "I would appreciate it you would leave us alone. The three of us need to discuss some things." David looked at Mark and Ramana. "And I'm not sure that we'll want you eavesdropping. We will fill you in on how things proceed and when you can access the lab. It was nice meeting you." David extended his hand to signal the end of the meeting.

Arthur's shoulders deflated. "Kicked out once again." He shook David's hand then the other two. "This is almost as tough as Congress." Arthur turned and slowly walked out of the lab, whistling a tune of his own design.

Chapter 17

"What do you think about this one?" Allison asked as she held a black dress in front of her.

"Looks good. It's pretty sexy," answered Rachel. "You'd sure get those professors all excited."

"Oh God! What am I gonna do? You really need to go with me, Rachel," Allison pleaded with her friend. "Come on, you'd have fun."

Rachel laughed. "Oh yeah, a biology party–sounds like a blast. What are you guys gonna do, dissect some cats?"

"Gross! Stop it," Allison said and laughed.

"Are you gonna bring a date?" asked Rachel.

Allison shrugged. "I don't know. It's a little too late, and I'm not even sure who I would ask."

A sarcastic smile came over Rachel's face. "Why don't you go with that freaky biology teacher of yours? He's already asked you out once."

"Rachel, stop." Allison shot her an ugly look. "That would be perfect, wouldn't it? Me with a Muslim, and him with his student. Eeeeeep!" She shuddered at the thought.

"Then just go by yourself; you'll be the hottest thing there," Rachel said. "Hey, take my car. I won't need it tomorrow. And wear that black one. You'll blow them away."

Allison rolled her eyes. "I'm not sure that's exactly what I want to do."

"Sure you do," Rachel argued. "It automatically gives you

an edge over them. Use it to your advantage, girl."

Allison remained silent as she looked at herself in the mirror, the black dress draped over her body.

"Trust me, beauty reigns supreme," Rachel declared. "No one can resist the power of it."

A spark of insight came over Allison's face. "Beauty, huh?"

"Beauty's the bomb," Rachel said confidently.

Allison slowly nodded her head as the idea began to grow. "I think you may be on to something."

Ramana sat at his terminal studying the DNA that he had extracted from one of the new bacteria. The code was literally miles long. Without the help of a computer analysis, he would be sitting there well into the next millennium. He was still in the work area of the computer analyzing what went on in the E.P. He stared at the message on the screen one more time: *No changes found, would you like to continue?*

Ramana clicked yes and the computer began another analysis on a different part of the DNA chain. Ramana watched in disbelief. "Where is the code that changed your membrane?" He knew that, in nature, there was no rhyme or reason to where specific DNA sequences were kept. No one had discovered its unique filing system, so he went straight down the line and took a piece at a time to compare it to the original sequence.

David quietly walked into the project room and dropped his things on the conference table as he studied his PDA. He heard a long sigh from Ramana. "Still nothing?"

"I don't understand it, David," said Ramana. "It's like somebody just stuck those cilia on their membrane without changing their DNA. If I can't find any changes in the DNA, I think it will be pretty evident that the results are invalid, and that maybe somebody is screwing around with us."

"Hold on there," David interjected. "I wouldn't be so sure about that. We need to play around with these guys a little more, put them through mitosis, and maybe send them through the evolution routine. It could be part of the process that we just don't see yet."

"Maybe," Ramana conceded, "but I've been through this DNA about three times, and still no changes found. You can't tell me that an organism can change its physical characteristics without changing its DNA first."

"I'm not telling you anything. We'll leave that to your little friends there." David pulled a paper and placed to the side. "Maybe the physical changes do precede the DNA changes. What's the problem with that? Maybe you should be analyzing the membrane and cilia programs."

Ramana squinted his eyes as he tried to process David's words. "Well, I guess I need to do that, but I just think that it is illogical for it to happen that way. To tell you the truth, after working with these things, I don't see how any changes except maybe degeneration could happen."

David shook his head. He silently laughed as he thought about his assistant. "Sounds like your letting Allison get to you."

"What?" Ramana barked.

"Well, I'm sure that's how she would explain things," said David. "She probably thinks her little God came down and made the changes to the bacteria."

Ramana tried to contain his emotions. "You haven't said anything to her about that, have you?"

"No," answered David, "but that doesn't mean that I won't. If she believes strongly in it, nothing I say will change that. I'm still not sure that I want her on this team."

"I don't think we have to make any drastic moves," Ramana began. "Anyway, after this semester she probably is off to medical school."

"You're kidding! What is she going to specialize in, faith healing?" David chuckled.

Ramana turned in amazement. "David, I would think that you could at least understand her point of view–I mean, with your background and everything."

"What is that supposed to mean?" David asked.

Ramana hesitated. "You are Jewish, aren't you?"

David was amazed at his blunt question and couldn't answer.

"I mean I don't want to get too personal," Ramana started, "but you had to be exposed to some of those beliefs as a kid."

"Listen Ramana," David said as a stern look came upon his face. "I was brought up with a bunch of that crap. I've seen first hand what it does to people. It closes their minds to reality. It makes them propaganda-spewing zombies. I mean, it's like they're all reading from the same script."

Ramana listened intently to David's first words about this subject. "If you don't mind me asking, what was it that made you reject a religious faith?"

David moved back in his chair in surprise.

Ramana saw his reaction. "I mean, you don't have to tell me if you don't want to."

"No, I don't have a problem with it," David explained as the realization made him contemplate his youth, "although my father has a big problem with it." David chuckled as he quickly reflected over his past. "My father is a simple man who let his whole life be dictated by myths and superstitions. From as far back as I can remember, we didn't agree on much, and you know how rebellious and ugly you can be as a kid. By the time I left for Texas, we didn't really even talk that much anymore."

Ramana listened intently to his confession.

David smiled as his hand scratched his face. He thoughtfully paused as he reflected over the many years.

"I just saw from an early age that it was all just a big show," David continued. "Then, I guess I was about sixteen, I remember reading a bunch of books by people like Ayn Rand, Jay Gould, and others like that. Did you ever read Atlas Shrugged?"

Ramana shook his head in confusion.

"Jesus Ramana, it's only the best-selling book of all time."

David turned his head slightly and chuckled. "I mean besides the Bible. Anyway, it set off something in me. I unloaded on my father with both barrels."

"I began using an intellectual type of logic on him–individualism, objectivism, the fallacy of altruism, that kind of stuff. He couldn't deal with it. He retreated to calling me names and trying to restrict what I could do. By that time I had all but made up my mind to pursue science and . . . well, here I am. I still talk with my brothers and sisters, but I haven't had a conversation with my father in several years. Anything else you want to know?"

Ramana was still trying to catch up to what he had already said. "Uh, no, I don't think so. I appreciate your being so honest."

"What about you, Ramana?" David turned the bright light of confession on him. "What made you leave your faith to pursue science?" he asked.

Ramana looked at his monitor and the recurring message: *No changes found, would you like to continue?* and hit the enter button.

"I think I can safely say that I have not left my faith . . . yet," Ramana tried to say in a non self-righteous manner.

"Ah," replied David.

Ramana looked indignant. "Seriously, there is nothing that I have learned in science that goes against what I learned from my father."

David suddenly became aware of the direction of their conversation. "By the way, Dr. Punjabi, have you read Arthur's first article yet?"

"What?" Ramana turned around. "He's finished . . . what . . . where is it?"

"Right here," David lifted up the three sheets of paper.

"When is it to be published? And where?" Ramana got up from his seat.

"It's published tomorrow, USA Today, and any local papers

that want to pick it up from the A.P.," David answered.

"Did you approve it?" asked Ramana.

"Dr. Green has read it. I wasn't really asked to approve it," David explained.

Ramana lifted the papers and started reading. He slowly grabbed a chair at the conference table and seated himself while he read. "Hmmmm."

David watched his facial expression change from surprise to anger then back again. He couldn't help but laugh as he watched.

Ramana looked up from the article. "What's so funny?"

"Oh nothing," David started. "It just seems so dramatic, like he's nominating us for a Nobel Prize."

"You're right," said Ramana. "I'm not sure that this is the direction I would take."

"It's the direction that Dr. Green wanted," David observed. "If this sparks some interest, there's already talk of bringing a camera crew in for a CNN piece."

Ramana kept reading. "Oh great, that would be just wonderful."

Ramana finished the article and set it down. "Whew, I didn't actually know we had such a significant piece of work down here."

David laughed. "I guess you'd better find out what made those changes to our bacteria pretty quick, huh?"

Ramana shook his head. "At least he kept the conclusions vague. I'm not sure I want to make the mistake of overstating our accomplishment."

"Well, you can set him straight tomorrow night then, can't you?" said David.

Ramana thought about the party. "So, are you going to wear a suit to the party?"

David grinned. "No, I'll probably wear slacks and jacket of some sort. How about you?"

"I really don't know," answered Ramana. "I don't exactly

have an extensive wardrobe."

David felt pity for his fashion-challenged friend. "I can always let you borrow something, if you need; maybe a nice sweater or a jacket. Why don't you come over about six, or so, we'll go together."

"Thank you David, that would be great," Ramana smiled.

Chapter 18

The University of Texas Ballroom, located within the student union, was elegantly decorated with linens and silver. The stage was being prepared for the band to play well into the night. The caterers hurriedly made the finishing touches to the tables as the bartenders opened their bottles of wine and organized their bottles of liquor. Around the room were various displays that highlighted the major research projects and their latest discoveries or news. Each display explained the importance of and future applications that the department and its benefactors could look forward to. On a strategically placed display was a diagram of the project room with an artist's rendition of the beast. Pictures of the virtual bacteria, some with legs, some without, accompanied the drawing. The biggest part, however, was the enlarged version of the article touting the accomplishments of the research team.

"UT Biologists Create R-Evolutionary Life," read the bold headline with a picture of Ramana sitting at his computer terminal and David standing behind him. The dateline read Arthur Lewis, USA Today, Friday-April 2.

All of the research team was invited to the party except the one most responsible for the latest development. The omega cell hung motionless where Ramana had left it after he found it in the work area. Kirk had no reason to move at the moment; the threat was over. The safety loop contained within its nucleus had even given control back to the E.P. , and this would continue as long

163

as the destruction had ceased. Over the past days, it was able to turn its efforts to nourishing and repairing itself. The exertion that Kirk experienced through that fateful night had brought it to the edge of destruction.

As the evolutionary routine started on its initial test, Kirk shook with awareness. The E.P. enclosed the test cell and began its supervision of the evolution process. The cells divided and were one by one exploded as the pressure within the enclosure was increased until only one remained. The Kirk cell leaped into motion in response to the slaughter, its mutated programming trying to correct the obvious problems. At the time, the activity was unnoticed by Mark, as the screen had isolated only the activity of the test process.

Kirk used the limited E.P. controls that it now possessed to move itself around the environment, searching for a way to solve the problem. The safety loop struggled to take over the operations of the experiment but found itself unable to. By the time that Mark had left the project room for the night, Kirk had found the entrance to the work area and opened the secure tunnel. Still aware of the activity in the E.P., Kirk tested its powers, trying to access the power to stop the destruction. Nothing was found.

Kirk proceeded back into the E.P. and moved next to the test enclosure, analyzing the process. It began to recognize the requirements of the process. The evolutionary routine stopped after each time mitosis was performed to determine if any changes were made to the cells. The result of finding changes would alter the decision to use these cells in the destruction routine. The safety loop continued to struggle with the E.P. for control as Kirk searched for a way to alter the dying cells.

Back in the work area, Kirk found construction routines loaded with the design of the new cilia programs that Ramana had developed. Kirk tried different ways to access these and put them to use. The beast tried to keep up with the flurry of conflicting data that was sent through its processors. While Kirk struggled to end the emergency, it was aware of the millions of cells that were formed then destroyed, its efforts increasing as the number of bad outcomes it detected grew.

Throughout the night, Kirk tried to combine the construction routine with the evolutionary routine as it processed faster than the speed of light. The safety loop grabbed at different access options to shut down the destruction. Hours went by while the integrity of the test cells were compromised by the endless mitosis activity.

At last, Kirk found a way to feed the construction routine into the evolutionary routine while it was still running. The destruction routine was replaced by the construction routine. The break allowed the safety loop to gain access to the main E.P. controls. The amended evolutionary routine now began to pump out new creatures, integrating cilia programs into the existing membrane programs. Just as this new process had formed these new inhabitants, the safety loop reached out and shut down the whole evolutionary routine and sent it back to the work area. Out of danger, Kirk no longer recognized any threats and went back to its mundane existence, content to stay in the new work area it had found.

David and Ramana were some of the first to show up at the ballroom. Ramana began looking around at the various displays as David headed for the bar to get a drink. In a stack next to the Ramana's display were dozens of copies of Friday's USA Today newspaper. He bent down and grabbed one to find his small picture on the top of the front page previewing the article to be found in the technology section. Ramana separated the sections until he found him and David on the front page and the same article that was prominently displayed before him. As he skimmed over the article again, fellow assistants and staff nudged him as they walked by, congratulating him and joking with him.

Across the room, Dr. Green spoke to a group of contributors when he spotted Ramana next to the display. He interrupted the conversation and began moving the crowd toward the unsuspecting Indian. Ramana began to hear footsteps walking behind him as the familiar voice got louder

"... And that's him right there," Dr Green said, "Mr. Punjabi and our research department's accomplishments announced to the world."

The contributors surrounded Ramana as some began to pick up copies of the paper.

"Ramana, this is William Randolph and his wife Betty..." Dr. Green introduced the group of people.

Ramana shook hands and greeted people, amazed that the names were forgotten from his mind as soon as the introduction was complete.

One of the contributors spoke up. "Tell us Ramana, what's it like to be a world famous scientist?" The group playfully laughed at the compliment.

Ramana laughed at the thought. "Oh, I'm not the famous one; this one is." Ramana pointed to the picture of the test cell.

The group responded with laughter.

"Seriously though," said Ramana as his gaze went around the room, "ours is just one of the many important projects in the department. I still don't understand why this project is the one to get such publicity."

"Don't be so modest, Ramana," said Dr. Green as he turned to the crowd. "I am absolutely amazed with what they are creating in this incredible computer. I've seen it for myself. I'm equally amazed at the cooperation that we have been able to cultivate within the computer science department. It is truly a phenomenal feat."

"Ramana? Do you need some help there?" David joked as he walked up to the crowd.

"Ah, David," Dr. Green shined, "you know most of my friends here."

Ramana watched the many greetings as he smiled at the prospects of reinforcements.

"David," Dr Green asked, "I know I will probably be asking you to do this all night, but could you give a brief description of the possible applications of this particular project?"

"Sure," replied David.

As David began to give his best sales pitch, Ramana scanned the room. He saw Mark standing with some other computer science comrades. Arthur was just now entering the ballroom, somewhat shyly, nodding his head at the guests around the entrance. After a quick look around the room, he spied Ramana standing near his enlarged article. He smiled at Ramana and gave a self-assured wave as he began to head for the bar.

" . . . The possibilities are really limitless when you think about it." Ramana turned back to the lecture and tried to catch up to what David was saying. "Research, teaching, testing, ultimately as this technology develops, there is no reason why we couldn't put together a completely functioning virtual human being someday. At that point, I think you can see, the knowledge that we could learn from it is unlimited."

"Thank you, David," said Dr. Green as he saw the faces of the assembled crowd soak in the project's significance. "We should let you two go. I'm sure there are many others who want to talk to you."

They said their departing words and began to walk through the ballroom that was now quickly filling up. David waved to a friend, patted Ramana on his back and said, "Have fun Ramana, and don't get in too much trouble."

David left Ramana standing alone in the middle of the room. He looked around at the gathered humanity, trying to see what would be his next move. His mind raced as he examined each small group of people talking, laughing, and drinking. He struggled to stay within the moment and not travel off to some distant world, which had been occurring too often these days. His thoughts began to analyze this event. What was this for? What did it accomplish? Was he strange for not understanding? He felt himself drifting off all alone in the middle of the room and struggled to set his mind back on the events at hand, twitching his head to regain a proper mind frame. He was becoming aware of the fact that he stood alone in a sea of small groups. He scanned the room to see if any group looked inviting.

Suddenly his attention was drawn to the entrance of the ballroom. Standing at the entrance was Allison. The moment hit Ramana like a crashing wave as her beauty engulfed him. She smiled as her eyes met Ramana's. He had to take a deep breath as her smile affected him physically. Ramana had only seen Allison in her jeans or shorts, sometimes with a hat on. He knew she was pretty, but this was unexpected. Her hair was curled and shined in the lights of the ballroom even more. Her dress revealed her slim body and bare shoulders with two thin black strands of cloth that held it to her body.

Ramana saw nothing else. Everything had disappeared. He knew that there would be no one who affected him as Allison did. The only thing that made it easier for Ramana was he knew he'd never have to find the guts to act upon these feelings. As she began to walk toward him, Ramana smiled with a quiet pride that it was him that she came to greet first. He held out his hands to grab hers as she finally made it to where he was standing.

"Hi Ramana," she said.

"Allison," he sighed. "You really look just . . . beautiful."

"Cut it out, Ramana," she laughed. "I feel like I'm way overdressed. You look very nice. That's a beautiful sweater."

Ramana looked down. "It's David's. I really don't have much . . ."

Allison interrupted him, "You look great Ramana."

They were staring at each other in silence when Arthur walked up to them.

"Wowee!" he said brushing his lapel, "you sure clean up nice, darling."

Allison shook her head as she smiled at his pitiful line.

Ramana struck a disapproving stare, which Arthur had already grown accustomed to.

"I see you've found the bar," Ramana shot at him.

Arthur's eyes widened and his hands stretched outward in wonder. "I don't know what I have to do to get on your good side. I mean, I just made you a nationally known scientist."

Allison's head turned. "What? Oh my God! Look at that."

Arthur smiled at Ramana as Allison began to walk towards their display. The two slowly followed Allison to the display and watched her from behind as she read the article. Ramana turned his head to find Arthur's stare had gone below the waistline. He smacked Arthur on the shoulder and scowled at him. Arthur was surprised at his reaction and smiled. He knew he had been caught.

Allison finally turned around and looked at her attendants. "Wow, I'm impressed, Arthur. That's great. I mean, that's in today's paper?"

"Yep," the reporter nodded.

"What do you think, Ramana?" asked Allison.

"Yeah Ramana, what do you think about the finished product?" asked Arthur.

Ramana weighed his response carefully. "You are definitely quite a reporter, Arthur. I was pleased that you didn't overstate the progress that we have made to this point. I must say your description of the project is somewhat dramatic." Ramana emphasized his point by bringing up his hands and flailing them about.

Allison laughed while she nodded her head.

"Well," the reporter said as he squinted, "I guess I'll take that as a compliment. Anyway, I think you guys work too closely to the project to see its appeal to the masses. I just tried to explain it in a way that Joe Schmoe could understand."

Ramana played ignorant. "Who is this Joe Schmoe?"

Allison laughed and turned away as Arthur tried to teach Ramana about slang. After the appropriate pause, she played her first beauty card. "Wow, I'm thirsty."

Both Neanderthals instantly turned into gentlemen as they

said in harmony, "I'll get it."

"What would you like, Allison?" Ramana won the race to that question.

"How about some white wine?" she answered.

The only problem that Ramana had about getting Allison a drink was leaving her there with Mr. Smooth.

"Are you old enough to drink, young lady?" Arthur quickly asked as Ramana made his way through the growing crowd.

"As of three months ago," she said proudly.

Arthur immediately yearned for younger days.

"How old are you, Arthur?" Allison asked.

"Too old for you," he automatically answered. "Hehe, just kidding. I'm forty-one."

The two paused in silence and glanced over to Ramana standing at the bar. Allison broke it with, "So, do you have your stuff printed in the USA Today all the time?"

Arthur nodded his head confidently. "Sure–USA Today, New York Times, Wall Street Journal–really it's put out on the wire for anybody to pick it up."

"I see," Allison started. "So this could run in local papers all over America? Even Oklahoma?"

"It's possible," answered Arthur. "Just between you and me, there's a strong possibility we are going to get a CNN crew down here also."

"Wow," she said as her glass of wine appeared. "Thank you, Ramana. Cheers."

The two gentlemen raised their glasses and toasted the moment.

As the night wore on and the bar was pushed to the limits of its inventory, the party started to resemble a full-on fraternity party rather than a faculty function. Dr. Green and other department elders said their goodbyes, and along with most of the older contributors, left the late hours of the night to the young people. The band played a mix of rock-a-billy and swing country that hit right at the heart of one's desire to wildly move different body parts. The dance floor became gradually more crowded as the clock passed, the shyness wearing off as the booze took its effect. Even David was caught up in the celebration, and let his count of drinks go beyond his tolerance and tact. Allison spent most of her time on the dance floor, being asked to dance by every scientific geek that could muster up the courage. In a multi-cultural gesture, Allison even tried, quite successfully, to teach Ramana the Texas two-step.

After the dance, Ramana and Allison walked off the dance floor laughing as his arm trailed closely behind her bare back, helping her through the crowd. They broke through the crowd and wound up right in front of David and Mark. Automatically they went toward them and joined their group

"You're quite a dancer, Ramana," David commented.

Ramana smiled. "Well, I must say, Allison had something to do with it."

Mark spoke up. "God Ramana, how many times have you had to explain the project tonight?"

Ramana laughed. "More than I could count. It's incredible. It's great to see so many people are interested in it."

David smiled proudly. "I think it's safe to say that Dr. Green left happy. It's a wonder what a national headline can do. We need to make toast to Arthur Lewis."

"I'll get the drinks," said Mark.

Allison nodded her head.

"I'll go with you," responded Ramana. "What do you guys want?"

After getting the drink orders, Mark and Ramana left David and Allison standing alone.

Allison suddenly realized this and gazed over at the long line at the bar. Her head raced through the issues on the table with this man and decided that this was not the place to go deep. David, on the other hand, was amused at the prospect of having this young, winsome girl all to himself for the next ten minutes.

As time used up all of its breath for one day and began to

make its way into the morning of the next, he examined the creature, his eyes quietly going down her exposed shoulders to the dress that was pressed to her body with the slight sweat that she had worked up dancing. She felt the heavy stare on her person and looked over to Ramana and Mark. His affected mind quickly fantasized of possessing her youth and vitality, then was mixed with the thoughts of "I've seen better . . . I've had better."

"So David," she forced out of her lips, "you really know how to throw a party."

Inside, he laughed at her irrelevance. "Why, thank you. I wasn't sure that you were into things like this. I mean, what would your father think?"

Allison kept smiling at him as she took the first blow and let it fly off the starboard side.

"Isn't this Good Friday?" David asked with a smile, gesticulating with finger quotations marks.

Allison decided not to be intimidated by this man. "Why yes it is. I really never understood why they call it Good Friday. After all, it's the day that Jesus was falsely accused . . . beaten . . . and mocked . . . and killed."

"Ah yes," replied David. "This Jesus fellow, he's the one that is responsible for creating everything, isn't he?"

Allison could feel her pulse rise and they proceeded down this dangerous path. "The way I read it, yes," she answered.

David nodded his head. "Seven days too, that's amazing . . . or I guess six really, if you don't count that one he rested. Let's see, and that was only what, about six thousand years ago?"

Allison's smile got bigger as she brought her hands up, palms showing. "Who can say? I wasn't there."

Her attitude began to make David angry and his tone began to change. "Let me ask you a question. Do you think it is Christian to use your pretty little face to wrap your teacher around your little finger?"

"What!" screamed Allison.

"Oh, don't give me that," David interrupted. "Don't sit

here and tell me that you're not trying to use your relationship with Ramana to your advantage."

Allison hesitated as her mind raced over her first day with Ramana and her conversations with Rachel.

"That's what I thought," David concluded by her momentary silence.

Allison stood speechless as she felt her frustration begin to manifest tears.

"You've already got him so confused that he's beginning to spout off some weird mumbo jumbo about the project." David glared at her as he took another drink. "That makes you a hypocrite; a hypocrite for using sex to corrupt this poor man's head, and a hypocrite for being involved in this project and celebrating here when you don't even believe in what we are trying to accomplish."

Ramana gazed back at the two from the line at the bar and noticed the stern look on David's face as he talked down to Allison. His thoughts went to terror as he wondered why he had left them together. Allison's watering eyes looked over to Ramana, which burned a hole in his heart. She quickly turned and began to run out of the ballroom. Arthur, sipping his vodka, instinctively noticed the scene and began to walk toward the door.

Ramana hit Mark on the shoulder as he left the line and struggled his way through the crowd to confront David. "What did you say to her?"

David smirked. "Settle down. I did you a favor."

"What did you say to her?" he said with even more force.

David took another drink. "Aa . . . I don't know. She started in on me with all of this Christian crap, and I gave her a little dose of reality. She couldn't handle it and ran out of her like a little girl."

"You jerk!" Ramana turned and shot through the ballroom after her. He ran through the entrance doors to the ballroom and looked to see if he could find her. His pulse raced as he turned and flew down the stairs, shifting his head from side to side to locate her. He reached the front entrance to the student union and ran to the top of the outside stairs, his eyes scanning the darkness for any movement. The lights of a car came on and he recognized Allison's black dress behind the wheel of the red BMW. The car began to pull out of its parking place as Ramana hit the bottom stair and sprinted toward it. He devised the best path to reach it on a dead sprint and ran out in the middle of the street. Allison saw him and slammed on the brakes as she swerved over near the curb.

Ramana stopped and walked over to the car, panting as he talked. "Allison, what did he say to you? What happened?"

Allison's head went down as she shifted the car into park, her hands slamming the steering wheel in frustration. She stayed silent, hiding her tears as she thought of what to say. Ramana came and leaned against the convertible, looking up into the night sky as he tried to regain his breath. The two sat silent, wondering how it had come to this.

Allison finally broke the silence. "Ramana, I'm sorry, but I'm not working on the project anymore, I'm never working with that man again."

Ramana turned to her. "Okay . . . that's okay . . . I'm not worried about that. I'm worried about you . . . are you okay?"

Allison's shoulders deflated with a sigh and she tried to talk without crying. "Why was he so mean to me? I don't understand, why did he have to say those things?"

"What did he say?" asked Ramana.

The reporter stepped out into the cool night with his pad in hand. He delicately moved into a position where he could view the action.

Allison turned her face away. She knew she couldn't talk about it. "It doesn't matter. Ramana, I've gotta get home. I'm driving back to Oklahoma early in the morning, and I . . ."

Ramana stepped away from the car. "Allison, I'm sorry. It's my fault. I told him about you . . . and I shouldn't have left you there alone with him . . . I . . ."

"No Ramana, it's not your fault," Allison started. "It's nobody's fault. You've been great. I really appreciate everything you've done. I had a great time tonight, and now I just need to go home."

Ramana grabbed for her hand. "Allison, you do what you have to do. Don't let this jerk make you feel small. Don't let anybody do that to you."

Allison looked at her teacher's hand on hers, then slowly moved her eyes to his. "Thanks, Ramana, I'll be okay. I'll see you on Monday. Have a happy Easter." She shifted the car into drive and slowly rolled away.

"Happy Easter," said the bewildered Muslim, his hand waving in the air.

Chapter 19

Pastor Wilson began his work at the usual 5:30 am, but this day his step was lighter, his strength was doubled, his purpose clear. Not only was this a day and a time to celebrate life, this was a time to celebrate family and all of the blessings they had received. His angel, Allison, would shortly be getting on the road to join the rest of her family in this time of rejoicing. He stopped and quietly prayed for her safe journey. His mind switched to the news he was to give to his daughter. For so long, he and his wife had kept this secret agreement to themselves. He had practiced delivering it to her many times in his mind, but this would finally be the occasion. She had reached graduation; the promise had been fulfilled. He smiled at the glorious morning full of new possibilities and looked to the rising sun that painted everything gold in the worn path that led to the barn.

Allison awoke a few hours later than her father, her body trying to convince her to stay where she was. As she stumbled across the room, stretching and wiping her eyes, she suddenly remembered the night before. She looked into the mirror, yawning and shaking her head at the events that took place. She looked over to her sleeping roommate and smiled at Rachel's peacefulness. Allison's mind then switched to the long drive home and the Easter celebration on the next horizon. She stood motionless in front of the mirror, unable to decide on a course of action. All of the deadlines and tests, the decisions and questions, the people, the family flashed across her mind, trying to find some resolution. She was able to break her stare away from the mirror and slowly walk over to the window. She got some fresh air and comfort from the birds singing and the spring wind rustling the tiny new leaves.

By the time that Allison got out of bed, her father had finished his chores and began to set up his tractor. On their 30-acre property, Charles had cleared and farmed half of it for the past 15 years. Although the work was more of a hobby than a business, it provided their family and other families with fresh produce in season. Peach trees, fig trees, grape vines, and blackberry bushes lined the farm and added to the variety and surplus of items they experimented with. Mrs. Wilson had made it her job to take the excess harvest and preserve it the way she had learned through the years of practice. She set up shop once a month on Main Street in town and usually was able to sell a good portion of their work to help subsidize the operation.

As the ancient John Deere cranked up and sent a cloud of smoke into the cool morning, Charles said a prayer for the corn he was about to sow. He shifted the tractor into gear and began the journey. His imagination went back in time to the original farm, the original farmer. *How Adam must have wondered at the garden God had created*, he thought. Every plant, pristine and perfect, cared for by its creator. Temperature, moisture, fertilization—all at optimal and perfect appropriations. At that time, God was the farmer. Adam or Eve hardly had to lift a finger to receive a perpetual bumper crop. His huge command of scripture began to intertwine with his imagination; the drama of God working among His virgin creation played in his mind as his eyes kept true to a point on the horizon. Soon his thoughts went to the tragedy of the inevitable fall:

> "Cursed is the ground because of you; through painful
> toil you will eat of it all the days of your life.
> It will produce thorns and thistles for you; and you
> will eat the plants of the field.

By the sweat of your brow you will eat your food until you return to the ground, since from it you were taken. For dust you are and to dust you will return."

Gen. 3:17–19

Pastor Wilson was amazed at the thought *Even man's curse has become a blessing to me.* The toil, the work, the knowledge all made him feel closer to God, a partner in allowing creation to try to regain a part of its original glory.

As the pastor contemplated his role in the process, he realized that it was he that was the less significant. All he did was stir up the ground, plant the seed, and give it food. The miracle was the seed: how it was made, how it became a mature plant, how it fashioned a fruit. These miracles still were as important to Charles as any miracle in his life. As he approached the end of the field, he lifted the seed drill from the plowed earth, executed a 180 degree turn, and picked another spot on the horizon.

Allison tried to quietly finish packing her bags while she went through her beauty ritual, although this morning she was content with "au natural." Rachel's head turned as she began to stretch and moaned an unintelligible, "Good morning."

Allison looked back at her and smiled. "Hey, sorry, I hope I didn't wake you."

Rachel shook her head and looked at the clock.

"Well, I think I'm just about ready to get out of here. I hope my car starts," she laughed.

Allison paused. "Have you decided what you're gonna do this weekend?"

"I going home," decided Rachel. "I'm kind of even am looking forward to it."

Allison smiled and finished stuffing her bag with a copy of the newspaper that contained the article about their project.

Rachel sat up in bed. "Allison, I don't think you really know how much you've helped me. I want to thank you again."

"Oh, I don't know about that," Allison said as she walked

toward the bed. "You have a great time and tell your family hello for me."

Allison leaned down and hugged Rachel. "Just to let you know, Rachel, I think I'm going to need a lot of help when I get back. I've kinda painted myself in a corner. I'm not really sure how I'm going to get out."

"You can count on me, girlfriend," Rachel said. She watched her friend walk out the door.

Allison walked out to the slumbering Oldsmobile that a parishioner had given to her father years ago. It creaked and moaned as she opened the heavy door and threw her bags across the driver seat. After a small internal combustion prayer, Allison turned the key and the sedan came to life. She stepped back out of the car and took a look around at the early morning life while she let her faithful steed warm up. Her destination lie five-and-a-half hours north, a journey she had taken countless times.

Although she tried not to think of the events of the previous night, her body couldn't shake the sense of dread that floated around her. She remembered telling Ramana that she was leaving the project. Would her conscience allow her to just abandon the project? Would her pride allow her to continue? Did she have the guts to write the paper that now began to form in her mind? What would Ramana think of her?

Ramana awoke and immediately his thoughts were a mixture of rage and embarrassment. His mind attempted to absorb all of the factors and events that had led up to the night before, without success. How had it gotten so complicated? He turned onto his back and stared at the water-stained ceiling above him. As the effects of the wine manifested in his belly, his eyes traced the shapes above him and his mind listlessly raced through space and time. He resolved himself to spend the weekend working to find the answer that had eluded them to this point. His concentration would focus on discovering the secrets that the beast had held tightly within its grasp. How could he get the computer to reveal its secrets? Ramana decided that he would try it from a different angle this time. He would initiate the evolution routine and track the results one step at a time.

The cool wind hit Pastor Wilson's face, and he struggled to keep his watering eyes on the target. The red soil of Oklahoma mixed with the wind to leave a scarlet vapor trail behind the green tractor as it made its way through the field. His thoughts once again turned to his daughter. He wondered how four years of college had changed her. College had so many temptations and alluring vices, along with endless calls to leave behind traditional beliefs for so-called "rationality and practicality." He was certain these worldly things had stained his daughter in some way; they were too powerful and our will too weak. As he tried to bring into words the solution to the problems that he imagined for her, they were stopped by others. He decided that it was best left to God's hand; He saw it clearly. The pastor brushed at the crimson tears that formed on his weathered face and made the last turn back towards the barn.

Allison's eyes stared at the never-ending interstate highway that slapped against her worn tires. She was deep in thought about her chosen fields of study. Could the two, faith and science, exist together? Was there a way to reconcile the two, or was she a fool to try? How could science have gotten it so wrong? Why did she feel that she was the only one who saw it for what it had become?

Science was the new intellectual religion. It was a religion whose god was a vague and nebulous force that had no power or reason to intervene or require anything from itself or the life it had witnessed take shape. As her mind developed ideas and words for her paper, she wished she could write them down and grabbed for a pad of paper out of her backpack. Her car veered to the shoulder of the highway as she leaned over, and when her eyes made it back to the road, she swerved to regain control of the old car. She shook her head at her stupidity and whispered thanks to the angels who kept the car on the road. Undaunted, she moved the pad up against the steering wheel and began to sloppily write an outline.

Ramana made it to the empty project room and surveyed the accumulation of data that he and Mark had generated. Neither of the two had proposed any plausible explanation for what happened. The data pointed nowhere. Ramana sat down at his terminal and cleaned up the mess from the previous night. He closed all of the open applications and moved to E.P. where the many bacteria continued swimming throughout the space. Ramana started to set up a new evolutionary routine using a bacterium of the original design. The process took several minutes as he attempted to corral the active bacteria into an isolated area and disable them to stop their movement. He placed the alpha and omega cells in a separate isolated area. He moved the group of new cells toward the back of the E.P. and placed them together next to the Kirk cells. The controls were set to slow down the process where it could be easily observed. Once everything was set, Ramana slowly moved his finger toward the key to initiate the process. "Okay, show me how you work," he mumbled to the beast.

Ramana hit the button and pushed his chair back. He placed the 3-D glasses on his face and watched the action on the screen. He had chosen to keep a wide-scale view of the operations. The screen showed the isolated evolutionary area along with the bunched together bacteria that were kept in stasis. The selected bacterium began its performance once again, transforming itself into a seething blob that duplicated the necessary genetic information and attempted to pull itself into two parts. Ramana watched intently, still amazed at the incredible process they had fashioned. Two cells now hung before Ramana's eyes and made the preparations to change again. Ramana grabbed for his cup of coffee that was now almost room temperature and downed the remainder. As he watched, his thoughts returned to Allison and the fool that he made of himself the night before. His eyes began to lose their focus as his thoughts blurred his concentration.

The routine worked its way through the mitosis stage and held its inhabitants, preparing the destruction stage. The omega cell hung motionless, surrounded by a mass of immobile cells. Ramana watched the transition from the mitosis stage into the destruction and squinted his eyes to gain focus on the process.

As the destruction routine started, the omega cell once again twinged with activity. Ramana watched the cells disappear one by one from the screen, unaware of the emergency that had been initiated. The omega cell had continued to go through changes since the fateful night. Its programming had begun to degenerate with the continuous replicating and changing it experienced. It fought to sustain its purpose through the array of tiny defects. The safety loop within its DNA took charge, and Kirk reached out to again stop the slaughter of its fellow creatures. It grabbed onto the E.P. and quickly moved itself into the work area. Ramana's eyes glanced over to see a flash of movement in the mass of cells and wondered what had happened. He moved to his terminal and checked the variables and data that were being generated. The information seemed strange and he began scanning for any other movement.

The movement was now in the work area. Kirk searched again for the construction routines and found them loaded with the cilia programs as before. The Kirk cell struggled to keep true to its mutated programming, the defects pushing the cell to confusion and chaos. It managed to grab the construction routine and feed it into the E.P. The safety loop tried to gain access to the E.P., but its failing programming couldn't coordinate the move. The construction routines began to override the destruction routine and the creative process began.

Ramana pushed back in his chair and looked to the screen. His eyes widened as the cells began to change. The cells continued to split and as they split, tiny hairs began to form on their membrane. Ramana's mouth opened wider as he began to witness the mystery of evolution for the first time.

Charles finished wiping down the tractor, put it away, and

closed up the barn as he went to survey the field he had just planted. The local weatherman had predicted rain for the first of the week, which should set in the corn and help it germinate. He tried to picture in his mind the entire growing season and what he would have to face in the coming months. Once he had come to an acceptable resolution, he turned back to the house and walked the worn path to find out how the preparations were going inside. He found that there would be enough food for two families, the house was dressed up for company, and Allison's room had been prepared for her with fresh linens and cut wildflowers. He retreated to the front porch with a glass of fresh iced tea, where he would wait and watch the horizon for his daughter's homecoming.

By the time Allison reached the Red River, the border of Oklahoma and Texas, she had outlined half of the essay. At the top of the page were the words *All This Useless Beauty*, the title of a song in which she had found inspired meaning. Her mind went through illustrations and comparisons that she tried to fit to the composition. The goal, in her mind, was to keep it simple, to only use what the simple observation of nature could reveal. Her eyes glanced over to the newspaper she carried with her. She pondered the various sacred cows of evolution: The circular reasoning of the fossil record and the geological column, radioactive dating procedures, a mythical meteor crashing into Earth and killing only the dinosaurs, and decided to leave these theories to their own impending death. Her words would be simple, truthful, and strike at the heart of the matter.

When she saw the first sign for Ardmore, Allison tossed the pad onto the passenger seat and tried to clear her mind of the whirlwind that had formed inside her head. She smiled as she thought of her home, her family, and realized again how lucky she was to have these things. She turned down the familiar gravel road that cracked and popped against the tires and sent a cloud of red dust high in the air. Pastor Wilson's head rose as he saw the dust rise on the horizon and set down his glass of iced tea. He stood up and squinted to focus over the long distance to make out the shape of the car. He felt a wave of warmth come over his body as he saw the old burgundy Oldsmobile turn down their road. He began to slowly walk down the steps of the porch, his mind travelling over the twenty-one years that he had been able to share with this angel. Charles turned and yelled towards the house, "Honey, Allison's made it home."

The car stopped next to their work truck and Allison smiled as she saw her dad walking towards her. She opened the door and laid her head upon his chest as their arms wrapped around each other.

"Hi Daddy," she sighed.

"Hi sweetheart," he replied.

Chapter 20

Ramana sat motionless as he watched the simple bacterium slowly change into an altogether different creature. His thoughts ran at light speed, trying to determine what was happening and what he was to do about it. No one had seen this process or even theorized how it actually took place, and he now had a private audience to the wonders of the universe. Maybe David was right; it looked as though the changes took place on the cell's exterior first, which must somehow affect the creature's DNA.

The omega cell stopped its frantic search as it determined that the life within the E.P. was out of danger. But the stress had finally begun to take its toll on the mutated cell. The number of flaws that existed in its programming were becoming too much for the cell to handle. Polypeptide production was constant and mostly unsuccessful as long chains of proteins were assembled then broke apart or mutated. The bonds within the cell were strained; the membrane proteins struggled to keep their integrity. The creator cell was near death. Sensing its own doom, the cell frantically reached out with its safety loop programming and shut down everything it could. With this last burst of energy, the membrane breached and the cell deflated. Its contents flowed out of the gashes in its shell and littered the work area.

Just as the first bacteria had finished receiving its new wings and was let go by the evolutionary routine, Ramana was startled as the E.P. screen went blank. He panicked. Not since the beginning of the experiment had the screen been turned off.

He raced to his terminal and began to access the controls. "What have I done?" he said aloud as he thought of how to regain control of the experiment. He accessed the display controls, the E.P. controls, and nothing worked. As his tempo became more frantic, the beast was overwhelmed and decided to lock up. Nothing worked. The small monitor screen in front of Ramana's eyes froze, and his hands rose in clenched fists as he contemplated slamming them down on the keyboard.

Ramana pushed his chair back and stared at the large blank screen, trying to figure out what he would tell his partners. He knew he would have to reboot the whole system and was close to hitting the appropriate buttons when he decided he had better wait until he consulted with Mark and David. He was unsure of what rebooting the computer would do to the experiment.

Ramana got up and walked toward the phone to contact David and Mark. How would he explain what happened? Did he even want to talk to "the jerk" as he called him the night before? He stopped with the phone in his hand and tried to find the words. His eyes went to the beast. The red lasers were still moving back and forth through the silicon gel; everything looked normal with the computer.

"It has to be the E.P. that has frozen up, probably due to a problem with the evolutionary routine," Ramana said to himself. His hand went to the phone as he dialed David's office number. David was not in his office so he began to talk to the voice mail. "David, this is Ramana . . . there's been a . . . a malfunction with the computer or the E.P. Everything's frozen and we may have to reboot it or something . . . we need to see what Mark thinks." Ramana's thoughts went to what he had witnessed. "It happened when I ran the evolutionary routine again . . . I . . . I saw it happen . . . I mean, a metamorphosis of the bacteria . . . it happened right in front of my eyes and then it just went blank. I'm here at the project room right now. Please give me a call or get down here . . . I'll get a hold of Mark also. Goodbye."

The Wilsons got their hugs and obligatory "How are

things?" questions asked and answered, and instinctively gathered in the dining room. The conversation stayed light until her father asked about the research project she had told them about. Allison excused herself from the table, grabbed the newspaper from her bags and handed the science and technology section to her father. He found the article and began to read it as she explained it to her mother and brother.

"This is what you have been working on this semester?" asked her father.

"Yep, pretty impressive, huh? That's my biology teacher. He's the one that got me involved in it. He's really the greatest guy," Allison said with a smile.

"So what's it supposed to do? The computer," her mother asked.

Allison looked up in the air. "Well, it's sort of a simulation program that lets you see how real live cells work and reproduce. They've also been using it to try to discover how evolution works. But personally, I think they are wasting their time. That's probably why I'm not working on it anymore."

"What happened?" her father asked.

"Well, the head of biological research is pretty much a jerk."

"Allison!" scolded her mother.

"Well, he is," answered Allison. "Just last night he . . . he . . . well, I don't want to talk about it. But I told Ramana that I was not working on the project anymore because of him."

"Did he do something improper," asked her father, "like sexually?"

"No, Dad," she answered. "It's no big deal. I'm sure most of the faculty would agree with his perspective."

"What do you mean?" he tried.

Allison set her fork down. "It's tough. I mean, about a quarter of my biology text is about evolution and I don't agree with it. It basically says we came from nothing, that we are descendants of a bunch of gooey slime."

"Oh, I see." Her father shook his head. "Aren't there other people who see it the way you do?"

"Not that I've seen," Allison answered. "Most people, even if they do, are not willing to take a stand. And I can understand why. I mean, you'd get laughed at, you'd fail the class–at least that section."

Allison's little brother finally looked up from his pot roast. "What's the big deal, Allison? We've all learned about that stuff in biology class. It seems logical enough. I mean it seems like all of the scientists are all in agreement about it."

Allison's face dropped as she realized the fruitlessness of her fight.

Charles saw her reaction. "You know I'm not a real smart, but I think I would tend to agree with the Bible rather than a bunch of stuffy scientists." Charles's gaze turned toward the open window. "Everything I see out there fits with what I read in the Bible. I've come to understand a lot of things about the Earth and all the plants and animals. I think of myself as kind of an amateur scientist, and in my opinion, I think it's pretty obvious that everything is waiting for its creator to return to restore life to the way it's supposed to be."

Allison smiled. "Don't kid yourself, Dad. You're a very smart man."

"Well, I guess the question is, what are you going to do about it?" her mother asked.

"I think I'm gonna take a stand," Allison answered.

Heads at the table nodded in response to the statement.

Mark and Ramana were sitting at the conference table when David walked in. He walked in front of the big screen to assess the situation and looked around the room. He shook his head and went to the table.

"What's the consensus?" he asked.

Mark started, "Ramana, tell David what you saw."

Ramana took a deep breath. "Okay, something was funny

about the whole situation. When I started the evolutionary routine again, I began to get funny readings from the E.P., but I went ahead and kept it going. It ran fine for a few loops, and then right in the middle of the process, one of the bacterium began to develop cilia on its membrane right in front of my eyes. I don't know how it did it; they just began to appear. Then right when it changed into this new bacteria, the whole computer screen went blank."

David was nodding his head. "Did you see any readings, any indications that could explain what was happening?"

"It all happened so fast," Ramana confessed. "I was so amazed at it all, I didn't see anything that could explain it. I can't think of any way to explain it."

"Well Mark," David started, "what do you think will happen when we reboot?"

"It's hard to say," Mark spoke up. "We could lose everything in the E.P. I think the work area is probably pretty safe. We didn't really plan for this type of situation, and I blame myself. How do you save these programs that are in constant motion and constantly changing?"

"We've got all of the cellular components in the work area," Ramana said. "Even if we lose them, we can rebuild them."

"Not the new ones," answered David.

"Sure we can," answered Ramana. "I have cilia programs ready to go in the work area. In fact, I was just about ready to construct some new bacteria . . ." his words slowed as his mind began to generate a theory.

Mark saw his reaction. "What is it, Ramana?"

Ramana remained silent as he tried to get through his thought process. His mind went through the strange happenings of the past semester: the dream at the coffee shop, the vision he had inside the Kirk cell. Everything began to converge in his mind.

"Ramana, what's the matter with you?" David asked.

Ramana awoke from his thoughts. "Uh, I don't know, I . . .

was just thinking that maybe the computer or something took the cilia programs and incorporated them into the evolutionary routine."

"How could that happen?" asked Mark.

"How could any of this happen? I'm not sure I understand everything that's going on in this computer anymore," Ramana confessed.

David quieted the two. "I guess there's only one way to find out. Mark, reboot it."

"Okay," he said as he got up from the table and walked over to the main controls. "This should take a few minutes, and to tell you the truth, I can't stay much longer. Dr. Meyers has me working on another three projects and I've got to get over to the main computer lab soon." Mark opened the panel and switched the power to the off position. The beast, which had been running non-stop for fifteen months, slowly hummed its way to a halt. Everyone looked to the beast and saw the red lasers turn off and the memory core turn black.

Ramana and David's attention went back to Mark in anticipation of him throwing the switch back to the on position.

"Okay," Mark announced, "here we go." He flipped the switch and stepped back to see the screen.

The motors began to wind themselves back to full speed and the gel core lit up with its familiar red glow. The beast hummed and clicked as it tried to decipher what was in its memory. The screen pulsed once as it received commands from the beast and waited for its instructions. The beast raced through its scattered circuitry and attempted to install the E.P. into the main partitioned space. It then opened up the saved work area. The whole process took fifteen minutes. David and Ramana paced, while Mark kept looking at his watch and waiting for the beast to reveal its results.

The screen pulsed again and slowly began to brighten to reveal an almost completely empty space. The only cell that remained had an alpha marking it in the isolated area where

Ramana had left it with the omega cell. The scientists looked in astonishment as the semester's worth of work and the subject of a national article was erased from existence.

After a long moment of silence, Mark was the first to speak. "Guys, I hate to do this to you, but I'm already late."

David looked at Ramana. "You think you can handle it from here?"

Ramana nodded.

"Okay, Mark, get out of here. We'll let you know when we need your help."

Mark started toward the door with a quick stride. As he opened the large metal door, Arthur appeared in the doorway and jerked with surprise as they almost collided. Mark shot to the side. "Hi Arthur, bye Arthur," he said, tipping off Ramana and David before disappearing out the door.

"Uh, bye," he responded.

David and Ramana quickly turned to the commotion at the door and tried to comprehend the situation they were now in. They looked at each other, looked at the monitor screen, and back at Arthur.

Arthur stepped in the project room. "Hi guys, uh, is it all right for me to come on in?"

David answered, "Yes," at the exact moment Ramana said, "No."

Arthur took a step forward and halted as he deciphered the commands. "Uh, okay . . . I . . ."

David took control. "Come in. We were just doing a little cleaning up. We . . . uh, are trying to see what . . ."

"We are examining the original alpha cell . . . uh, trying to evaluate its condition." Ramana's voice cracked as he improvised.

Arthur made his way to the group. "I see. How's the little bugger doing."

Ramana lied in a child-like voice, "Seems to be doing fine. No problems."

"Where's all the other cells, the ones swimming around?" the reporter asked.

"Oh," Ramana continued with David's blessing. "They're put away for now."

Arthur nodded his head in understanding. "Have you made any headway in figuring out how those swimmers . . . uh, came about?"

"You could say that, I guess," Ramana stammered.

David began shaking his head. "Uh . . . nothing concrete. We have maybe some indications, but nothing definitive."

Arthur smiled. "Well, let's get a move on. I need some info to get started on the next piece."

"The next piece?" asked David.

"Yeah, we had such a response to the first one, my editor has asked me to stay here and lead the CNN crew."

David peered over to Ramana. "Uh, when again is the CNN crew to get here?"

Arthur instinctively looked down at his watch. "Should be sometime Monday. They probably won't start shooting until Tuesday though. Not to put on the pressure, but it would be great if there were some theories about how this happened to put in that piece. We would definitely like an interview." Arthur paused and smiled at his power. "Yeah, you think that article gave you some publicity, just wait until you go on TV."

The two scientists' stomachs cringed at the thought of what was taking place. Ramana slowly moved over to the conference table and sat in the closest chair.

"You okay, Ramana?" Arthur asked. "You don't look so well. Don't worry, I will make you look great."

Ramana looked up at Arthur, ready to explain what had happened.

David interrupted quickly. "Arthur, I hate to do this to you again, but we need to discuss some rather important matters . . . privately."

Arthur rolled his eyes. "Geeezh, you guys always treat me

like I'm bringing you bad news or something. You know, I don't need this from you guys. I could get plenty of this crap working at the political desk." Arthur laughed at his wit and began to walk out of the project room, shaking his head.

After the reporter left, David joined Ramana at the table and stared in silence as their minds spun in circles. They stared at the alpha cell that hung above them in judgment for their stupidity and deceit.

"Well, we've got to create some more bacteria with cilia just like those others," David proclaimed.

"Do you propose that we use the evolutionary routine?" asked Ramana.

"I don't care how we do it!" David barked. "Just make some dang swimmers. Can you do that?"

Ramana recoiled at his response. "Uh, yes, I think so. I mean I'm sure I could construct some in the work area. But what will we say about them?"

"Let me take care of that," replied David. He took a deep breath. "Okay, sorry Ramana. Let's see, I want you to work to find out the problems we've been having and start the construction work. I'm going to track down Dr. Green and talk to him about this. We need to handle this very carefully. This could really blow up in our faces." David got up and started blindly walking toward the door. He stopped and turned to Ramana. "Ramana, do you think you can handle this alone?"

Ramana laughed as he shook his head. "Sure, I'll take care of it."

Ramana watched David walk out of the lab and immediately wished for his trusted assistant's help. He stopped and tried to visualize what she was doing at this moment, then traveled in a daydream to what their life would be like if they were together. His mind explored the feeling of touching her soft skin, kissing her lips, holding her body close to his. The thoughts only served to depress him more as his shame eventually transformed the visions into vulgarity.

Ramana woke up from the daydream. He shook his head to clear the thoughts and pushed his chair up to his terminal. He looked up to the fuzzy vision of Kirk from where he sat and said, "Well, Captain Kirk, looks like you're the only one left. Once again you have beaten the odds. I wish you could tell me what's going on."

As he wondered about the omega cell, Ramana remembered finding it in the work area after the last episode. He quickly hit the appropriate buttons and began to examine the different areas. When he entered the operating room, he gasped at the sight before his eyes. In the middle of the operating room was the omega sign. Littered around the area were what he determined to be the remnants of the other Kirk cell. He looked down at his keyboard and tried to theorize what happened as a wave of sadness came over him.

Unable to find a plausible scenario, Ramana started rummaging through the various pieces of Kirk. The nucleus was almost completely intact, and he moved it to a somewhat clear area with the joystick device. The outer membrane looked like a torn and soiled sheet, which he grabbed and tried to consolidate in a ball. Cytoplasm was covering almost everything in the operating room and he hit the button for the suction device. As he cleaned up the area, he continued to re-examine the events from the beginning, trying to understand it all. He remembered the movement he saw out of the corner of his eye when he initiated the evolutionary routine. Ramana realized that the omega cell had somehow moved or was moved into the work area just like the first time. The answer had to be in its DNA.

Once Ramana had finished cleaning up, the nucleus was prepared for surgery. The tedious process of finding the chromosomes, then unraveling them for examination was accomplished after an hour's work. He initiated the analysis program to decipher the DNA code and left to get a beverage, his thoughts trying to determine how he would next construct the new bacteria they needed.

The Wilson family finally began to comprehend Allison's research project by the end of dinner. They asked relevant questions as each of them helped clean up the mess. Her younger brother, Josh, acquired the keys to the family car and was off for the chosen hang-out for the night, pummeled by statements about when to be back and cautious warnings. After the dishes were done, Allison and her parents walked to the back porch and gazed at the beauty of what their little parcel had become.

"What are you planning to grow out there, Daddy?" Allison asked.

"I planted corn this morning on about half of the field. The rest of it will be up to your mother and what she wants–probably some onions, tomatoes, peppers, cucumbers, that sort of thing."

Charles took his favorite chair. "Allison, have a seat. Let's talk."

"Okay," she nervously said.

"There's something that I need to tell you about, before you graduate on us." He scratched the whiskers on his weathered face. "Maybe it can help you decide where you go from here, so to speak."

Allison looked at her mother to try to understand.

"You know, I look back now and again on your mother and my early years. All of the places we have been, all of the things that we've done–it's really amazing to me how we were able to do it all." He moved in his chair and his head bowed as he pondered his direction. "But recently I've begun to see another side of things. I've begun to look at it through other people's eyes, namely yours and your mother's." His gaze came up from the floor to their eyes. "What I put her through, what I put you through. I can only imagine the things you guys had to deal with. There's no question in my mind about whether or not it was worth it, but I've begun to realize now that I never gave you guys much of a choice." He paused as tried to remain steady.

"What do you mean, Dad?" Allison tried.

"Let me finish," Charles said softly and cleared his throat.

"A lot of good was done by this family. More importantly, a lot of good was done for this family. The people that I . . . that we preached to, the people who gave of themselves to support the ministry. I . . . I get thinking about all those people and it . . . it just makes me . . ." A hand went to his face to stop a tear that had found its way to his cheek.

Allison's eyes began to water as she listened to her father.

"I guess one of my regrets is that I feel I never did enough to pay back those people. I never was the person, the example, the comfort that I think I should have been for them. I wonder if there wasn't something more that I was supposed to do, something I never saw. I look back over time and see some of the things I said or didn't say, the people I didn't try to reach, and some of the questionable things I did that only I know about that I will have to answer for."

"Daddy?" Allison said through her tears. "Why are you doing this to yourself? You're my hero . . . both you and Mom. You always have been."

Charles shoulders deflated with a sob. "I guess what I'm trying to say then is . . . that I wouldn't be half the man I am without you two. I wouldn't be anything. And, I want to apologize for the way I may have treated you or neglected you through all this. But I especially want to thank you for everything you have done for me."

Allison sobbed and made her way over to her sobbing father. "Dad, I don't want to hear that from you again. You have nothing to apologize for. You allowed me to be a part of something great, something beautiful, and it'll always be a part of who I am." She grabbed her father and hugged him as he cried.

Her mother wiped away her tears and waited as the two shared their sorrow and joy. Allison then got up and did the same with her mother. The confession had left the three exhausted and worn. They sat trying to recover their balance and let the spoken words sink into their souls.

"Is this what you wanted to tell me, Dad?" Allison finally

asked. "This is what you were talking about?"

Charles blew his nose in his hankie. "No honey, there's something else I need to tell you."

"Oh great," she said. "Let me get some more tissues."

They laughed at the thought and resumed their places.

Charles went through the different ways he had practiced this moment. "Do you happen to remember a man named William Stroud?"

Allison shook her head. "Uh, no, I don't think so. Should I?"

"Well, I don't see any reason why you would remember him, but he was someone who has always been a special friend to this family." Charles continued, "It was in Dale that we first met him. We spent a lot of time there, and he was always there. He gave his heart to Jesus at one of our first meetings. He spent most of his time confined to a wheelchair."

"So what about him?" Allison asked as her mind began to drift to her dreams.

"Well, he passed on . . . I guess about seven years ago," Charles started. "That's when we got this letter requesting that your mother and I go to Dale and be present at the reading of the will."

"Yes," Allison responded.

"Well, as you can imagine, we didn't know what to expect," Charles continued. "Apparently, he was a man of significant wealth, though you really couldn't tell. We listened as most of his large estate was parceled out to his small family, and then at the end the man pulled out a hand written note and began to read it."

Charles lifted his hand to his shirt pocket and pulled out a worn piece of paper and began to unfold it. Allison's eyes were glued to it as he carefully handled the old letter.

Charles grabbed his reading glasses and began to read.

"*I, William Benjamin Stroud, being of sound mind, add these words to my last will and testament. Having acknowledged* *my family and given to them enough to sustain and keep them, I wish to acknowledge another family. I think the words of Paul express my feeling the best: '... Whatever was to my profit I consider loss for the sake of Christ.' The man who taught me this scripture, Charles Abraham Wilson, I can only hope is sitting in this room with my family right now. I ask that each one of my family members listen to this man and pray with this man today, for my sake. I wish to make a covenant with this man today. That he should receive the amount of $50,000 for the care and education of the precious angel they call Allison. He will promise to use this money for her education and upon her graduation from college, inform her of this covenant."*

Tears once again began to run down Allison's face as the old man from her dream came to life. Her bottom lip began to tremble as she watched her father.

"*It is this person, of all people, in whom I have seen Christ. The care and comfort that this little girl has brought me, in my final days, is beyond my understanding. I pray that the day that she hears these words, she will understand the tremendous impact she had on my life, and it may serve some purpose in helping her find the path God has chosen for her life. I know that day I will be with my Lord, hoping to someday return the priceless gifts that she shared with me.*

Truly, truly, be with me as I try to be like thee. Take this sickness far away, make your children well today.

Signed William Benjamin Stroud."

Allison's face fell down to her lap as she cried out loud. Her mother and father watched in tears. The moment was more than they ever expected. They got up and hugged each other, feeling the undeniable hand of the Lord holding them.

Chapter 21

Ramana returned to the project room armed with a bottle of root beer and two packs of Fig Newtons. The flashing icon on his terminal immediately grabbed his attention. "DNA changes detected, do you want to continue?" flashed in a window on the screen of the work area. Ramana's breath rate increased as he ran to the keyboard and tried to determine how he would proceed. He instructed the computer to highlight the location, and then clicked the button to continue. Immediately the process halted again, and Ramana followed the same procedure. For the next twenty minutes, he went through the same thing until finally the analysis was complete. The beast finished and waited for further instructions.

Ramana scanned the highlighted areas with the discrepancies and looked for a pattern. Although the changes were scattered throughout the polypeptide chain, there seemed to be two distinct areas that contained the bulk of it. He cut and placed these areas in isolation. Finishing the first pack of cookies, he opened the other and popped one in his mouth. He scanned the structure and wondered about its makeup. It wasn't like the rest of the DNA structure, yet it was familiar. Realizing his time constraints, he decided to begin working on creating the new bacteria that David requested before examining the strange DNA further.

After cleaning up the rest of the mess in the operating room, he loaded up the construction routines with the proper information. His plan was to program it just like it had been for the original Kirk cell, except he would insert the proper routines for the cilia programs. The process was tedious and took most of the night. The construction routines had to create everything within the cell, so he took great care to set everything in place. When he finally looked at the clock on the wall, it was close to morning.

Ramana's hand hovered over the button to initiate the process, and his mind began to wander. If the process was unsuccessful, he realized that he could be there well into the morning trying to fix it. His hand came back to his body as he decided to wait and create the new creatures with a fresh start tomorrow. He looked around the now disorganized project room and began to imagine what lay in store for Allison just a few hours away. He saw her in a beautiful white dress with her family entering a church for Easter. He wondered how so many people could be wrapped up in this idea of this man coming back to life and escaping the fate we know awaits us all.

Ramana's eyes moved to the big monitor screen and looked at the fuzzy alpha cell. Immediately another wave of sadness flowed over him as he reflected over the events of the past semester. He struggled to determine the root of the sadness. There was nothing he could single out that caused it. Sitting alone in the project room, his mind tried to answer question after question. *Why am I really here? Why do I keep obsessing over this girl? Is it worth it? When will I be happy with this? Shouldn't I be back at home with my family?* The last question hit hardest and caused him to take a deep breath. His palms hit the desk as he decided he would rather leave the room for the night than try to field these questions. He gathered up his things, tried to clean up a little, and headed home for the night.

After church, Allison decided to saddle up her horse, and sometimes best friend of 12 years and visit her secret get-away spot. She took the outline that she had started on and her portable CD player and headphones. This was her chance to sit by herself out in creation and figure out how she would accomplish her task.

When he saw Allison, Prince snorted and scraped his hoof in anticipation of the long awaited reunion. Allison hoisted the saddle to the wooden fence and walked to her old companion. Her mind went back to the years that they had spent together. She hugged the horse's head and squeezed in appreciation as Prince licked her white shirt and finally jerked his head out of the grip. She happily wiped the grass and spit off of herself and began to brush the silver-gray coat of the animal. Her father watched from the window of the house, smiling as he tried to make the most of the short time that she would be present. Allison swung the heavy saddle onto the blanket on Prince's back and started the intricate weaving and buckling procedure. Prince moaned and snorted as Allison tried to tighten the main strap across his belly.

She hopped on the old horse, put on her headphones, and started him walking down the familiar path. She headed down past the abandoned barns and well houses a mile behind their property and made it to the small creek that still ran with spring water from deep underground. She took Prince down into it and let him feel the cool water, in which he dropped his head and began to drink. She gazed around the place that used to be her sanctuary, each sacred element revealing a distant memory as her eyes picked them out. She brought the horse over to her big tree and swung her legs off and onto the ground. She started to tie Prince to the tree and decided that he wasn't going anywhere, so she dropped the reins. He remembered the familiar ritual from the past and found a nice patch of grass to consume until his master needed him again. Grabbing her pad of paper, she headed for her throne at the base of the grand oak tree that shaded the creek. She set her things aside and looked up to the sky for insight.

Sufficiently content, Allison picked up her things and allowed her pen to scribble and doodle on the outsides of the pages as she tried to regain her thoughts. She let her eyes travel around the picturesque scene that was before her. The creek sang its comforting song as it splashed cool water on the rocks that littered its bed. Minnows, tadpoles, and crawfish scurried around the clear water, trying to find food to fill their permanently starving bellies. Bluebirds and cardinals swooped down to get a drink of the precious liquid and splashed vigorously with their wings, sending a spray into the spring air. Butterflies danced on the wildflowers that were fed by the bountiful creek. A feeling came over her as she watched these creatures in this wonderful setting. With her inner acknowledgement of the creative artist responsible for what was in front of her, she felt a sense of invulnerability that started her pen.

"Beauty is one of the greatest attributes of life." Allison wrote the first sentence in bold letters. She stopped and gazed at the words, feeling that they had come from somewhere unseen. She smiled as the words and ideas started to flow through her mind. As creation looked on, her hand attempted to keep up with her thoughts.

Chapter 22

"I just think that we should delay the news crew until we have time to sort things out a little," David said as he glanced around Dr. Green's office.

"It doesn't work that way, David. You should know that," Dr Green replied. "Either the story is done now or not at all. They will not wait around until we think we have a story. They think we have a story right now, and that's the only reason they're coming down here."

David stared at his boss silently, trying to determine the proper course of action.

"Tell me what the real problem is," Dr Green inquired. "Is it Punjabi again? Is he losing it again?"

David knew he couldn't go down that path. "No, it's not that. We're just having problems with the beast, you know, the computer. Funny things are happening and we've lost some of the more significant cells that we developed."

"What do you mean 'lost'?" Dr. Green inquired with a wondering grin. "They died or what?"

"No," started David. "We had a problem with the computer. Like I said, we had to reboot everything and we lost a lot of information. This is brand new stuff we are doing."

"You've got to be kidding me," Dr. Green snorted. "You didn't save your results? That seems like a sophomoric mistake."

David shook his head at the aging doctor. "It's not that

easy, Wallace. It's not like a normal computer, and they're not normal programs. It's all still so new . . . we're still learning and making mistakes . . . and well, we made a big one."

Dr. Green took off his glasses and rubbed his eyes. "Okay David, I have a feeling you haven't told me everything yet."

David inhaled deeply and stared blankly into the vastness of the office. Not wanting to beat around the bush anymore, he said, "We've lost all of the cells except the original Kirk cell. Right now, unless Ramana has changed our situation, we have nothing to show our CNN crew."

"What?" Dr. Green said even though he heard every word.

"Ramana was attempting to repeat the original experiment that created the new cells and that's when the computer locked up."

Dr. Green remained silent, wanting David to complete the thought.

David interpreted the sign. "We went back and forth about how to proceed. We knew it had some risks, but rebooting the computer seemed like the only way to fix it."

Dr. Green nodded his head, understanding David's concerns regarding the news crew. "Was Ramana able to determine how the . . . the new cell's origin . . . where they came from?"

"Well, we have some indications," David generalized. "But, in all honesty, we're still unclear about the exact process."

Dr. Green sneered at the obvious dodge. "Well, why don't you run the evolutionary routine again? It worked the first time. There's no reason to believe that it won't again."

"We're attempting that." David looked down at his watch. "But we're also trying to construct some similar cells to the ones that were created in the experiment. So chances are good that we could have something soon, but tomorrow–I don't know."

"Well, Dr. Levin," he looked down at his subordinate as he devised his strategy, "I suggest you make sure you do have something to show the world tomorrow. I don't have to tell you how important it is that we represent ourselves well on national TV for the regents, the faculty, the alumni, and so on. I suggest that you do whatever it takes to put on a good show for the cameras."

David turned his head and squinted at his fellow scientist. "I . . . I know, I'll take care of it. I'm sure Ramana has everything worked out by now. Don't worry, we'll be able to put on a good show."

"David," Dr. Green started.

"Yes?" David stood up as he prepared to depart.

"I don't want that crazy Indian saying something stupid or messing this thing up. You need to make sure he keeps his comments guarded . . . and to a minimum."

"Don't worry, Wallace," David assured him, "I'll take care of it."

"I'm confident you will. Your name is as much on the line as anyone else's," Dr. Green politely threatened. "I tell you what, though. I will meet with the crew first to give you some time. They should be getting here around one o'clock."

David nodded. "Sounds good. We'll be ready, don't worry." He turned around and left the office, developing options in his head.

After spending the morning together in heated interaction, the beast alerted its master with the results he was anxiously anticipating. "Construction routine successful, do you want to continue?" flashed across Ramana's monitor screen. He stared at the message halfway through taking a bite of his sandwich and tried to determine which was more important. After a quick choice, he set the battered sandwich down and moved toward the beast. He hit the appropriate buttons to take him to the operating room and gazed upon their creation. Ramana's eyes gave away the success of the experiment. The new creature lay motionless in the work area, a beautiful specimen waiting for its creator to give it the breath of life. Ramana looked closely at the membrane, which had the hair-like cilia in neat and organized rows completely around the cell.

Looking back down to his keyboard, he hit the key to transport the cell to the E.P. Once the cell appeared next to the remaining Kirk cell, he paused, hesitant to do anything to destroy his intricate masterpiece. Again his hand hesitated above the button to activate the cell as he heard the door open.

David quickly made his way into the room and immediately appraised the situation. "Ramana, you did it! Ha! I knew we would be all right."

Ramana looked at him confidently. "What did you expect? I was just about to start him up."

"Wait," snapped David. "Uh . . . let's think about this. Why don't we go ahead and make some copies of the cell before we do anything that could harm it."

Ramana shrugged his shoulders. "I don't even know if it works . . . I mean, if it will come alive."

"Still, I think we should go ahead and make copies now, just to be safe." David moved close to Ramana's terminal.

"Okay, I guess you're right," Ramana relented. "It did take quite a while for the beast to construct this guy. But we did it, first try."

"You guys make quite a team, don't you?" David laughed.

Ramana began to set the beast to duplicate the newly created cell. "How many do you want?"

"Oh, I don't know," David began. "I'd say a dozen or so."

"You got it." Ramana entered the data and the beast set off to work. "It should take around thirty minutes or so. I have it processing the duplication very slowly and methodically."

"Good." David took a seat at the conference table. "One problem solved."

"How'd your meeting with Dr. Green go?" Ramana asked.

"Oh, fine. He's gonna meet the reporters first. We may not see them until tomorrow." David looked into his palm computer. "I assured him that we would put on a good show for the university."

"What do you mean?" asked Ramana.

"Oh, you know." David grinned. "Television is very powerful, and reporters can be . . . well, let's just say that we need to be careful about how we present our work and what we say."

"I got an idea." Ramana grinned. "How about I keep my mouth shut and let you do all the talking."

David smiled at another problem solved. "That sounds good. I think I know how to handle these guys."

David's face turned serious again. "Tell me, Ramana, have you been able to determine anything regarding the new cells produced from the evolutionary routine?"

Ramana's face flashed with insight. "Yes . . . I mean, well, no. I did find the remains of the omega cell in the work area, and there were some pretty unusual mutations in the DNA. I haven't been able to classify them yet, but I'm of the opinion that it may reveal something that could help us determine the cause of the membrane changes."

David looked at Ramana in confusion. "What? I don't get it. How does a mutation in the Kirk cell have anything to do with the evolutionary routine? The Kirk cells were not even involved in the experiment."

"Yes, but," Ramana raised his finger, "both times that the evolutionary routine has been run, the omega cell ended up in the work area. This last time, well, it really ended up in the work area, like torn up, destroyed."

"What do you think it means?" asked David.

"I don't know, but while the cells are being duplicated, we can take a closer look at the mutations." Ramana moved to the isolation area that he place the chains of DNA and magnified them on-screen. "See, here are the areas of the omega's cell that were different. I haven't been able to determine their makeup or origin, but the structure seems very familiar."

David stood up and placed the glasses on his face. "Can you put a piece of normal DNA next to it?"

Ramana looked down at his terminal. "Sure, here, I'll use the construction program to make a put together a small chain." He quickly programmed the beast to construct a tiny piece of Kirk's DNA. They stared at the process as the double-helix came together before their eyes.

"Ah, I see what you mean," David observed. "Yeah, it doesn't look like normal DNA. Has Mark taken a look at it yet?"

"I haven't seen Mark since he left on Saturday," said Ramana.

"Well, he should be in today," David said hopefully. "We've been working him pretty hard."

Ramana tried not to scowl at his boss. "Mmm-hmm."

"Speaking of that," started David, "don't you have a class to teach about now?"

"Oh crap!"

Allison tried not to giggle as Ramana made it through the doorway of his classroom three minutes late. He quickly made his way to his desk and laid his things upon it. Since the afternoon at the creek, her mind was alive with innumerable thoughts regarding this course, her teacher, and the essay that was halfway complete. As she watched Ramana prepare to speak, she wondered what the last few weeks of school had in store for the two. Ramana's eyes scanned the classroom and eventually met up with hers. She smiled with a warmth that he had never seen before, and it forced his lips to smile in response. His head immediately dropped down to hide the involuntary reaction that occurred. He turned back to chalkboard and began to write: "Final Exam-Last day of class, Friday May 14."

Ramana turned back around and cleared his throat. "As you can see, our final is only a few short weeks away. I will be using the remainder of our class together to review what will be included on that exam and help you with any problem areas that you are experiencing. Let me also say on a personal note . . ." Ramana paused as he felt a wave of emotion run through his body. "As many of you know, this has been my first experience teaching students on the university level . . . well, really on any level, this class and my morning class. I wanted to say that you people have made it very easy for me, and I appreciate that, more than you know probably."

Allison's smile grew bigger as she saw this man struggle to confess his feelings to their group.

"Truly, I have learned as much from you students as I have attempted to teach to you. I can only hope that I will continue to have students and classes that are as fulfilling and special as these. I thank you from deep in my heart."

Somewhat red-faced with his voice quivering, Ramana turned back around to the chalkboard and walked towards it, wondering if he had just made a fool of himself. His ears then heard the familiar clapping of Allison's hands that again was joined with the many that were in the room. Ramana turned around in surprise as the sound and faces of his students affirmed his performance more than any of his peers or department heads would ever be able to.

Ramana stood watching the spectacle, feeling guilty for maybe manufacturing it, but nonetheless, soaking up every ounce of this precious substance that he could.

After the review session was over, both Allison and Ramana knew they had to discuss what had happened since Good Friday. She nervously walked to his desk as the classroom emptied.

"Hey," she said.

"Hey," he replied.

Silence quickly replaced the words.

Allison's hands and fingers began to fumble in front of her. "So, how is everything?"

Ramana squinted and searched his brain for the proper response. "Complicated."

Allison couldn't respond and stood in silence.

Ramana changed the subject for her. "How was everything at home, your family?"

She jerked in response. "Oh, it was great, fantastic even. I ... I got some incredible news ... really got a good start on my paper. It was great."

"That's wonderful." Ramana tried not to sigh as he said the words.

"How was your weekend?" Allison asked, realizing as she finished the question that it probably wasn't the right one to ask.

Ramana scanned it in his head, which worked slowly due to the lack of sleep. "Hmmm, long, eventful, depressing, and to top it all off, we have a CNN crew due here any minute to report on our revolutionary project that, to say the very least, is in shambles."

Allison stared at him speechless, confused, and began to feel guilty.

Ramana finished packing up his materials and said, "I'm sorry, I don't mean to dump that on you, Allison. Really what I want to tell you is how much I appreciate your help on the project, how much fun I had at the party Friday, and how happy I am for you. I mean, you're about to graduate and start a brand new life. This is a joyous time and I'm glad I get to share even the smallest part."

A switch clicked in Allison's head as she listened to this man. Decisions she had made two days earlier started flying out of the window. "Ramana, I'm not gonna let you do this alone. Are you going over to the project room now?"

He turned his head back to her and nodded. "Why?"

"Because, I'm going with you and will do whatever I can to help you."

"But David is going to be right there. You don't have to subject yourself to this," he said.

"Screw David," Allison barked. "I'm not worried about

him anymore. I'm worried about you and I'm not going let you go through this alone, Ramana."

The smile on Ramana's face began to grow. The feeling of confusion and weariness began to transform into power and determination as he stared at this angel of beauty.

As soon as his face reached its zenith, it was replaced with concern. "There's some bad news I have to tell you, Allison."

Allison's face changed too. "What is it?"

Ramana paused as he thought. "Kirk is dead . . . at least one of them is dead."

"Oh my gosh. What happened?" Her face showed her concern.

Ramana looked down at his watch. "Let me fill you in on the way to the project lab."

"Okay," she said as all of her prior plans were erased.

The two left the empty classroom and headed for the lab. Everything in their path disappeared with the intensity of the words they spoke.

Chapter 23

"And coming up next," the veteran anchor said as he stared into his teleprompter, "Scientists at the University of Texas have developed a computer-based life form that has the potential of replacing laboratory test animals and could tell us more about our own primordial origins, after these messages."

Allison looked over to Ramana with excitement in her eyes. "Oh my gosh, here it comes."

Ramana's head poked out from his kitchen. "It's on?"

"No, not yet, after the commercial," she answered.

"Oh, good," he turned back to finish his task. "I'm almost done."

"What are you doing in there?" she asked.

Ramana remained silent.

"You'd better hurry," she warned him.

"You need some more wine?" he finally spoke up.

"Uh, sure," Allison answered once again, wondering about the position she had gotten herself into. She looked around his apartment and realized how organized things had become, and how much Ramana must have struggled to get it this way.

Ramana emerged from the kitchen with a bottle of wine tucked under his arm and two Caesar salads in his hands. He awkwardly arranged them on his coffee table. "Cracked pepper, ma'am?"

Allison laughed and played along. "Please, sir."

They sat down and began to eat as the commercials came

to an end. Their eyes focused on the archaic television as the TV anchor forced a serious look into camera one. "Thirteen civilians were killed today in another suicide attack . . ."

Both Allison and Ramana tried to deflect the horrible news away from the enjoyment of moment while trying not to seem insensitive.

"Wow, this salad is great," Allison said, successfully changing the subject.

"Thank you." Ramana smiled. "It's an old family recipe."

Allison's face went from confusion to appreciation of Ramana's developing sense of humor.

" . . . Scientists at the University of Texas in Austin, Texas have developed a computer that has spawned the emergence of a completely new form of life." The TV pulled the two to the edge of their seats. "Two biology researchers are working on a single celled life form that exists in a world similar to ours, the only difference being, this one exists in the memory of a highly experimental computer. Science reporter Arthur Lewis has the story."

They looked at each other and couldn't help but laugh. "To Arthur," Allison toasted.

The camera took them to the familiar room in which they had worked countless hours. The room looked strange from the lens of the camera, distorted and small.

"A completely new basis for life and corresponding new life form has been created in the laboratories of the University of Texas. One made completely of a new trinary computer language and millions of hurling electrons in an amazing computer using the latest in experimental storage technology. This life is every bit as complex and real as the life that we see around us. The computer that makes this possible, the beast as it is called, is a one-of-a-kind computer itself and uses a highly experimental solid core for storage instead of the common two-dimensional silicon disk. The creators of this world's newest inhabitants, Dr. David Levin and Ramana Punjabi, say that the most significant use for this new creature and ones to come will be the research that can come from them. Medical, genetic, even evolutionary testing should provide answers that, to this point, have eluded science. The creature you see here is the product of a routine that tries to replicate our own world's evolution at a remarkably faster pace. It has developed the means of locomotion on its own and could presumably, given enough time, evolve in a similar fashion to ourselves."

Ramana looked down at the last sentence as he felt Allison's wondering stare upon him.

"The advancements that this research team made in this area have truly placed the University of Texas and its research department among the leaders in artificial intelligence and biological research. Reporting from Austin, Texas for CNN science and technology, I am Arthur Lewis."

Allison's stare made it back to the TV as the anchor led them to another story about the upcoming election. She waited for Ramana to say something as she resumed eating her salad.

Ramana followed her lead and started eating once again, aware of the rest of the meal that he still needed to finish. "Wow, that's definitely the first time my name has been mentioned on TV."

Allison smiled. "You're famous, Ramana. You guys are on the cutting edge of science, for sure. You're life may change now that you're a celebrity."

Ramana frowned. "Celebrity, huh? I don't think so. Anyway, you're as much a part of it as anyone else."

Allison looked down with a puzzled look on her face.

"What's wrong, Allison?" he asked.

Allison paused. "Well, the story wasn't exactly accurate."

Ramana shrugged his shoulders. "Yeah, I know. I kept my mouth shut as David explained things to Arthur and the rest of the news crew. I knew he was misrepresenting things a bit, but I couldn't . . . I didn't want to . . . I don't know." He got up to take his empty bowl to the kitchen and prepare the rest of the meal.

"I hope you don't think badly of me."

Allison still looked puzzled. "Ramana, I just don't understand why you didn't tell the truth about what you know and what you did."

Ramana's stomach began to churn as he reached the kitchen. "It's not that easy. There's a lot of pressure on the project now. Dr. Green and the department have so many expectations and desires for this project . . . or any project really. This one just seems to have so much momentum behind it right now."

"Well, you have to admit, what they said on the news piece was a lie," Allison pushed.

Ramana tried to put off the question as his dinner preparations began to look worse in his mind. He stayed silent while his thoughts raced.

"I'm sorry, Ramana." Allison tried to relieve the pressure. "I know it's not your fault, but really, that cell that they showed was not a product of the evolutionary routine. You made it. You told me you did."

"It's no different than the ones that were made in the evolution routine," Ramana defended.

"That's not the point," she shot back.

"Okay," Ramana walked back out into her sight, "what exactly is the point?"

"Okay, well for starters, you still don't know how the original cells changed, do you?" she asked.

Ramana tried to change the subject. "Well . . . let me ask you this."

"Uh huh?" she responded.

"Do you like grated parmesan on your pasta?" He looked around the corner for her reaction.

"Ramana!"

"Let's talk about it after dinner. Why don't you tell me about your paper?" Ramana used the diversion to his advantage.

Allison relented and decided to let him off the hook. She

angrily laughed and said, "No."

He tried a long shot. "Well, Miss Wilson, if you would like a good grade in this class, young lady, I think you should be a little more forthcoming."

Allison smiled at his misguided courage. "You better watch it there, professor. You could get yourself into some big trouble with me."

Ramana entered the room with two plates of pasta. "I fear I already have."

Allison let the comment go unchallenged. "Wow, that smells great. I'm very impressed."

"Well, you'd better taste it first," he said.

"I'm sure it's wonderful," she responded.

The two ate until their plates were nearing emptiness and stained with the tomato sauce that Ramana had created. Allison got up and began to take her plate and things to the kitchen. Ramana stared at her as she moved, imagining what it would be like to have this play out every night for the rest of his life. For some reason the remoteness of the possibility did not depress him. The short time of this strange relationship had produced enough emotion for a lifetime. He got up and followed her into the kitchen, where they cleaned up the mess that Ramana had made.

"So, where do you go now?" Allison vaguely asked.

Ramana crunched his brow, trying to determine what she meant. "You mean about the project, right?"

She nodded her head as the lines of confrontation began to take shape again.

He took his seat again at the couch and brought the nearly empty bottle of wine with him. "Well, I would assume we are going to continue developing different cells throughout the summer, continue to experiment with the evolutionary routine, and hopefully create something useful out of this thing. How about you? What do you plan on doing after you graduate?"

Allison's eyes lifted to his as she thought. "You know, I

haven't decided yet . . . still. She paused and thought twice about revealing what happened over Easter. "Though I kinda got a sign when I was home for Easter, but I really don't know what to make of it."

"A sign? Like from God?" he asked.

"Well, I guess you could say that," she confessed. "At least it felt that way, but I've been feeling that way a lot lately. I just haven't put everything in place yet."

Ramana nodded his head. "I feel the same way. I've been having crazy dreams and visions and I don't know what they mean."

"Like what?" she asked.

Ramana proceeded cautiously. "I'm not sure I should tell you . . . but before I put Kirk together. Before I put any cell together, I had this crazy dream or vision at the Quackenbush."

Allison laughed. "I'm sure you're not the first . . . maybe somebody slipped something in your coffee."

Ramana took offense. "I didn't think I should tell you."

Allison pouted. "I'm sorry Ramana, I was just kidding. Really though, I think you should tell me about it. Maybe I can help you interpret it."

With a frown, he said, "Well, I haven't told anybody about this, and I don't want it told to anybody else."

"You have my word," she promised.

"Okay," Ramana started. "It was early in the morning. I hadn't been getting any sleep, and it's not like I'm getting a whole lot right now. I must've fallen asleep or something, but I dreamed harder and more real than I ever have before. I was alone with the beast, and we began building cells together, piece by piece. Then we began connecting them together to form all sorts of creatures. I saw how everything came together to form these complex organisms using thoughts and instincts–it was incredible. By the time we finished, the place where we stood was overrun by hundreds of creatures . . . animals."

Allison listened intently to his story. Sufficiently satisfied with her reaction, Ramana continued.

"It all happened so fast, too. We went from tiny plankton to wolves, and birds, and monkeys. It sounds crazy, I know, but I was putting them together . . . I saw how it was done. I mean, the next day, I knew what to do to produce Kirk . . . and I did it."

"That's incredible, Ramana." Allison smiled with wonder. "Really, I've never heard anything like that before. Is that where it ended?"

"No." Ramana paused. "It went on and the last part really confuses me . . . I don't know what to think about it. It seemed like things happened without me doing it . . . I mean, it was like I was a spectator. It was quite embarrassing, too."

"How so?" she asked.

He looked up to her eyes. "It ended up with me waking up in the middle of a scream . . . to the surprise of everyone in the coffee shop, me included."

Allison couldn't help but giggle. "You're kidding."

Ramana shook his head.

"So what was the end of the dream?" she asked.

Ramana took a deep breath. "I remember contemplating what it would take to take the last step, to give to a human organism what it is to be human: Sentience, self-awareness, and a will of its own, whatever you want to call it. I couldn't grasp it; I tried for what seemed like a long time. It seemed like my inside was turning itself outward as I got closer to what my own existence was revealing."

Allison's eyes widened as his words and her imagination took her to his dream.

"In an instant, light and colors were all around me and I saw myself as I was. I realized that I was the answer. It was inside of me." Ramana paused again as he felt his pulse rise. "The next thing I know, I had pulled the panels off of the computer and was sticking my hands inside to grab the main power grid. I swear I felt the electricity flowing through my body when I touched it. It felt like every cell in my body was being ripped apart and I screamed. I screamed like I've never screamed before."

"My God, Ramana, that's wild," she concluded.

"Yeah, I thought so," he said. "What do you think it means?"

Allison drew back in her chair. "Man, I have no clue. But you said you learned something from the dream, didn't you?"

"Yeah, after the dream, it seemed like everything was clear. I knew where to go with the first cell, how to finish it." Ramana's gaze went out into the distance as if he was trying to look back to the past.

Allison looked at Ramana, unable to say anything at the same point that he had run out of words. They sat in silence trying to determine the meaning of their visions, their dreams, their signs, and their lives.

Chapter 24

Arthur Lewis had suspected something was wrong after he watched his news piece air just hours earlier. Something about seeing the final edit aired on TV made his mind began to replay all of the events that had transpired. Though he had given the scientist the benefit of the doubt, Arthur felt that David was not being completely honest with the findings and conclusions that he had just reported to the nation. The possibility of being used as a pawn began to make him extremely angry, and created within him a desire to delve deeper into the project and the people that were responsible for it. He was able to track down Mark at the computer science lab as he worked on one of the many projects to which he provided technical assistance. After completing the standard introductory small talk, he inquired about the project, which he hadn't been involved with much in the last week.

"Did you see the piece on CNN?" the reporter asked.

Mark turned his head. "No, how'd it go?"

Arthur tried to be humble. "Well, it went fine. We've gotten a lot of response from it. The story behind those cells and how they evolved has a lot of people intrigued. David said that the phones at his office are ringing off the hook."

"So they recovered them?" Mark asked.

The reporter's instincts began to work as he sensed an opportunity. "Um, yeah they did," he responded, not knowing where the conversation was going.

Mark looked up from his work. "Wow, that's really surprising. I thought we lost all of them when we rebooted the computer."

Arthur put on his poker face. "Oh yeah, they said something about that . . . but it was kind of confusing. I have such a hard time with all that technical stuff." The reporter's hand automatically grabbed for the note pad in his pocket as he easily manipulated the unexpecting novice. "Do you think you can explain it in a way I can understand?"

Mark laughed. "Sure. Man, that scared the crap out of us. While Ramana was running the evolutionary routine again trying to figure out how the new cells formed, the computer locked up. It had never happened since the computer was developed. We didn't even think it was possible. So once we tried everything we could, we decide to shut the computer down."

"Hmmmm." Arthur sighed, unraveling in his head the game that the two scientists had played.

Mark continued, "Once we got everything restarted, all the new cells appeared to be gone–except for that original Kirk cell. I guess we should have saved . . . or separated some of the cells that changed. We just didn't think that far ahead. I'm not sure it could even be done."

Arthur nodded his head, trying to get Mark to elaborate further.

Mark continued, "I haven't talked to David or Ramana about it, but they must have gone back and recovered those cells somehow."

Arthur's mind went back to the day that he barged in on the trio where they were acting so strangely. The only cell visible then was the Kirk cell. He was now sure that he was the victim of some sort of deception by the research team. Arthur laughed inside at the inept skills that these scientists possessed in relation to his investigative talents.

The anger that burned within Arthur led him down another road. "Let me ask you another question. What do you think about the relationship that Ramana has with that one girl . . . um, Allison, isn't it?"

Mark laughed at the suggestion. "I think it's pretty innocent. You know, he's probably not had a date since he's been in America, so I can completely understand it. It's really more common than you'd think."

"So you think something's going on then?" Arthur continued.

"Well, let's just say . . ." Mark got a look of concern on his face. "This is off the record, right?"

"I'm done with this story."

Mark hesitated as he tried to determine what the reporter's statement meant. "Come on, Arthur, you really think a pretty girl like that would have anything to do with a guy like Ramana? I think it's a case of wishful thinking on Ramana's part. It's always nice to think a pretty girl like her could fall for one of us science nerds. I would be very surprised if anything has come from it."

Arthur nudged him. "Yeah, you're probably right. She is one cutie though, isn't she?"

Mark laughed. "Jeeesh, I guess I'd be more disappointed if Ramana didn't at least try, you know."

The two continued to laugh. Arthur got up from the side of the desk. "Well, I've gotta get out of here. I guess I'll be seeing you around, Mark. Take care."

"Yeah, see ya, Arthur," he said as his attention went back to his work.

The reporter's mind now began to weigh options for pursuing a story that detailed the obvious scandal that was unfolding before him. At the very least, he decided that a subtle yet more in-depth investigation was in order.

The longer Mark sat at his terminal, the more he wondered if he had said too much to the reporter. As he went back over the conversation he just had, he began to worry about his loose tongue and decided to head to the project room. He found Ramana alone with the beast and walked in. Mark looked around at the room he hadn't seen in a week.

"Mark," Ramana turned and smiled, "good to see you. I was just about to call you and see if you could come check out a few things."

"Hey Ramana, no need. I'm here," he replied.

Ramana sighed, "I want you to look at something," just as Mark said, "I have something to tell you."

They both looked at each other, hesitating in silence until Mark said, "Go ahead."

"Well okay, it's been such a whirlwind around here for the last week that I don't feel like I've accomplished anything," Ramana said as he punched some buttons on his terminal. "I've found a strange mutation in one of the Kirk cell's DNA, and I was hoping that you could help me identify it."

Mark grabbed a pair of glasses on the table and stepped back to get a good look. "A mutation, huh?"

"Yeah," Ramana replied, "I found the omega cell in the work area, blown apart, all over the place. And when I analyzed the DNA, I found several areas that were unlike anything we asked the construction routines to build." Ramana pulled up the isolated area containing the pieces of DNA. "There are all the areas that were mutated. Let me magnify, um, this part first."

Ramana put his glasses on, grabbed a remote control to manipulate the screen, and joined Mark in front of the big screen. "You see, this is a different structure than any of the other DNA that the Kirk cell, or any other cell contained."

"Hmmmm." Mark squinted as he gazed at it. "You know, it looks like . . . hold on a second." He headed for his old terminal.

Ramana bent his head down to peer out of the space above his glasses. "What?"

Mark remained silent as he punched on his keyboard. Ramana slowly began to walk towards him. Mark stopped typing and then turned his head to Ramana. "It has the same structure as the safety loop."

"What?" Ramana shrugged. "The safety loop? How could

"... what is ... Oh my God." Ramana's eyes got wide as he started to unravel the story.

Mark went back to his terminal. "You're right though, it is mutated ... it's quite a bit different from the original."

Ramana's mind was still trying to understand. "Do you see any indication of how it got into the DNA structure?"

Mark stayed silent, looking intently into his monitor.

Ramana moved over to his monitor. "Let me pull up the other DNA mutations and let you take a look at them."

"Sure," Mark replied.

In a few minutes, Ramana had pulled up two more large portions of the programs in question, and they stepped back to examine them.

After analyzing them for a few minutes, Mark looked at Ramana. "You know what that is, don't you?"

Ramana looked at Mark and then back to the large screen. "It appears to be some part of the E.P. What do you think?"

Mark nodded his head. "It looks like the controls–the controls to the environmental program."

Ramana's eyes squinted to see closer. "What is happening here?"

"Is this a joke, Ramana?" Mark asked. "You found this stuff in Kirk's DNA?"

Ramana's mind was working. "I'm not sure how it got there, but I think I may have an idea about what's been happening around here."

"Tell me what you think," Mark requested.

Ramana paused. "Well, I want to check some things first. It would probably sound crazy anyway."

The two stared at the screen in silence until Ramana broke it. "By the way, what were you going to tell me earlier?"

A chill hit Mark as he remembered what he had come there for. "Oh yeah ... Ramana, I'm not sure, but I think I may have screwed up big-time."

Allison sat in front of Rachel's computer trying to plug into the same inspiration that pumped out the few pages of words at home. Her first instinct, like anything related to schoolwork, was one of aversion. She forced herself to sit there and read the words that she had transcribed from her notepad, trying to leap back into the train of thought. Rachel lied on her bed trying to read the textbook that held the answers to the test that loomed over her head. Their room was identical to countless others around the country at this time. An open pizza box, Starbucks coffee cups, papers, texts, and the two clothed in boxers and t-shirts, hoping that this universal tradition of cramming up until the final moment held the key to their success.

Allison sighed, as the words seemed to be locked behind some unseen door.

"No luck?" Rachel looked up from her text.

Allison's head went down. "I'm stuck. I know what I want to say, but it's just not coming out."

"You still have a couple days on that, don't you?" she asked.

Allison's head turned around, "Yeah, but I'd sure like to wrap it up so I can think about it before I turn it in. You know, work out the kinks and everything."

"Anyway," Rachel began, "don't you have a final in Spanish tomorrow?"

Allison laughed, "Si, senora."

"I'd think that'd be what you'd be working on," she observed.

"You're probably right, but this is the only thing that I'm really motivated to do." She sized up her performance. "And, geeeez, I'm not doing crap on this."

Rachel looked at the clock. It read 1:30 am. "Well, it's not surprising. I think I've had about enough." Her book popped loudly as she slammed it closed. "That's it for me, girl. I think I'm calling it a night. I'm gonna leave it up to St. Gregory from here on out."

Allison turned again and laughed at her friend's suggestion. "Rachel, what am I gonna do without you?"

Rachel's face changed to a sad smile. "Maybe we can stay in college forever."

The girls laughed at the inviting thought to ease the pain of their ever-approaching farewells.

Allison hit the appropriate buttons and got up from the computer. "I guess you're right. I can't even think straight anymore. Let's go to bed. We'll clean up this mess in the morning." She turned on her lamp and shut off the overhead light. She went to Rachel, sat on the side of her bed and looked at her.

"What do think is gonna become of us?" Allison asked as she grabbed her hand.

"Not a clue, Ally. I wish somebody could tell us," she said.

Allison nodded her head as her gaze fell to the floor. "I think we'll be okay. Goodnight, sleep well."

"Goodnight." Rachel pulled for her covers as Allison moved to her bed.

Allison set the appropriate alarms and turned out the lights. Her body was so tired, she was sure that she would be out cold as soon as she hit the pillow. She lied down and looked at Rachel, who seemed to already be in dreamland, then turned on her back and waited for sleep. Sleep did not come. The moment her eyes looked toward the ceiling, her mind came alive. Thoughts that began four months ago twisted through the events of the last semester. Allison's eyes never closed as she thought of Ramana, her parents, and her paper. Just as she thought she had wrapped the thorough process, she looked at the clock that now read 3:30 am. Her stomach felt queasy at the prospect of having little or no sleep to face the day with. Her mind raced with thoughts about the paper, and the words came forth in all sorts of combinations. She knew she had to get up and put them down before they were lost forever. She pulled the covers off and headed through the dark room toward the computer. When she hit the button on the monitor it clicked, followed by the pulsating sound of the tube firing up. She glanced back at Rachel, hoping that the noise and ever brightening glow didn't wake her. Content that her friend was not bothered, she stared once again at the last words she had written.

"This creation, intricately interwoven with these transcendent laws, results in an unequaled and incomprehensible beauty." Her fingers began to silently type on the next paragraph. "Modern science attributes this beauty to a constantly broadening balance of chaos and phenomena. It attributes these strict laws of nature to nothing, no one. They are random statutes that conveniently fell into place as the elements of our reality: space, matter, time, light, gravity, energy, and the rest appeared suddenly from a mysterious void." Allison smiled as her thoughts became clear and the words began to flow from her fingertips.

Chapter 25

When Mark left the project room, Ramana sat alone in the quiet trying to place all the seemingly scattered pieces of his life in some order. He wasn't angry with Mark; he was angry with himself. He wasn't even angry with David. He saw, looking back, that everything could have been different if he had chosen a better path on which to travel. All the problems that he found himself in now were caused by shortcuts, lies, and inappropriate behavior.

A confrontation with Arthur had to be the only answer; a confessional, a plea to do what was right and honorable. That was the only thing to do from here on out, Ramana decided. He began rummaging through notes and finally found Arthur's mobile number. Reluctantly, he dialed the number and had a short conversation with Arthur. Both he and Arthur knew that what had to be said could only be done face to face. The time was now for their troublesome relationship to be ironed out one way or another

After the phone call, Ramana turned his attention back to the discoveries that Mark had made about the DNA mutations. Content to delay his confrontation with Arthur for a few moments more, his mind tried to piece together the story of how the cellular changes were made and the fate of the omega cell. His thoughts went back to the night that he and Allison had set up that fateful experiment. Immediately a twinge of despair was added into the equation, as possible scenarios of his outcome flashed in his mind. He shook his head to release them and went back on the trail.

Ramana determined, just by chronology, that the Kirk cell mutations were most likely to have taken place prior to the first evolutionary tests. He remembered, after the first experiment, the spike in the E.P. and the attempt to determine its origins. His hand started to write on the pages in front of him. "Initial anomalies in E.P. caused by omega cell, possibly initiated by actions of the evolutionary routine." It began to fit in place as he realized that the safety loop inside of the Kirk cell would attempt to gain access to the E.P. "The destruction sub-routine was interpreted as a threat, and Kirk attempted to shut down the program."

Ramana paused as he contemplated this possibility. If this were true, Kirk was forced to react as thousands of its own were slaughtered in their quest for answers. As Ramana pondered this thought, he wondered why it made his stomach strain against the rest of his body. This was not unlike any other bacterial experiment; millions of life forms are experimented on for the sake of science. He was not opposed to this practice, and he never would be; it produced much greater benefit than the cost. It was one of the backbones of science. Why would this be any different?

As his mind settled his stomach, his hand continued to write the possibilities on his paper. "Kirk somehow gained access to the construction routines within the work area . . ." He stopped as he realized he hadn't answered how Kirk had gotten into the work area. Ramana's pen tapped the paper as he looked at the list of controls that were contained in the mutated DNA. After a few minutes of sifting through them, he determined that it could have been possible for Kirk to move and open the secure passage to the work area.

Ramana kept working, continually aware of the impending meeting with Arthur, trying to keep focus on the story unraveling in his mind. Just as he began to reach his final conclusions and place the reality of the meeting out of his mind, the door creaked on its hinges and the reporter walked in.

"Ramana," Arthur began, "You ready for me? Am I allowed to come in?"

Ramana stood up from his terminal. "Yes, Arthur, come in, please." He made his way to the conference table with his notes and motioned for the reporter to join him. Arthur noticed the change in Ramana's face as he shook his outstretched hand. He was amused and empowered by the obvious position of strength that he now possessed.

"So Ramana, what did you want to talk to me about?" Arthur coyly asked.

Ramana went through a checklist in his head and said, "First, Arthur, I believe I need to apologize to you for the way I've treated you during the time you have spent here."

Arthur smiled as this confirmed his suspicions. He deduced that Mark had been there already.

"I've had a chance . . . and I guess an opportunity to look back over the past weeks, and I am somewhat disgusted with myself." Ramana had to clear his throat as his voice cracked with this first confession. "I've not only been . . . let's say inhospitable to you. I think I may have recently allowed you to be misled."

Arthur allowed his face turn to a feigned surprise. "Misled? How?"

Ramana began to speak then stopped. "Let me start from the beginning, if you will allow me."

Arthur nodded his head.

Ramana recounted the events that brought about the new bacteria accompanied with the facts that he had just uncovered. He explained his theory of how the original Kirk cells had mutated and taken over the operation of the environmental program, therefore corrupting the experiment. He told of how the computer had locked up and had to be rebooted. As a result, all of the new cells had disappeared, and the ones shown on the news report, although similar, were not as they had presented, a result of the evolutionary routine.

Arthur once again displayed a disapproving frown at the realization of the misrepresentation. "Tell me, who else knew about these things?"

Ramana's mind reviewed the path that he was on and he immediately made his choice to lie again. "No one. Once the cells were lost, I assured David that I had some saved and would use those for the interview. It was my choice. I . . . I thought it was the best way to proceed. I made a decision, and I think now that it was a bad one."

Arthur listened to the confession and stared at Ramana, "What exactly is the purpose of this meeting, Ramana?"

Ramana pursed his lips as he kept thinking. "Well, I guess to lay my cards out on the table and to find out how you would handle being told this information."

Arthur remained silent, not wanting to play his hand too early.

Ramana continued, "Although I rationalized my deceit then, and in my mind, I still can, I am not going to try to rationalize it to you."

"Mmhmm. I appreciate that," Arthur replied self-righteously.

"I guess what I am asking is how you are going to handle this information?" concluded Ramana.

"Is this all of the information that you need to tell me?" the reporter asked.

Ramana looked around the room as he thought. "I . . . I think so. I mean I can go into more detail if you want me to, but that is it in a nutshell. Why? Do you have something else that you want to know about?"

Arthur contemplated his direction. Something inside him couldn't resist the feeling of power the confession gave him. He felt the need to go further. "Well, since you are in the confession mode."

Ramana looked confused. "Yes?"

"Well, I don't know how to put this lightly, Ramana, but

". . . well . . . I guess I'll just say it. Are you or have you ever been involved with any of your students?"

"Involved?" Ramana asked innocently. "I'm very involved with my students."

Arthur shook his head. "No, Ramana. I mean personally involved, like sexually?"

Ramana's face turned to surprise. "Oh my God! No! What are you saying?"

Arthur dismissed his protest. "Listen Ramana, I'm not stupid. I've seen lots of things around here. I've heard even more things. You guys have not been completely honest with me around here. I'm beginning to believe some of the rumors I've heard."

"What? What have you heard?" pleaded Ramana.

"Well," the reporter started, "for starters, there's a rumor out there that you propositioned one of your students on your first day of class."

Ramana's eyes turned from his inquisitor. The surprise of the question forced them away and made his shoulders sink.

Arthur knew he was on the right track. "Well, Ramana, is that accurate, or just a rumor?" He began again without an answer. "And I have to be honest–I have seen you in a number of compromising situations with one of your assistants."

Ramana's gaze fell to the ground as he felt trapped in a cage; he couldn't speak.

Arthur went for the kill. "It's Allison, isn't it?"

Her name was enough of a jolt to return his stare back to Arthur's eyes.

"She's the one you've been involved with, isn't she?" He turned into a prosecutor.

Ramana's face turned pained. "Involved? No, we're not involved in anything but the project. We're friends but nothing else."

Arthur continued to frown at his answer. "How can I be sure that you are not lying again, Ramana?"

Ramana gathered his composure. "Truly, I am not lying to you, Arthur. She would have nothing to do with me in that way," he said with emphasis.

Arthur's stare examined his witness. He remained silent, trying to decipher the truth. "Mmhmm. Well, I guess that's not the big story. Anyway, I'm sure that kind of thing happens quite a lot around here with all of these pretty young girls."

Ramana's mind cringed on the words "big story" as he tried to calm his breathing and think about how to proceed. He tried not to let the accusation develop again into contempt. They remained silent in the project room until Ramana spoke up. "Again, I go back to my question before; how do you plan to proceed with this information about the project?"

Arthur scratched his face. "Well Ramana, it would be negligent of me not to follow up or report further on what I have uncovered."

Ramana was close to arguing the fact that he didn't uncover anything, but thought better of it. He just nodded his head, acknowledging the reporter's ethics.

"On the other hand," Arthur started, "the biggest part of the story would've been some kind of cover-up behind the scenes, and I guess, to your credit, you've eliminated that."

Ramana breathed deeply as Arthur continued.

"As for your relations with students, well, I'd say that's your business anyway," he said as he gave Ramana a smile and patted him on the shoulder. "God knows everyone is pretty tired of that stuff."

It was Ramana's turn to remain silent and let the reporter finish his thoughts.

"I'll probably sit on this one, Ramana." Even Arthur was amazed that the words came out of his mouth. "I will keep my eyes on this. However, I think you have some other people to inform of these things." His face lighted up as a thought came to him. "By the way, I think it would be appropriate that we also have an understanding that I have an exclusive on anything else on this story and deserve better treatment by everyone involved."

Ramana smiled at the agreement that was on the table and forced out the words, "Arthur, you can count on that."

Arthur smiled back and wondered from where this streak of generosity came. "Well okay, let's try this thing out then. I want you to sit here and answer my questions until . . . I have no further questions."

Ramana thought of his schedule, then said, "Fire away."

Chapter 26

Allison was halfway through her test before she encountered the first question regarding evolution. Her pencil left the paper and the eraser made its way to her mouth. Her face raised and looked around the silent room. Her immediate reflex was to peer at the pile of notebooks and papers under her desk. Stuck between the pages and peeking over the top of her biology text was her finished essay. *What was the point?* She thought to herself. *How can I answer these questions in a way that contradicts what I have decided to be true?* She thought about her grade. She knew from talking to Ramana that right now she had a high B. She'd be lucky to squeeze out an A on this test if she answered these according to the text. The extra credit essay might generate some pity points with Ramana, but she knew that he probably couldn't give it much.

The scales of her mind began to examine the weight of each option. She pondered first the weight of strict scholarship, the attention to the cumulative findings and opinions of the men and women of history that had been presented to her in her textbook. The overwhelming amount of work, intelligence, and consensus overflowed the fanciful scale in her mind, pressing until it landed with a resounding crash. She shuddered as the imaginary, but highly visual scene began to tear at her resolve. She physically turned her head away from the picture in her mind. Her eyes closed tightly as she tried to visualize what it held. To her surprise, what she saw was a simple scroll, rolled and tied with a flimsy ribbon. To her surprise, the ribbon untied and the scroll started to unravel, but she already knew what it contained, what it said. It read "Integrity." Her soul reached for the perfect integration of everything that was absolutely true. It had no compromise. As she watched, the flimsy scroll of paper began to press against the hard metal of the scale until it lifted the accumulation of human knowledge high into the air.

The decision was made. The significance of the grades began to fade as she felt she had to integrate her beliefs into everything that she did. "No compromise," she whispered as she woke up from her daydream and went back to her test.

The multiple choice question read: 25. The atmosphere on early Earth consisted largely of a. water vapor b. hydrogen c. carbon dioxide d. nitrogen e. all of the above. She had seen the question, and the description of the now-famous experiment in her text and on a previous test, but now for some reason it seemed completely absurd. There was no clear way to answer this question according to her new strategy.

Her eyes once again lifted to peer around the room and caught Ramana's. His face continued to have a look of sadness she had seen when she entered the classroom. She could only imagine what was causing it. She gave him a comforting smile and went back to her test.

Allison's lips tightened as she decided what to do. Her pencil began to write in the space under the exam question: "Improper question based on an unfalsifiable theory that makes assumptions to fit the desired outcome. It is biased speculation and not science." She went on, answering this group of questions in a similar manner. They ended and she was able to answer according to the text once again. As she made it to the last page of the exam, other students were now getting up from their chairs, gathering their things, and leaving the class for the last time. She watched as they dropped their exams off at Ramana's desk and headed out the door. A few set down their extra credit essays, earning Ramana's approving smile.

As she closed in on the end, an essay question stopped Allison in her tracks. 61. Describe the meaning of altruistic behavior in nature. The statement was followed by a large blank space for writing the answer in the student's own words. She looked up again at her teacher, wondering why he had chosen this tact. She smiled and began to write. "According to our text, altruism is an action that imposes a cost on the performer while benefiting another. If one believes that survival is the ultimate goal in nature, then altruism should not exist. Altruism is sacrifice; it is the purest form of love in our world."

Allison completed her test and made her way to Ramana's desk. He pushed his chair back and began to rise as she laid down her test and essay. They slowly walked toward the door until they stood together outside the classroom. In a whispered voice, Ramana spoke. "So . . . I feel I don't know where to start . . . I . . ."

"What is it?" she asked.

"I have a few things I must tell you," Ramana started. "I've talked to Arthur and hopefully straightened things out with him . . ."

"Good for you, Ramana. I'm proud of you," Allison inserted.

Somehow, the words were painful to him. They sounded patronizing. He knew they weren't meant that way.

"How did he take it?" she asked.

Ramana recovered and said, "He was pretty mad at me, but I don't think he is going to report anything on it–at least not yet. We talked for about an hour, and I explained everything he wanted to know."

Allison nodded her head.

"But there is something else I guess I need to tell you," Ramana sighed.

Allison turned her head and gave him a questioning look. "Uhuh?"

"He asked if there was anything going on between you

and me," Ramana said while he stared downward.

"What!" Her voice raised enough to attract attention. The two reacted with a quick look around the hallway. "What . . . why did he . . . what did you tell him?" Allison managed to ask.

"I told him no . . . nothing . . . I mean we are just . . ." Ramana's voice trembled as he tried to explain. "We are just deeply involved in this project, and . . . there is nothing else."

Allison raised her brow. "You told him like that?"

He looked at her in confusion.

"If you told me like that, I'm not sure I'd believe you," she said. "Why was Arthur asking about that anyway? I mean, what does it have to do with the project?"

"He's a reporter," Ramana replied. "I guess he just looks for that kind of stuff. Anyway, I said it better to him. He doesn't suspect anything." Ramana quickly realized what he had said from Allison's reaction. "Not that he should . . . Oh God, Allison, I feel like such a jerk."

He looked back up to see Allison's comforting smile. "It's okay, Ramana. I know it's been tough on you. Still, I'm very proud of you . . . and actually I feel I need to explain what I've done, although you'll know soon enough." Her eyes went back to the classroom and his desk.

Ramana's followed hers. "Was the test too difficult? What is it?"

"No, well I mean it wasn't easy, but I answered some of the questions kinda . . . oddly, and well, in my own way. I hope you're not too offended." She smiled cutely, trying to win his approval.

One of Ramana's eyebrows rose as he tried to understand. "I see, and I noticed you have finished your extra credit essay. I am assuming that you have accomplished that in your own way also."

Allison giggled at the notion. "Uh, yeah."

"Hmmm, well, I look forward to seeing your final thoughts." Ramana got a look of concern on his face after the words. "I guess this is the end of our . . . time together."

Allison nodded her head with a sympathetic frown. "Yeah, I guess so. You'll be at my graduation, won't you? I'd love to introduce you to my parents."

"Sure, I'll be there. I wouldn't miss it for the world," said Ramana as he turned back to his classroom. "Well, I must get back in there. Hopefully we'll run into each other before then."

"I'm sure." Allison smiled. "Thanks Ramana, I'll see you later."

"Bye Allison."

Little did they know that fate would work to make sure they would never meet again.

Chapter 27

Ramana sat at his desk among the throng of graduate students and teachers. Although everyone in the big open room had piles of work to finish, the noise of papers shuffling, printers clacking, and people talking was anything but conducive to productivity. However, the fact that everyone was racing to the vacation finish line made such distractions inconsequential. Ramana saw David walk through the room and his eyes went back to the exam he was grading. After he had checked up on his other graduate students, he began walking toward Ramana.

"Hey Ramana, you hanging in there?" he asked with a laugh.

His head came up from his work. "Oh, hi David. Yeah, what else would I be doing?"

"How much you got left? Anything I can help with?" He grabbed the small stack of essays on the corner of his desk. "What are these? 'All this useless beauty'? Oh, by our friend, huh? What has she done here?"

Ramana stood up from his chair and moved to grab them away from him. "They are essays that some of my students wrote for extra credit. Please, David."

"Don't get so touchy. Extra credit?" David put a feigned look of disapproval on his face. "I don't remember you telling me about an extra credit project."

Ramana sat back down and placed the essays on the opposite side of the desk. "I was unaware that I was required to."

David stepped back in surprise. "Well okay, I guess I'll just leave you with your work then."

As he began to walk away, Ramana stopped him. "David. I'm sorry; I just have a lot on my mind . . . and my agenda. I appreciate your offer for help, but I think I've got it under control. I'll probably drop everything off in your office Monday or Tuesday."

"That'll be fine. And by the way, I'd like to read some of those essays, just to see what your students have to say." David headed for his office and Ramana went back to work.

He eventually made it to Allison's exam and started down the key. About fifteen questions down, Ramana made his first mark. "Aw, come on Allison, you should know that one." His pen started again down the exam as he nodded in approval. As he turned the page, the handwriting under questions 25 through 30 immediately caught his eye. He squinted and picked up the exam to read the small writing. "Improper question?" His lips mumbled the rest of her declarations as he read through them. Five times she had purposely avoided answering his questions and left a somewhat accusatory excuse for not answering them.

Ramana held the exam in both hands as he determined how he would treat the situation. He flipped through the rest of the pages to see if there were any other of her modifications. After finding none, he went back to the five in question. He knew that anything but an incorrect finding on a standardized exam would reveal a bias for this particular student, especially this student. Realizing this, he placed the exam back on his desk and began marking the five questions as incorrect. He went back to grading with his key, but the reasoning behind her objections was nibbling at his mind as he checked the line of multiple-choice questions.

Ramana made his way to the short answer question he had left at the end of the exam. He stared at her neat cursive handwriting as a twinge of desire leaped through his heart. He began to read her answers and was stopped at the unusual words. "Altruism is sacrifice; it is the purest form of love in our world." Ramana stared at the sentence, trying to figure out how he would grade a statement like that. She had gotten the answer correct, but added together these things were, at the very least, up to interpretation. He decided to let her slide. His conscience prodded him to do so. Once again, Allison's words had made an impact on his thoughts. He finished grading her test and began to add up the damage. He wrote at the top of the front page, "85, B." He quickly made a mental note that he would unfortunately have to award Allison with a B for her final grade.

The stack of exams shortened throughout the night until there were none left. Ramana sighed. Not only was his desk was empty, but the large room also. He sat in a much different environment than the one in which he had started. His thoughts shifted into a self-analysis as he sat alone on the last Friday night of the semester with no plans. His eyes went to the small stack of essays left on his desk and he picked them up. Allison's was still on top and he was tempted to start reading it, but the idea of staying in this room another minute persuaded him to place them into his bag to be taken home. He organized his things, headed out of the quiet building and walked into the hot night outside.

When Ramana made it to his apartment, he grabbed a glass of wine and lay out on his couch. His eyes went from the TV to the bag with the essays and back, trying to pick the appropriate one. He made a compromise and decided that he would read Allison's, then turn on the TV and forget everything. In fact, it seemed comforting to bring Allison into another one of his Friday nights however he could. He leaned and grabbed the papers out of the bag and resumed his position. The bulk of the essays were placed on his coffee table. Ramana stared at the neatly typed essay in front of his eyes. "All This Useless Beauty, by Allison Wilson." He turned the page and began reading.

"Beauty is one of the greatest attributes of life. It has inspired mankind from the beginning of time in matters of

love, art, music, literature, philosophy, and every other noble endeavor. Beauty is transcendent; it has countless definitions and descriptions while, at the same time, it is beyond the grasp of words. Beauty can be found anywhere: in a person, in a song, in a sunset. I've found that my appreciation of beauty goes hand in hand with my recognition of the one responsible for creating that beauty. I choose to recognize a soul, an artist, a God. Now, as I have endeavored to pursue truth and knowledge, science, the guardian of these precious things, tells me that I am a fool.

"I choose to believe in God. I choose to pursue truth and knowledge because I believe that there is ultimate truth and knowledge. I choose to believe that we were created perfectly and wonderfully by a perfect and wonderful God. I believe that it is this God who is responsible for creating space, matter, energy, time, life, and death, and is, therefore, the one who personally wrote the laws that govern them. Mankind, through science, has begun to unravel creation to discover and marvel at these laws: Laws that demand truth. Laws that cry out for an omniscient Lawmaker. Laws that are both simple, yet too complex for our simple minds to fully understand. These simple minds have slowly begun to uncover a universe intricately interwoven with these transcendent laws, resulting in an unequaled and incomprehensible beauty.

"Modern science attributes this natural beauty to a constantly broadening balance of chaos and phenomena. It attributes these strict laws of nature to nothing, no one; random statutes that conveniently fell into place as the elements of our reality. Space, matter, time, light, gravity, energy, and the rest appeared suddenly from a mysterious void. We're told that this universal nature is a balance that promotes and encourages a continual upward progression of life. Through its domineering struggle, life begat itself. Seething and gasping in a primordial slime of rotting ooze, primitive life began. Whether on this planet or some planet billions of light years away, science tells us that we owe our very existence to this primordial slime. As this prim-

itive life created itself, it fashioned for itself bodies with useful and balanced limbs, intricate eyes for sight, diverse organs for metabolism, and infinitely complex brains for thought. For each success, we're told, in this evolutionary process were innumerable failures. Mutations that resulted in horrible deaths of inadequate and inconsequential life. If a new life form was able to survive its own fragile body, it had to then enter an immediate fight for its existence against the rivals in its environment.

"Amazingly, each step that this self-forming life took, it did so making compatible male and female organisms or life could not reproduce. And reproduce it did. This mysterious life process ultimately produced mankind, of course, after it relegated us to living in caves for a few hundred thousand years, hunting and gathering and painting cave walls. Through a fluke of evolution, we gained sentience, purpose, and reason. We learned to question and experiment and began to create technological advancements and change our world. Now through this power, we have taken over the leadership of this mysterious life process and hold the keys to our own destiny. Mankind has triumphantly dragged itself out of the primordial slime and thrusts its mighty fist high into the heavens for the entire universe to see.

"While I can offer no satisfactory proof for my belief, I listen patiently for a scientist to discover the mechanism for the incredible and physical law-defying process of evolution, and give it a name. Name the unseen mechanism that wrote the volumes of information that makes up the code that tells matter how to form itself into an organized and living creature. Ironically, we scan the universe with our radio telescopes for signs of the simplest organized message to point to an intelligent life form, while we dismiss this infinitely complex and diverse message and attribute it to no one.

"I can, however, offer you a glimpse into a unique exploration of creation and beauty. For the past semester, I have been privileged to work with some of the brightest minds I'm sure I will ever know. These minds have endeavored to duplicate the *complexity of life within the framework of an environment of man's creation, the computer. Mountains of research and information went into the creation of this primitive life. A primitive life that, in all reality, is infinitely simpler than organic life. This process was lined with great triumphs, incredible discoveries, and of course, disappointments. In the end, these minds created a life that was ultimately too complex for them to fully comprehend. In the process, many truths have been learned or confirmed: the intricacy of life, the significance of life, the tragedy of life, but most of all, the beauty of life. I offer this project, this incredible triumph, as my only scientific observation that validates my belief. We watched in amazement as this life form was literally knit together by its maker and came to life. Imagine the shock and disdain we would have for the one who would come years after us and attribute this creation to the random electric pulses and bits of information coming together by itself in this computer generated environment. We would laugh amongst ourselves, trying not to be offended by their misguided explanations, watching as they relegated our work to a fluke process of chaos and phenomena, saying to ourselves, "Only a fool would believe something like that."*

"As for the explanation that the consensus of science gives us for the origin of life, I submit to you, science is wrong. It has embraced a theory by a man who saw variation and adaptation and called it the creator rather than the one who wove these incredible things into His creation. As for the upward progression that science has theorized exists around us, I submit that the overwhelming amount of scientific observation shows us that nature's progression is downward. Creation, subject to the laws that govern it, is becoming less organized, going toward chaos and confusion, not away from it. Mankind is less perfect than he was originally created to be. We have infinitely more knowledge now than ever before, though everyday, it is more and more evident that we are no smarter or rational. In fact, some could argue that we are less rational than ever.

"*As for the mechanism that governs this process that science has theorized created man, I will name it for you. Death is its name. Death is this creative force that makes life possible. Death has pervaded this creation to the extent that we see it as commonplace, the logical end to the cycle of life.*

"*It has become, for many, the necessary process that weeds out the weak and the sick from spreading their foul genetic code into our pristine world. We no longer see it for what it really is—the result of our selfish and blind rebellion toward our Maker and His beautiful creation. Sadly, in our attempts to evolve beyond the necessity of a maker, we have fashioned a god out of the primordial slime that we are slowly becoming. It is to this god that I pose the question, 'What shall we do, what shall we do, with all this useless beauty, all this useless beauty?'*

Ramana stared at the paper in his hands, oddly aware of everything around him. His mind tried to shake her words off as the ramblings of an obviously less schooled mind. The reasoning that she used was faulty, wasn't it? It was late and hard for him to concentrate, so he lied back on the couch. Soon his weary, confused mind was overtaken by sleep. The waking dreams soon began.

Chapter 28

Allison and Rachel decided to stay in town together until graduation, when both of their families would make the trek to Austin for the ceremony. They woke up and made their way to their favorite bakery to share coffee and muffins. They were waiting until 9:00 a.m. when the bursar's office opened and they could pick up the final grades of their college career. The day was a little overcast, the clouds hiding the morning sun and keeping the temperature at a comfortable level. They hit the campus in their flimsy summer garb and sunglasses, trying to soak in their last time to walk the grounds as undergraduates. They walked silently through the sidewalks lined with budding trees and sweet smells of the May blooms. Allison's mind went through each of her classes as they walked, trying to predict the grades that she was about to receive and calculate what that would do to the grade point average that she would live with for the rest of her life. After she sufficiently worked herself up into a nervous state, she tried to tell herself again that it wasn't important. Whatever happened, happened.

"Allison," Rachel started, "do you think we'll ever walk this campus again . . . together?"

Allison looked down and smiled. "Well, if you come visit me."

Rachel turned her head toward Allison. "What? What are you talking about?"

She wrung her hands nervously and looked back at her

friend. "You're gonna kill me, but I haven't told anybody yet."

"Allison, what have you done?" she quickly inserted.

Allison stopped walking. "Okay, I went by the nursing school the other day . . . and I filled out the application and, you know, talked to a counselor . . . and I think there's a good chance that I may enroll for next semester in the graduate program. I think I can even get a scholarship." She finished her sentence and waited for Rachel's reaction.

"Oh my God!" she said in a falsetto voice. "What made you do that? I mean I think it's great, but I thought you wanted to be a doctor."

She laughed. "Yeah, I weighed it back and forth, and I think I'm supposed to be a nurse. When I was home for Easter I had kind of a guardian angel point it out to me in no uncertain terms. To be a doctor, I would have to pick a specific field and only be able to help certain people. I don't want to limit myself like that. I want to help everybody."

Rachel nodded her head as they began to walk again. "I can see that. Of course you could make a killing being a doctor, but yeah, I can see it. I could only hope that if I need a nurse you will be there for me."

Allison and Rachel made it to the door of the bursar's office and joined the big crowd huddled outside. They made their way into the appropriate room and separated to get in the proper lines. Waiting in line, Allison's thoughts were racing from the decision she had just revealed to Rachel and her reaction to it, to the results that she was about to receive and how, if necessary, she would explain it to her parents. As she got closer, she convinced herself that it would at least be a B average. That wouldn't be a problem, but what if . . . ? She finally stood, flashed her student I.D. to the indifferent worker and received her small computer printout. She quickly folded it in half and got out of the crowded line. Her eyes immediately tried to locate her friend who was near the exit waving her hand. Only then did she open the paper to discover the news.

Rachel watched as she walked with her eyes glued to the small paper. She tried to read the look on Allison's face with no luck. Allison's eyes slowly lifted from the grades as she stopped in front of Rachel.

"Is it that bad?" Rachel asked.

Allison looked back down as if to check it one more time. "Uh, no, actually it's great . . . better than I had hoped. It's just . . . I mean it looks like there's a mistake."

"A good mistake, I hope. What is it? Show me," Rachel replied.

Allison turned the sheet around for her friend to see. "Here, Advanced Biology 304. I got an A."

Ramana walked up the stairs to the faculty building, trying to keep the feeling in his body contained. He tried to keep from sweating and quickly peeked down at his shirt to check for any visible signs, but the more he tried the more it seemed inevitable. He rubbed his hands on his pants to keep them dry and shook his head as he tried to determine the cause of his anxiety. He made his way to his large open office and scanned the room for occupants. People were scattered around the room, and he waved and nodded his head to his colleagues as he passed them. Once he got to his desk, Ramana sat down and looked through his desk drawers. He picked up the envelope he had prepared and leaned back in his chair, trying to calm himself. His mind went through all he had done in the last few days and the effects that it would have for the rest of his life. He went through the plans that he had set in his mind and wondered how they would play out. Once he had thoroughly prepared himself, he stood up again and headed for the faculty mailboxes. Placing the envelope in David's box, he made his way out of the faculty building and to the project room.

The walk wasn't far, and Ramana tried to take in all of the colors, smells, and sounds that he experienced along the way. As he approached the research building, the preparations lost their effectiveness and the feelings of moist hands and body resurfaced. The attendant at the security desk recognized Ramana and let him pass without asking him to empty his pockets. The girl behind the front desk quickly located his badge and presented the sign-in book as he stopped. Ramana smiled at the familiar face and went through the normal routine without any words spoken. He started through the large research lab, looking at all of the project tables and the handful of students still present and attending to them. The room looked different now.

Ramana pressed through the double metal doors to the rest of the lab on a mission. The steps of his feet echoed as he trotted down the stairway until he stood outside the door to the project room. His mind fluttered as he wondered who he would find there, if anyone.

After a deep breath, Ramana opened the door and walked in, happy to find that the room was deserted. He quickly made his way to his terminal and began to punch the keys of his keyboard. Finished with the first task, he stood up to grab his polarized glasses and gazed at the contents of the E.P. As he looked at the screen, he made his way to the main terminal and pulled his laptop computer from its case. He connected the small computer to the beast with a USB cable and as he opened it up, the laptop sprung into action. As the laptop went through its boot-up routine and tried to decipher the strange language that the beast was pumping through the small wire, Ramana returned to his familiar monitor station. Once he propped his glasses on his head, he began to punch commands into the super computer. The beast went into action and responded to the instructions of its master. He turned in his chair to see the laptop screen. Ramana was surprised to see that no error messages had appeared and the two computers were communicating without any difficulty. All of his plans executed, he awaited the eventual confrontation.

The wait was not long. David shortly appeared through the door of the project room and walked toward Ramana. "Hey Ramana, got your call. What did you want to discuss?"

Ramana's mind raced as he tried to respond to such a simple question. "I've been doing a lot of thinking lately . . . and I think I need to tell you about it."

"Uh oh," David spoke as he smiled, trying to diffuse the determination on Ramana's face. "Just kidding, Ramana, go ahead. What have you been thinking about?"

"Well, it has to do with a lot of things." Ramana stood up as he began his prepared speech. He noticed that the screen of the laptop was open to their sight, and he quickly moved over to close it before David could see what was taking place. He lost his train of thought with the action and began again. "It has to do with many, many things: the project, my classes, my future, everything."

"I see. Good, we need to discuss this," David said as he took a seat for the dialog, wondering why Ramana's computer was hooked into the beast. "What is that computer doing?"

"Nothing." Ramana twitched, angry with himself for not removing it before David arrived. "I wanted to see if it could communicate with the beast."

"Can it?" David asked.

"No," Raman lied.

David began to rise from his chair. "Well, can I see . . ."

Ramana moved quickly between David and the laptop. "David, this is not what I wanted to discuss. I would appreciate if you would sit down and listen to me."

David fell back into his chair and watched Ramana disconnect the two computers. "Okay Ramana, go ahead please."

Ramana's eyes lifted to his superior and he continued. "David, I have a lot of concerns . . . and reservations about the direction of the project and what we've done. It has taken a life of its own and we don't seem to have control of it anymore."

David shook his head slightly. "What do you mean?"

"Well for one," he started, "I think it was wrong how we deceived Arthur for the news piece."

David frowned. "Oh Ramana, is that what this is about? I thought we had already discussed this. It's nothing, and I can't believe that you are worrying about it."

Ramana's eyes went downward as he went straight to the point. "I have to tell you David, I told Arthur everything."

"You did what?" David barked. "Tell me you're joking, Ramana, because . . . you have got to be kidding me . . . what the hell did you tell him? Why the hell didn't you talk to me about it first?"

"David, it's okay." Ramana held his hands out defensively as if to hold David's anger back. "He's not going to do anything about it. I spent about two hours explaining things to him and we have an understanding."

David scoffed at his naiveté. "You have an understanding, huh? Well understand this, Ramana. You may have just jeopardized everything that we have worked for, everything that this biology department has accomplished, and possibly your and my future here at this university." David got up from his chair and started to pace around the room.

Ramana waited until he saw David slow down his pace and turn his focus back to the conversation. "Don't worry about yourself, David. I told him that I was the only one who knew about it, that it was my idea."

David lifted his head with a look of confusion.

"I told him that I was under a lot of pressure and I made a huge mistake. Rather than telling anybody, I covered it up and manufactured the other cells." Ramana waited for David's reaction.

David sat back in his chair with the look on his face unchanged. "I don't understand you, Ramana. What do you expect to accomplish with this move? Is this some kind of martyrdom complex or extortion, or what?"

Ramana shook his head at the suggestion. "I don't expect you to understand my motives, David. I am only trying to communicate to you my conclusions."

David's face turned from confusion to one of surprise. "Oh, there's more? Well lay it on me."

Ramana tried not to show his contempt for David's insolence. "David, I don't expect you to understand what I'm about to tell you, but I hope that it will explain things." Ramana took a deep breath as he felt his anxiety level rise again. "I have had quite an experience this semester. I'm not really sure how to explain what I've gone through, but I will try."

David turned his head in wonder. He no longer knew where the conversation was leading.

"I have had time to see things from a completely different perspective than anyone has ever shown me before; different than any text that I have ever read. I have had the opportunity to create a life form from scratch and watch it come alive." Ramana's countenance fell. "Having created this life form, I feel I have also failed it miserably."

David wanted to speak and question these strange words, but he decided to remain silent and let him finish his thoughts.

"The responsibility that came with what I have done was not something that I was prepared for. I think I understand what has happened in the environment that we created . . . and I am somewhat disgusted at the world and life that I gave these creations."

David couldn't remain silent any longer. "Ramana . . . hold on. You sound like . . . what are you talking about?"

"Please David, let me finish." Ramana regained his train of thought and continued. "We created a form of life . . . a beautiful form of life. And the first thing we do is . . . is kill it, torture it over and over again to try and get it to reveal some secret that we think is hidden from our view, when, in all reality, everything we want to know is right before our eyes."

David's look went further and further toward confusion. "My God, Ramana, what are you talking about?"

"The changes, David!" Ramana lost his composure. "The changes in the cells. Do you know what caused them?"

David's mouth opened and closed as he paused before answering. "Well, Ramana, the evolutionary routine . . . I would think had something to do with it."

Ramana stayed silent to let the scientist elaborate further.

"Um, I'm sure it had something to do with the cell's need to move around the environment to gather needed resources." David looked into Ramana's eyes. "What do you think happened?"

"Does the word altruism mean anything to you?" Ramana calmly asked.

David laughed. "Sure, Ramana. What does that have to do with anything?"

"The Kirk cell turned out to be altruistic, after some pretty monumental changes." Ramana began to pace. "Part of the E.P. controls along with the safety loop somehow got incorporated into the cell's DNA structure. Somehow, the cell detected a threat when we began to destroy hundreds, thousands of its brethren flippantly, for no comprehensible reason. It then tried every way that it could to stop the slaughter that we had started. It finally was somehow able to insert the construction routines that were loaded with the cilia programs in order to stop the destruction, and created the new cells."

David's jaw began to lower with the revelation. As soon as he realized it, he quickly twitched his head to stop it. "How did you find this out? How come you haven't told me until now?"

"You're the first one I'm telling, David." Ramana waited for him to respond. David's attention went to the screen as he processed the information that he had just received. He stood up and grabbed a pair of polarized glasses. His voice changed to a softer tone. "And you're sure of this? I mean, you have checked all the other possibilities and this is what you believe happened?"

"To tell you the truth," he started, "besides just blatant espionage, I think it's the only plausible explanation. We were the ones that built the new cells all along, David. Us!"

"What do you mean the only plausible explanation?" David took his glasses off and turned his attention to Ramana.

"How can you be convinced that these changes wouldn't have eventually occurred?"

Ramana stopped as he saw the threshold that was before him. "I . . . I guess I feel that the probability of that happening is beyond . . . beyond the realm of possibilities."

David crunched his brow as he looked at him. "What are you talking about? Beyond the realm of possibilities . . . what are you trying to say, Ramana?"

"Just what I said." Ramana cleared his throat. "I believe that we could run that evolutionary routine for days, weeks, months on end and not see anything but the cells degrading to the point of destruction. It's the only possible outcome that I can see."

"Okay," David started, "so what you're saying is that you don't believe that we have duplicated the natural world very well."

Ramana's hand went to his chin. "To the contrary. As you've said, I think we have done pretty well in duplicating nature. In fact, I think that is our greatest triumph, and it is what I'm most proud of. In awe may be the best way to describe it."

David looked at him incredulously. "I don't understand, Ramana. It's like you're beating around the bush here. What is the point of all of this?"

Ramana took another deep breath. "After I have had some time . . . and insight, I have had quite a change of heart . . . or mind regarding my studies and my future."

David looked relieved at the statement. "That's normal. Tell me how your thoughts have changed."

Ramana's face took on a matter-of-fact smile. "I'm not so sure you want to hear everything."

"Well, it's a little late for that now," he replied.

Ramana retreated to the conference table and his notes. "You know David, this field of science is quite a minefield. You think everything is okay where you stand until you take another step and the facts blow up in your face. Everything we do is trial and error; nothing is mapped out. It's just a shot in the dark every time until we hit the right spot. Then when we hit the right combination and nothing blows up, we come across as geniuses."

Once again, David's face strained in confusion. "That's not true."

Ramana shook his head at his former mentor. "Sure it's true, David. Everything we do is the work of someone else. Everything that we know is the knowledge of someone else. We pile up tenets of findings and conclusions and say that they point in one direction until someone else comes around and convinces us that they point in another." Chuckling, he continued, "Then someone comes along and proves the piles of findings and conclusions were false to begin with, and we start all over again building up theories that will eventually suffer the same fate."

"You're talking crazy, Ramana," David interrupted.

"Crazy?" Ramana found a second wind. "I'll tell you about crazy. The craziest thing about all of this is that our brains, our minds, as incredible as they are, cannot even come close to comprehending the questions that we spend so much time on. Yes, we have been able to determine how some things work . . . but not why. Oh yeah, we egotistically postulate how these things came to be and how they acted in some incomprehensible past. My god, David. I'm twenty-eight years old and I'm making conclusions and comments on something that supposedly happened five, ten billion years ago. That's what's crazy, and what's even crazier is that people will listen to me and believe me because I'm a scientist."

David laughed nervously. "So, every field of study is like that. Better that we give them the truth than some nut case."

Ramana's eyes lit up. "But what happens when we are the nut case, when we give them theories and interpretations labeled as the truth, then find out later that they were all mistakes? Who do we answer to when we do that?"

"Nothing is absolute," David began. "It's implicit in everything that we do. Everyone can see how the view of the world has changed over time based on the different discoveries science has made. We're used to it by now. It's the price for all of the improvements that science has given the world."

"Ah," Ramana sighed, "improvements."

"What, you're telling me you don't believe that science has improved life on Earth?" David sat back and waited for the attack.

"Hard to say. I would have to say that medically we have improved things." Ramana continued, "But I think that we lose sight of how much our own body is responsible for our healing, like it was built into it. Medicine can only do so much; the body itself does most of the work. As for the rest of science and technology, so we have created bells and whistles that allow us to supposedly improve our existence if we have the right amount of money. Most of the world knows nothing of these so-called improvements."

David smirked at his sophistry. "And you think that people absorbed into some kind of fanatical religion are better off?"

"It's not that easy to distinguish the two anymore, David," Ramana shot back.

"That's just crazy." The objection ran across his face. "Religion has caused more destruction and misery on this Earth than any other idea conceived."

Ramana paused as his thoughts went to Allison. "You don't really believe that, do you David?"

"What?" David couldn't believe his words.

"First of all, science is basically a product of religion, until it began to break its ties and became a religion of its own." Ramana continued at David's silence. "And this thing about religion causing all this misery, I guess you're right. I mean people do kill in the name of God, but come on, look at this twentieth-century alone, this scientifically enlightened century. More people have been slaughtered by their own secular or atheistic governments in the last hundred years than all of history. Much of it based on these new tenets of science. For god's sake, David, more lives have been extinguished in the name of convenience than religious crusades or wars could ever kill."

David waved his hand, dismissing the words. "Come on, Ramana. That's a load of crap."

Ramana, not knowing where to go from there, stayed silent.

The two sat silent as the beast watched them, humming and clicking. David's eyes were fixed on the red lasers moving back and forth in the silicon, hypnotizing him. He finally woke up from the daze and stood up quickly out of his chair.

"I'm about finished with this conversation, Ramana. I'm not gonna sit here and argue about this. I'm not sure what you're trying to say with all of this, but if you are trying to communicate something, let's hear the bottom line."

Ramana's mind had been racing through his time in America, and his time with Allison and the many others who had meant so much to him. He stopped it to utter, "I don't believe anymore."

"You don't believe what anymore?" David asked.

Ramana picked up the text that sat upon the table and lifted it into the air. "This, David. I don't believe in this anymore."

"That's funny, Ramana." David scowled and repeated, "That's real funny. The only reason I'm not laughing is that you are about a breath away from being escorted out of here."

"I'm sorry, David." Ramana's eyes turned to David's. "But I don't believe in you anymore either."

David's hands went to his hips as he burned with anger. "You can't expect me to allow you to teach under me with this confession of yours. You understand this, don't you?"

"Yes, I do," Ramana sighed as he picked up his computer. "You'll find my resignation in your mail box. I'm flying back to India on Saturday."

Chapter 29

The tremendous number of graduates generated by the University of Texas each year necessitates that the ceremonies are divided up into the different schools and scattered over a number of days in May. Each school organizes and plans its particular service and ceremony. A similar scene plays out day after day as the thousands of graduates are hurled out into the real world or into another advanced state of the theoretical. Emotions ranged from gleeful pride to a certain sadness that most know, which accompanies any step into a different stage of life. Very few students, however, felt the sadness yet. It would come when they realized that they were no longer protected by the label that they held for these formative years, a label that deflects the disapproving stare of society when one's college habits extend into the real world. Most of them believed that their years of learning were finally over. Seventeen years of practicing, watching, and building themselves into towers of knowledge would now be released into an all-out assault on society. Only a select few understood that their real education began when they picked up their diplomas.

People began to appear and congregate around the Frank Erwin Center a little before lunchtime. This was Austin's greatest auditorium, the only one really, and it housed everything of size and consequence that occurred in this capitol city. It was part of the magnificent university architecture along with the Royal Memorial Stadium and the famous UT Tower. The first burnt orange cap and gown showed up and signaled that it was okay for the other eager but hesitant graduates to make their appearance. Mothers, fathers, and other family members were easily detectable, gathered around their gowned loved one. Cameras clicked and hugs were issued as paper programs of the day's activities were rolled up and slapped in the hands of impatient fathers. The grounds soon became a sea of the smoky orange colors, engulfing the blues and browns of the spectators. Though most of the graduates did not know the ones in the same vicinity as them, the spirit of the day made them smile and nod as they passed each other; simple congratulations and a feeling of kindness pervaded the morning air.

This spring morning decided to grace the school of natural sciences graduation ceremonies. Though the clouds hid the beautiful sun, they also kept the moderately humid temperature in the eighties. Every so often the clouds allowed the sun to send its heavenly rays of light to illuminate the grounds of this elaborate celebration. Allison's father pointed the sight out to his wife and son as they drove into the city of Austin. They exited off of the upper deck of Interstate 35 just in front of the grand auditorium and weaved their way through Martin Luther King Boulevard to the campus and sorority row. They were lucky enough to find a fairly convenient parking place and made their way to the front door of the majestic mansion that Allison called home. The housemother greeted them and led them to the parlor where they waited for the girl of the hour. Josh took a seat on one of the uncomfortable couches, trying to catch the eyes of any girl that walked through the room. His parents walked around the parlor methodically examining the pictures and tasteful decor. The sudden smiles on their faces signaled the appearance of their precious angel.

"There she is," Mr. Wilson spoke up.

"Hi Daddy, hi Mom." Allison walked down the stairs and hugged her parents. Her eyes finally caught her little brother still sitting on the couch. "Josh! Wow, I didn't expect you." She said laughing. "I'm really happy that you came down for this."

Josh got up and walked towards his sister as their parents smiled at the moment. "Parents made me," he joked and turned their faces from smiles into objection. He waited to achieve the proper amount of disdain, then said, "Just kidding. I figured that I should come and see my big sister have her day in the sun." He walked up and gave her a hug.

"Well, I appreciate that little brother." She noticed his eyes follow two of her scantily clad sisters walk past them and out the door. She giggled and shook her head.

"Joshua Wilson!" Mrs. Wilson spoke up. "You keep your eyes to yourself."

"Anyway," Allison said as they laughed at the situation, "are you guys hungry?" Heads nodded from all directions. "Well, I know the perfect place. Let's go."

Ramana stared at the packed bags lying on the floor of his apartment. A broom was clutched in his hand as he stopped from his cleaning to examine the small space he had called home since he came to this new world. As he contemplated this, he noticed how his mind seemed to work differently now. He seemed more aware of things, all things, especially his senses and his emotions. It had almost taken him to tears a couple of times through his eventful few days. He wondered how he would ever explain that one night of words and thoughts and dreams to anyone, and if the need would ever arise. The change was so recent that his thoughts took him back and forth over the fence many times a day. He went through a list of people in his mind and how he would explain his sudden departure. They didn't need to know everything, but his leaving so close to earning his doctorate would arouse a certain degree of curiosity. Mainly, he thought of Allison. It had gotten to the point of an obsession and he knew it. It was one of the reasons that he thought of leaving without seeing her again.

If Ramana did see her again, he would likely say something that made her uncomfortable and ruin the memory that she would have of him forever. At the very least, it would not go as he hoped, and his last memory would be forever tainted. No, it would be better this way, a mystery. Allison would be hurt maybe, but hopefully it would be interpreted someday as an act of valor. He wondered what effect it would have on her to know that she was, in no small part, responsible for the change that was taking place in his brain. Would it be an intellectual victory that she would chalk up on her mental scoreboard of achievements, or would it mean more? Whatever her reaction, he was sure that he would be unable to express it in a way that garnered respect. So it was decided that he would flee without notice, without goodbyes, back to his home to start experiencing his homeland with this huge paradigm shift he now carried with him.

The moment he decided this in his mind, it circled around on him and began down another road. Why not be open and honest about what had happened? Admit it and be proud of the decision that he had made and the path he now walked. Allison couldn't be the only student that held these beliefs, and surely there were more faculty members working within the hierarchy and various denominations of science that held within them a similar objection to this doctrine. A rational discussion of these things may act as a catalyst for these others to come out of hiding, maybe even to stand with him.

Ramana's enthusiasm faded as he saw in his mind the slaughter that would fall upon any scientist who spoke out against one of the "central dogmas" of the church of science. Not only would he face excommunication, but ridicule. It seemed strange that now the long-held tradition of faith standing in the way of knowledge had shifted. It was now science that held the power to execute the heretics and blasphemers. How the Galileos of history must be turning in their graves as they see the reformation that science established start repeating the same mistakes of its arch-nemesis, The Church of God. Once he began to equate himself with these characters of history, the validity of his course waned in his mind. He wasn't Galileo, and this wasn't an earth-shattering discovery; it was an idea rejected by a society that seemed indifferent to its imperceptible effects. Again, his mind circled as he saw his confession and questioning of one of science's core beliefs, resulting in nothing more than a more thorough filtering process for candidates applying to the school of natural sciences.

"I can't believe he would have the audacity to abandon the department at a time like this." Dr. Green wrung his hands as he looked at David. "After all we've done for him. I have at least ten schools waiting to come to Austin to view what we have accomplished. I just don't understand. What would have made him resign, David? The pressure, the media attention; what was it?"

"You've seen him, how he acts. You know that he was, at the very least, unstable." David looked again at the letter of resignation, which told nothing of what he and Ramana had discussed. "He lost it. He couldn't handle it. We should have . . . I should have recognized the signs before it got to this point."

"David," started the senior scholar as he checked his watch, "the best scientists have always been unstable, aloof. I feel that we have lost a great and creative mind. Are you sure there's nothing we can do to change his mind?"

David's countenance fell as he felt the jealousy begin to burn in his belly. He wondered at how this man had seemed to suddenly change his mind about Ramana once he had lost him. "Wallace, I think you're wrong about him. He's not the great mind that you think he is. In fact, I think you'd be surprised with some of what he believes."

"Really?" Dr. Green grunted. "What are you talking about?"

David shifted his head as he chose his words. "It seems he has let his superstitions and religious beliefs take precedent over his work."

Dr. Green remained silent for a moment, waiting for David to finish his thought.

David continued, "Basically, he has rejected the text that we use . . . I guess, mainly, because of the parts regarding evolution."

Dr. Green nodded his head as he raised his hand in front of David. "Ah yes, I know the disease. I have seen it fall upon some of my closest colleagues. Something snaps in their mind and they become like . . . like imbeciles on a mission; their bias becomes burdensome. Actually, I think there are a couple of them still in the faculty. They keep their . . . their creation beliefs to themselves so no one will really be able to detect it, but you can usually spot them."

David watched, fascinated by his words.

"Don't get me wrong David," he inserted, "I don't have problem with any of the faculty being church people . . . or pursuing whatever spiritual quest they want. But when they start pushing it and talk about forgiveness and personal saviors, that's when it's gone too far. It completely destroys their credibility, and that's when it starts reflecting on the university."

"I completely agree." David slowly nodded his head as he spoke.

"Well, it's the right move, then, to let him go his own way. I don't want somebody like that being the lead on a project like this." Dr. Green's head popped up as a thought came to him. "Speaking of that, do you have anybody in mind to take the lead? We need to move pretty fast here."

David crunched his brow. "I've been thinking about it. I've even approached Mark about it, but he refused."

"Refused it–why?" he asked.

"Well, he's become kind of . . . freaked out by the project, if I can use his words. Anyway, he doesn't have knowledge base to do it. We need someone from the biology department. Maybe I can talk one of my other graduate assistants into it."

Dr. Green slightly frowned. "David, let me remind you,

we have a number of schools ready to come and see this creation of yours. I don't want it to appear that some greenhorn is in charge around here. I want you to become the lead. Spend some time with this one and get to know it inside and out. Once you have it wired, then you can begin to train others in it."

David's body visibly flinched as it reacted negatively to the suggestion, but he controlled himself enough not to say anything.

"Anyway David," he quickly said, "we have a graduation to attend."

The Wilson family took Rachel with them to eat and to the graduation ceremony. Rachel's parents were spending the summer in Europe and were unable to attend the event. Despite the absence of Rachel's family, the two girls radiated as they walked together with Allison's family toward the auditorium. Allison's graduation ceremony was the first of the day with Rachel's scheduled in the evening. Due to the size of the graduating classes, the process was one of expediency and not necessarily pomp and circumstance. The throngs of graduates assembled in the lower bowels of the huge, drum-shaped building, anticipating the grand entrance into the awaiting auditorium. Since they had arrived early, Allison took Rachel with her to the mass of graduates as a remedy for the anxiety that welled up inside her. They walked through the great air-conditioned hall, happy to stop the sweating before it affected their hair and makeup. Allison waved to the few people that she recognized and stopped to give a few hugs and goodbyes. She nervously anticipated seeing Ramana walking down the hall or congregating with other faculty. Allison stopped and peered on her tiptoes at the small group of assembled faculty, trying to spot him with no success. Immediately, she lowered herself and slightly shrugged her shoulders.

"What is it Allison?" she asked.

"Crap. David's right over there. I think he saw me, like, hide from him. God, I'm such a dork." She smiled at the irony and shook her head. "I don't wanna deal with him today–not this day . . . I wonder where Ramana is?"

Rachel giggled at her friend as they scanned the room. "Don't worry about him, girl. He's got nothing on you. You should just walk right up to him and thank him for all that he and the school have done." She paused and laughed as she heard her words. "Wow, that doesn't sound like me at all. What's wrong with me?"

Allison smiled.

Rachel continued, "But, it's the right thing to do. I know it is. And if he's any kind of man, he'll congratulate you too."

"Yeah, you're right. Anyway, he probably knows where Ramana is. I'll be right back."

Allison walked over to the group of faculty in front of David and began talking and shaking hands with the project staff that she had worked with. Similarly, David stood talking to some of his students and graduate assistants when he spotted Allison. He kept his eyes on her as he talked with the people around him, examining her. She kept her eyes anywhere but toward him; she wanted the meeting to be an apparent surprise. As she continued the small talk, David excused himself from his group and approached her.

"Well hello, Miss Wilson. I guess this is your big day," he snorted.

She used her prettiest smile. "Oh, hi Dr. Levin."

An unpleasant silence lingered in between them as the group diffused in the larger room.

Allison fumbled for the words. "I . . . I wanted to thank you, Dr Levin, for the opportunity . . . for all the opportunities that you and the school have given me."

David gave her a smug smile. "Well, I guess congratulations are in order for you . . ."

Allison smiled as the conversation went perfectly as Rachel had said. Her head bowed as she thought how to quickly wrap up the conversation.

" . . . And I guess you won you a little convert to boot. I guess it still remains to be determined if it was a physical or mental victory."

Allison froze as she tried to understand his words. Her head snapped upwards to look at him. "What?"

David rocked back as an angry laugh shot out of him like a sneeze. "I hope you find a whole lot of satisfaction in helping Ramana throw away everything we have worked so hard for, because–"

Allison stepped toward him to interrupt. "What are you talking about? Where is Ramana?"

David looked at her in disbelief. "You don't know?" A wicked smile began to appear on his face as he realized that it was true. "What a coward. He didn't even tell you . . . how sad. This gets better all the time. Well let *me* tell you." The two instinctually walked out of the crowd for the confrontation. David paused. "It seems that you have some strange power over our little friend. He's gone back to India." David talked slowly to get the most enjoyment out of it.

"Me? What are you talking about? He left? When is he coming back?" she returned.

"He's not coming back. We don't want him back!" David's temper began to rise. "He quit the school. He quit everything. Don't you get it?"

"He quit?" she repeated. "Why'd he quit?"

"Listen, I'm not gonna spell everything out for you here. Anyway, I've already told you more than I should." David began to turn to walk away.

Allison's mind raced as she tried to figure out what to do. She reached out her hand and grabbed his shoulder. "Where is he?"

David turned around in surprise at her courage. He paused and looked down at his watch. He looked back at her, wondering if he should tell her. "You've probably missed him. His plane leaves sometime today. He's probably already left." He looked up at her and smiled. "Happy graduation." David turned and walked away.

Allison's body snapped rigid, her mind fluttering in between thought and faintness as hundreds of fuzzy people swirled around her. Rachel was watching the confrontation and made her way there when she saw David leave. She stood in front of Allison, but her eyes were off in the distance and her face had become ashen.

"What's wrong? What'd he say?" she asked.

Allison's eyes still looked out into space as her thoughts left the auditorium, her friend, and her parents.

"What'd you say to her?" she yelled at the group that David joined, not really expecting an answer. She turned and put her arm around Allison and began to lead her out of the area. Allison went where she was led but remained silent. "You'll be okay, Allison. Don't worry about him. Let's get you a drink or something."

After walking through the lobby and listening but not hearing Rachel's words, Allison's mind clicked in gear and she made her decision. She stopped and turned to Rachel, who was pleased to see that she was coming back to earth. The color began to come back to her face as the words came out of her mouth. "Rachel, I need your keys."

Rachel immediately changed her opinion of her friend's condition. "What?"

"Give me your keys. I've got to go . . . I've got to go find Ramana."

"The ceremony is going to start in like twenty minutes, Allison. You're not going anywhere," Rachel tried.

"You don't understand. Ramana is leaving on a plane back to India . . . and I have to see him."

"Back to India? I thought . . ." she stopped.

"I don't have time to explain. I have to go. Now!"

"You're just gonna leave your family here? They're expecting to see you graduate, you know." Her hands went up in frustration.

"You're gonna have to cover for me. They won't even notice. There's too many people here. Hopefully I'll be back in time to . . . to . . . I don't know; I don't care. Give me your keys!"

Rachel could tell it was no use. "Okay, okay, here. I'll do my best to cover for you. Meet us back at the sorority house. I'll tell them you rode back with somebody else or something. Just be careful."

"Thanks Rachel." She hugged her friend and kissed her on the cheek.

"Uh, good luck . . . I guess." She watched Allison fly out of the auditorium, her burnt orange cape trailing high behind her. "What the. .?" Rachel laughed as she contemplated her options.

Chapter 30

Allison sped to the airport on autopilot. It wasn't until she pulled onto the highway that she realized she didn't remember making any of the turns and stops it took to get there. Images and memories of the past semester wound in her mind, trying to compete with the whine of the engine and the gust of the open air. Most of the feeling had now forged into anger focused on swerving and accelerating Rachel's nimble BMW through the scattered traffic that lined the route. It was anger at Ramana, anger at herself, anger at the biology department, anger at the injustice of life, anger at whatever came into her mind. Each type of anger was different, yet burning the same, an empty, unquenchable heat. Right now she didn't want anything to douse the flames; right now it seemed to give her the excuses and explanations that she needed for the situation. It also kept her from thinking about what she was going to do when she got there and if she found him.

Allison's parents sat next to a now nervous Rachel, unaware of their daughter's dramatic quest. They followed the meticulously rehearsed recognition and ceremony as they attempted to locate Allison in the sea of graduates. Rachel pointed and feigned as she assured them that she was sitting on the opposite side with her back to them. The beautiful music presentations acted as the prelude for the main speaker. She was a doctoral student from the School of Natural Sciences and spoke of their research and accomplishments in environmental biology and ecology. Though interesting and well meant, most attendees were glad when she summarized her charge and finished up. As Rachel mentally checked off each section in her program as it happened, her pulse quickened while she developed a plan to implement after another twenty minutes.

There is no easy way to do this, Allison mused. She drove through the loading zone of the Austin Bergstrom Airport and stopped the car to gaze into the terminal. She weighed the possibility of leaving Rachel's car in the tow-away zone; she parked the car and turned off the engine. When she scrambled out of the car, she couldn't help but laugh at herself. Her graduation gown was still on, mocking her decision to flee and causing passer-bys to stare and smile. She quickly unzipped the gown, stepped out of it, and ran into the terminal. An overweight security guard stared at the spectacle and yelled towards her as she ran. After entering the terminal, she knew she couldn't go any farther. Her eyes quickly scanned the visible areas for Ramana and in desperation she called out his name.

"Ma'am . . . ma'am!" the guard caught up to her. "You can't leave your car there."

Allison silently turned to the man and walked to the car. The parking for the airport would delay her at least another ten to fifteen minutes. There was no choice. Her anger at the situation again rose from the depths. She squealed the BMW's tires in front of the guard as she was forced to leave the loading zone, leaving the guard yelling impoundment threats. She eventually looped around to a space in the parking garage that sat at least a quarter-mile from the terminal. With a slam of the car door, she began to run toward the airport, her heels echoing through the cavernous parking garage.

Rachel watched in dread as thousands of graduation caps flew into the air. Allison's parents looked wonderingly as they tried to understand the confusing ceremony. Rachel laughed nervously as she heard Mrs. Wilson say something about how she never saw Allison take the stage. They turned to Rachel, who wore a pained smile as she began her improvisation

"Okay, there's been a change of plans . . . um, see Allison wanted to meet with . . . or really, drive over to the research lab with some of the people she was working with, and will meet us back at the sorority house. And, well, I let her borrow my car, so I'm supposed to go with you guys back over there."

The two adults looked at this girl in confusion. "What?" Charles spoke up.

"Yeah, see, they were having a small party or something for the assistants that were graduating today." Rachel continued fabricating. "It shouldn't be long. It's just a quick thing and she wasn't gonna stay long."

Mrs. Wilson frowned at the idea. "Wha . . . why didn't she say anything about it?"

Rachel's laugh interrupted her. "That girl, she's about half brain dead today anyway. She probably forgot to tell you . . . she reminded me when we went downstairs."

"I see. I was under the impression that she wasn't working on that anymore." Charles spoke into Rachel's eyes.

Rachel helplessly smiled and raised her hands, signaling the end of her explanation.

The two parents looked at each other in frustration, accepting the possibility that they were being deceived.

A cool gust of re-circulated wind hit Allison's face as the automatic doors of the airport burst open in front of her. The hurried walk from the parking garage left her winded and contributed to the frantic feeling that bubbled within. Thoughts of her present circumstance flashed through her mind, leaving no room for the obvious obstacles that lay in wait for her. She walked toward the sparsely populated checkpoint until a security official donned in a blue sport coat stopped her.

"May I see your boarding pass and I.D.?" the guard asked.

Immediately, Allison returned to the reality of the present world with a quick shake of her head. "Oh yeah, I'm sorry, I don't have a ticket. I'm looking for someone who's supposed to be leaving today and . . ."

The guard interrupted her with a raised hand. "I'm sorry, ma'am. You can't enter the concourse without a ticket."

"But you don't understand," Allison pleaded. "He may be leaving right now. I have to find him and . . ."

The disinterested guard interrupted again. "Ma'am, please step away from the security area if you don't have a ticket. I would suggest that you go over to the information desk and ask them to page your friend, but you are not entering the concourse area."

Allison tensed at the suggestion and quickly turned to locate the desk. "Oh, thank you," she sighed. She made her way to the semi-circle counter that surrounded a woman wearing a similar blue sport coat.

"May I help you?" the attendant asked while Allison was still a few steps away.

"Yes," Allison answered as she laid her hands on the counter top. "I need to page someone right away, please. It's an emergency."

"Okay," the attendant responded as she grabbed for a pad of paper. "Please fill this out."

Allison's face tightened as she grabbed a pen and began writing as fast as she could. The attendant began to help another person as Allison held the finished form toward her and let out a lady-like grunt.

The attendant slowly made her way back to Allison and took the form from her. Staring at it, she said, "Can you pronounce that for me?" After Allison coached her several times, she continued, "Okay, see that white phone over there? Go pick it up and wait. I will page him and if he is here, he will be connected to that phone."

Allison took a deep breath. She looked at the plain white phone mounted to the carpeted wall that suddenly seemed like her only hope. She reached out and picked it up, wiping her hand over the mouthpiece in a futile attempt to sanitize it, and slowly sank her shoulder into the carpet covered wall. She could hear a faint hum over the resonant noise of the airport. Allison's head rose as the mechanical voice of the public address system announced her message. Her hopes faded as the barely intelligible voice seemed to diffuse unnoticed in the massive complex. Allison shot a dissatisfied look to the attendant, which had no effect, and then leaned squarely against the wall and prepared herself for a long wait.

David left the graduation ceremonies before they ended and headed straight for the project lab, though it was the last place that he wanted to go. His gut still burned with the words that Dr. Green had uttered. He couldn't devote all of his time to salvaging this project. He had let Ramana take on such a leadership role that he didn't even know where to start. With the expression of Mark's desire to leave the project also, the prospects of accomplishing anything of any consequence quickly enough for presentation to other scientists and universities seemed beyond the scope of possibility. He gazed through the door of the project room, which was more cluttered and messy than he had ever seen. Notebooks, papers, and trash were scattered around the dark room. The only light was from the never ceasing, weaving red lasers of the beast. The light switch was hit and revealed the empty, sullen lab drained of its life and creative force. David strolled slowly to the conference table where they had dreamed of such grand discoveries and slouched in one of the chairs. He tapped his fingers on the table in time with the noises of the beast that pulsed behind his back. His hand grabbed a set of polarized glasses and placed them on his face. The screen came to life, lunging out into the emptiness of the lab, with the remaining bacteria swimming and darting back and forth. He surveyed them, at first with wonder, then with contempt, knowing that he had little to do with their intricacy and design.

Thinking about these things brought a tightness to his head and neck. David's hand traveled up to the back of his neck and began to squeeze the muscles that held up his exhausted mind. He grabbed the thick instruction manual that Ramana had written and began flipping through the many pages, trying to find the appropriate section to get quickly acquainted with the beast. The text was a combination of biology and explanations of the experimental trinary computer language that was being used. As he skimmed over the material, he was again taken by Ramana's intellect. All of the information that he needed was there, organized and thorough, but it was the size of the biology text that sat next to it. It would take weeks, maybe months, to decipher everything necessary to regain the momentum that Ramana had developed. He sat for several minutes, browsing and skimming over the various chapters and headings until the enormity of the information took its toll on his continually tightening muscles. He closed his eyes and slowly closed the manual, setting it next to the biology text.

  David's mind switched from the operations of the project into another direction. It headed toward his other options, the ways he could solve his most immediate problems. He thought of ways he could buy time. As he weighed each idea that came to his mind, his eyes lifted to the active screen hanging in front of him. The bacteria quietly moved through their virtual world, hunting and exploring to find the nutrients and compounds they needed. One of the bacteria was unable to keep up with the endless struggle for survival and had begun a downward spiral. It twitched as its functions began to degrade. Tiny holes in its membrane began to appear, and cytoplasm slowly spilled into the E.P. The yellowish liquid stained the local area around the cell. The drama caught David's attention and his eyes locked onto the dying cell. As the immediate area was filled with the contents of the cell, the roving bacteria closed in to absorb the nutrient-rich cytoplasm. They huddled around the withering bacteria, trying to absorb the life that this creature was releasing. David watched with fascination as new ideas were being sparked by the reality of life playing out in this strange world.

One idea remained at the surface of David's thoughts. It had the easiest implementation and the quickest explanation. Once it had taken root into his mind with these thoughts, other reasons began to give it the appearance of the best and only solution. His eyes never left the spectacle before him on the 3-D screen. Even this somewhat gruesome end to one of their creations seemed to confirm his growing confidence in the idea. He pulled his eyes away from the scene and looked to the manual he had placed back on the table. He opened it and immediately went to the index to search for the appropriate section. Pages flipped and tore as he hurried to find the proper place in the thick, poorly bound manual. His finger outlined the sentences on the pages as he sped through the text. Knowing that he now was headed in the right direction, he picked up the manual and made his way to the main terminal. He instinctively looked back at the humming beast that tirelessly worked behind him. He sat down in the unfamiliar seat that Ramana used for the entirety of the project. His hands grasped the keyboard and mouse and moved it to a comfortable position. He set the manual in the book holder above the terminal and began to type.

Within a few minutes, David reached the appropriate level of programming and rechecked the instructions next to the terminal screen. His eyes went up to the fuzzy 3-D screen as he contemplated his actions. Making the final decision, his attention went back to his terminal and he typed in the simple command. The beast went into action and immediately had a response for its new master. "If you initialize the memory core, all current information will be lost. Are you sure you want to initialize the memory core?" David hesitated at the question and reflected on the many implications and effects. As thoughts of aborting the process began to bubble in his subconscious, his finger moved to the enter key and pressed down.

The beast went into action, and the lasers flowing through the silicon gel now took on a new role. Rather than its role as provider and protector, the beast assumed the role of destroyer. Its red lasers that once held the environment together now began to disrupt and dissolve the bonds that enabled the incredible order. David stood up and stepped away from the terminal as the computer started to utter new sounds. He pulled down the polarized lenses propped on his head and looked toward the big screen. The bacteria jerked wildly in space as they slowly began to fade from view. David watched as words went through his mind, moving his lips to mouth them. He grabbed for the phone on the conference table and hit the button for Dr. Green's office. He knew the department head was not in and prepared for his voice mail beep. "Uh . . . Dr. Green, this is David. I'm down here at the lab right now . . . it appears that we have a new problem . . ."

Chapter 31

As the minutes passed, Allison held the white phone to her ear. Her eyes stared into the seemingly endless space of the airport. She had prodded the attendant at the information desk to page Ramana again, but the uselessness of her efforts began to dissolve the thoughts of actually finding him. Allison wondered how long the airport staff would let her remain glued to the paging phone. She knew she would eventually have to hang up the phone and make her way out of the airport. But, no one seemed to even care about her plight, which added to her frustration. Her hand twisted the cord to the handset as her backed pressed into the soft wall. Finally, she realized that she had not uttered one word to request help from the One that makes all things possible. She shook her head in disgust with herself with a desperate laugh.

"God, I'm sorry I forget about You when it seems that I need You most." She bowed her head and closed her eyes as she spoke. "Thank you for being with me today, this day, this wonderful, screwed up day. I don't know what to do or what to say to Ramana if I find him, but I need to find him. I ask you Father, if it is Your will, direct Ramana to the this phone and bring him to me. In Your name, Amen."

Her eyes rose slowly to the information desk. She saw the female attendant speaking on her phone and turn toward Allison. Her head nodded as she reached for a button on her terminal. Immediately, she heard a click on the phone and a change in the monotonous tone of the earpiece.

"Yes, this is Ramana," Allison heard through the warm phone, unable to speak. "Hello . . . this is Ramana Punjabi."

A shot of anxiety through Allison's body made it difficult for her to respond. A combination of disbelief and the instantaneous answer to her prayer made her tremble and freeze.

"Is anyone there?" Ramana asked with an impatient sigh.

Feeling that he might hang up soon, she let out a trembling cry. "Ramana!"

Again, silence hung on the telephone line as Allison tried to regain her composure and wondered if she had waited too long to speak.

"Allison?" Ramana's voice quivered over the line.

"Yes . . . yes it's me, Ramana," she answered.

"Where are you? Why are you . . . how did you know where to find me?" Ramana tried to piece together the situation.

"I'm here, at the airport," Allison started. "I'm right out here by the entrance. Come out here, now."

Ramana fumbled for words. "Uh, my plane leaves soon . . . I don't know if I can make it, I mean, let me see . . ."

Allison interrupted, "Ramana, you have to come out here. I've come all the way out here and I'm not letting you . . ."

"Okay, okay, let me check with the gate and I will be right out." Ramana said, "I'll meet you by the security point."

He looked down at his watch and hurried to his departure gate. "What time are we boarding?" he asked the attendant, interrupting an on-going conversation.

The disturbed attendant turned her head to Ramana. "We will begin boarding in twenty minutes."

Ramana thanked the attendant and quickly turned away. He wondered if she would be there; or was it another of the many visions that plagued him? If he made his way to the security point, would she be there? How could it be true anyway? Her graduation ceremonies were taking place at this very moment.

With his bags in hand, Ramana jogged the 10 gates back to where he had entered the concourse and scanned the area beyond the metal detectors. He swiftly passed the security agents and guards and out the only exit into the main area of the airport. His motion stopped the moment that she came into view.

His eyes met hers and they were softer and warmer than he had ever seen, slightly red and dampened by tears. They enveloped him like a warm blanket until the truth of the situation hit him. The warmth was replaced by terror, fear, and guilt as he searched for the words to use, for the look to wear on his face, for the courage of the moment. She started toward him with a lunge and an anxiousness that he could see. As they approached, the strangeness of the situation began to slow them until they silently stood before each other. Allison looked deep into his eyes and her mind became clear. Her first instinct was to ask why he would leave without saying goodbye, but it seemed like an unanswerable question, or one that would make too harsh an opening. Instead, feeling his anxiety and shock of the meeting, she tried to keep the air light.

"So, where do you think *you're* going?" she asked with a trembling smile.

Ramana's tension faded at her playful question. He chuckled out loud along with Allison but said no words. After they quieted, Ramana sighed, "I'm sorry Allison . . . I don't even know where to start. I guess you know I'm going back home."

"Yeah," she replied, "David told me."

"David?" he asked. "Uh, what else did he tell you?"

"We didn't talk long," she started, "and I don't remember much more . . . I was kinda in shock, I guess."

"Oh," Ramana replied, wondering what she meant. As soon as he reflected again on the situation, his countenance fell. "Oh Allison, I'm so sorry. You shouldn't be here. You should be at your graduation. Your parents."

"Don't worry about it, Ramana," she assured him, "I couldn't let you leave without . . ." She paused as her words outpaced her thoughts.

Ramana crunched his brow, wondering if he should ask the obvious question. After an extended silence, he saw no reason not to. "Without what?"

Her thoughts caught back up when she began to speak. "Without . . . knowing why you gave me an A in your class."

Ramana shifted his gaze away from her inquisitive eyes. "Oh . . . that." He looked around the lobby as he wondered what to say, where to start. "Can we sit down, Allison? This may take some time." They said no words as they made their way to a nearby row of chairs.

"Would you like something to drink?" he reactively asked.

"No, Ramana!" she barked, as he shuttered in reaction. Then she softened slightly. "No thank you. I just want to know what's going on here."

"Okay," he said as he sat down with her. "I guess I owe you an explanation."

"I think so," she replied.

Ramana closed his eyes as he felt like he was starting a journey over a vast crevasse. He silently asked God to help him find the right words as he inhaled deeply.

"You were right," came out of his mouth, and then he contemplated his words. "I mean to say, you are right . . . at least *I* think you're right."

Allison looked at him with confusion. "Wha? What are you talking about?"

"Your paper," he replied.

"My paper?" she said in surprise. "You . . . you think I'm right?"

Something inside Ramana did not want him to go any further. It pulled at his gut and his vocal chords, warning him to stop the confession. He sat silently as Allison's brain was processing the new facts about the situation. Immediately, she recalled David's comments about winning a new convert. Ramana watched her as he fought with his pride until it gave in.

"Allison, your paper . . . sparked something in me. You've sparked something in me to be honest. Ever since we started–with the beast, I mean. I've had visions and dreams, you know, like I've told you. And well, after I read you paper, I had more. I think it is the only way I can explain what has happened"

Allison listened intently, nodding her head.

Ramana continued, "That night, it seemed like I was fighting and struggling with something or someone as I tried to sleep. I woke up many times in a sweat and in a daze, but I kept going back in and out of sleep, and I began to see things like I've never seen them before. The first thing I can remember was seeing these . . . these living things; I guess you'd call them. These magnificent, multifaced, strange living creatures. The intricacy and craftsmanship was amazing. It was beyond even anything I've ever seen . . . beyond the beauty that we can see now. It was perfection, pristine, absent of any defect. No struggle for survival, no hunger, just perfectly sustained existence radiating from the one who created it.

Allison's eyes grew wide. "Wow."

"It was a thought process that I never experienced before. It didn't look for answers, or guess at a direction. It knew all of the answers . . . or I should say, He knew." Ramana shook his head to clear it. "I don't know Allison, it has been so strange."

She said no words, but her eyes begged him to go on.

Ramana breathed deeply again and tried to regain his thoughts. "Then I saw the perfection start to fade. It was so painful . . . so sad; I felt sick, like I was going to throw-up as these things faded away. A veil . . . or a curtain seemed to separate the vastness of creation from its maker. Separated, its only option was to try to sustain itself. It sought to survive and death was now the rule. The strong began to feed on the weak and small to ensure its continued existence. Everything began to place survival above everything else. The thoughts changed too. They became scattered, barbaric, and empty." Ramana paused as he heard his words. "Allison, am I going crazy?"

Allison's expression went from wonder to a warm glow. "I don't think you're crazy, Ramana. I think it's incredible."

Again, Ramana wondered at her remark. "Do you want me to go on?"

"Please," she replied.

"Okay, well where was I?" He began, sounding a little more encouraged. "Like I said, the thought process at first was primitive and barbaric, but it eventually started to develop and become more organized. Slowly the ideas, observations, and concepts of reality began to appear again through the struggle of reason, but it was different than before. The process of getting the ideas was different. It was trial and error, hit or miss until a concept or truth was discovered. Then it sparked into all out quest for knowledge and began to move quicker and quicker, with an almost religious zeal. I saw how the modern tenets of knowledge were put together. Really, it was chance, flukes, and mistakes all the way; hardly an original flash of insight throughout all of time. It was usually hitting us over the head by the time we figured out some great truth about our world. Then at some point, it began to change again. It started as an attempt to look inside itself, to understand itself. For some strange reason, this seemed to turn into a desire to elevate itself. It looked to take the . . . the essence that was inside itself and elevate it to a position of . . . of worship, I guess. Peeling away layer after layer of its workmanship and finding more reasons to adore it, worshipping itself to the point of deceit. Deceiving itself to the point of believing that this faded shadow of reality *was* the perfection. It placed these ideas at the center of its knowledge, not understanding the decaying effect it had on itself. But, the wisdom that it accumulated looked like foolishness compared to the earlier perfection." He paused.

"My." Allison was still riveted to his words. "Please go on."

"Well, it just kept going and going like that, until finally I was given a choice." Ramana's speech slowed.

"What choice was that?" she asked.

Ramana looked for the right words. "Where to stand, I guess."

"I see," she inserted.

"The decision seemed obvious at that point," he began. "I saw no other choice . . . I chose as you did, to believe in the perfection; to believe that what we are now is not how we are intended to be."

Allison struggled to keep up with him. "So . . . that's why you gave me all that extra credit . . . and an A?"

Ramana silently nodded his head.

"I still don't get it . . . did you resign? Did David fire you? What happened?" she rattled off.

"I resigned," he said as his face fell. "It was a cowardly thing, I know, but . . ."

"No . . . No Ramana," she interrupted. "I understand. Geeeez, I feel like I should apologize to you Ramana . . . for . . . for . . ."

"Good god no, Allison!" he interrupted back. "No, Allison, you don't understand. You have given me . . ." He faltered at how far his confession should go.

She fired her own question. "Given you what?"

"Well, you have given me . . . a new chance, a new life. You have opened my eyes to a world that I might have never seen . . . a beautiful world." Ramana stopped to look down at his watch. In his mind, he couldn't have scripted a better last meeting. She truly cared for him; he knew that now. He could leave with some sense of victory, but she needed to be back with her family now. He tried to end things. "Allison, I'm sure my flight has begun boarding now. In a bold move, he reached out his hands and grabbed one of Allison's. "I can't thank you enough for all you've done for me, and coming out here to see me off. It means so much to me. I will never forget it or you . . ."

Allison's heart began to pound in her chest as she thought

about the words on her tongue. She had little time to decide how to proceed.

"Don't go, Ramana."

Ramana looked at her with surprise. "What? Don't go? What do you mean?"

Allison gathered her courage. "I mean don't go. I mean . . . I mean I think I'm falling in love with you, Ramana."

Silence hung over the two as they tried to figure out how those words seemed to change everything.

Ramana's head started to spin. He began to feel light-headed and lose his awareness of the things around him. Their hands remained outstretched and clasped at the table, though his grip loosened and shifted as he wandered through oblivion. It was the last thing he expected to hear, but at the same time, the one thing he had longed for the most. Some part inside told him to just hang on, to try to act normally while he attempted to regain his faculties. He stared at the glow that his blurry eyes painted around her face but could not hear her words as she started to speak.

"I don't know exactly what your intentions were with this relationship that we have. I don't even know if you considered it much, but I . . . I can't seem to get you out of my head." She stopped to try to read Ramana's face, which at the moment wasn't giving anything away. "It seems wrong, I know, because you're my professor and all . . . but you're not my professor anymore. I know that people would probably think that something was going on while you were my professor if, you know, we had something going on now. And that wouldn't be appropriate for a college professor to be dating a former student . . . but now, you're not a college professor anymore."

Ramana's subconscious tried to decipher her words but was unable to. It tugged at his nervous system to awaken from his stupor and take in the moment that was happening without him. Fortunately, Allison's rambling outburst was one that only would have confused him further. Ramana struggled his way back to awareness as Allison's message became more focused.

"I know that you've had some strange things happening, and well, I'm not exactly sure that I've figured everything out that has happened this semester. And, I know it's crazy for me to tell you to miss your flight, but I think there's something bigger at work here." She stopped to gather her thoughts and finally saw a spark of recognition in Ramana's eyes. "I just feel like I was led to you, that this semester was planned, that you and I were meant to go through this time together. And I don't want to miss out on it because of some . . . some *thing* that doesn't really matter. I mean, I don't care what you believe about this stuff or what David believes. All I care about right now is . . ."

Like surfacing from a great depth of water, Ramana awoke with a gentle gasp and firmly squeezed her hand. The sound of her words faded as Ramana regained his ability to speak.

"All you care about is what?" he asked.

Allison's eyes looked into his, and she softly said, "You."

The word made Ramana's chest pound with warmth. A smooth wave of anxious nerves flowed over him as he tried to speak. "To hear you say that, Allison, makes my heart melt. You'll have to forgive me; I'm a little bit shocked that you have these feelings . . . for me. It truly wouldn't be an overstatement to say that I have had feelings for you since the moment I first saw you." He paused as he carefully planned the words. "I have loved you since that day."

Allison smiled at the thought. The two quickly turned their heads to security gate.

"Ramana, you can't leave me. I need you," she pleaded.

He looked into her eyes and sighed, "What about your father? What would your parents think?"

She shook her head. "I don't care about my father right now!" A twinge of hurt shot through her body as she heard those words echo through her mind. For the first time since she made it to the airport, she thought about her parents. She wondered how Rachel had handled the situation and what she would find when she eventually made it back to the sorority house. Ramana saw the effect that her words had on her and made his decision.

"Allison," he started, "I need you, and I . . . I do love you. But, I must go home. My family needs me and, as silly as it sounds . . . my country needs me. I came here to find that out, I think. I didn't know what it was I was supposed to learn then, but I think I have learned it now. And, you have been the one who taught it to me."

"Then I will go with you," she said in desperation.

Ramana looked down. "No, Allison. My country is not a place where I would take you." Things began to become clear in his mind. "You know, I think you're right . . . I think we were meant to go through this time together. It is a gift that I will always cherish and look to for inspiration, but I think our paths from here on out are . . . different. I wish they weren't, but I feel they are. Anyway, Allison, you don't know me . . . not all of me."

"But I want to," she said.

"No, I don't think you would like what you see. I know I don't. The past couple of days, I have been able to see myself as I really am, in comparison to . . . uh, I guess you would call it perfection. I am a beast inside, ugly and vulgar. It is not something that I would want to expose you to." He looked to Allison for her reaction to his confession.

"What are you talking about?" she asked. "You are one of the sweetest, most gentle men I know."

Ramana shook his head. "You don't know me, Allison, and I don't ever want you to see that side of me. You would shriek in horror."

Allison couldn't help but giggle at his words. "I don't care about all that stuff. I'm the same way inside; everybody is. That's what love and forgiveness are all about."

Ramana wondered at her words. "Nevertheless, I wouldn't want you to ever see that part of me. I think if you ever did, you would fall out of love very quickly."

The strange conversation left the two silent, wondering how they would spend their final moments together.

"I don't know what to do, Ramana. I can't let you go away and out of my life. Will you at least call me, or write me, or email me or something until we can figure this out?" asked Allison.

"Religiously," he answered with a smile. "Allison, I do want you in my life . . . forever. Maybe someday when we . . . or when I figure things out, we can try this again. I just have to go home."

Allison's shoulders deflated as she heard the familiar words she spoke on the day before Easter.

"I guess I understand, but how can you leave everything behind?"

"Everything?" he asked.

"Well, school, your Ph.D., me–you're even leaving your creation behind," she added.

Ramana squinted at her stare. "I'm not exactly leaving Kirk behind."

"What? Where is he?" she asked.

His hand went to his black bag. "He's here." Ramana placed the bag on his lap and pulled out his computer. "He's right here, the alpha cell that is."

Allison smiled. "Oh my God! What did you do? How can he fit on that thing?"

Ramana stared at the disk. "Well, I had to erase everything on the hard disk, and I installed the transfer stasis platform. And well, I downloaded him right in here." He opened the computer and screen began to light up. "I'm not exactly sure what is happening in there, but it seems that Kirk is alive and in there somewhere. I will keep him there until I can find or create a computer that can house him. I believe I owe it to him."

"We will now begin general boarding of Northwest flight 437 to Houston . . ." Ramana looked up, and Allison knew that it was his flight.

Allison ripped a piece of paper from a pamphlet left on

their table and started to write. "Ramana, I'll never understand or will be able to tell anyone, and hopefully I will recover from the fact that I was rejected in favor of a bacterium."

Ramana chuckled.

She continued, "But, if you don't write me, or if I don't see you on my computer, when I get one, I will come to India and hunt you down and—"

"Don't worry Allison," he interrupted the thought, "you will never get rid of me." Thoughts began falling in place for him. "You know, Allison, I think I'm beginning to understand the dream I had at the Quack more."

"You think you've figured it out?" she asked as she looked up from her writing.

"Yeah, I'm beginning to think it has something to do with sacrifice." His eyes squinted as he pondered further. "It's an idea that I really haven't thought much about . . . I . . . I can't really say I fully understand it, but I feel it has something to do with why I must go home."

Allison's gaze fell back to the piece of paper as she thought about his words.

She handed him the piece of paper. "What are you gonna do? I mean the flight to India must be way long."

"It's okay," he grabbed into his carry-on. "I've brought a book to read." He pulled out a thin black book with gold leafed pages that Allison immediately recognized as a Bible.

She smiled and looked back into his eyes. "Oh, I know that one . . . it's good. It's a love story. I think you'll like it."

He nodded his head. "You know, I am very interested in that 'In the beginning' thing."

"The ending's pretty good too. It's all *about* sacrifice," she said.

He pushed the book back into his bag. "Well, Allison, look's like this is it." He stood up and gathered himself, wondering what was to happen next.

She stood up with him and they moved slowly toward the

security checkpoint. Ramana grabbed her hand and squeezed it tightly as he felt his emotions start to rise. Allison stared at his face as they walked toward the security agent, feeling her eyes begin to water. The line had had cleared of passengers when they stopped and turned to each other.

"Never forget me Ramana," she sighed.

He smiled lovingly at her. "I will never forget you, Allison." He reached out his hand and touched her soft cheek. Ramana moved his thumb gently across her skin as she closed her eyes. He began to move closer and she opened her eyes, inviting him in. Slowly, their faces glided through space until their lips touched for the first time. Allison closed her eyes and her body shuddered at the sensation. Their lips brushed and Ramana moved his hands to Allison's hips as their bodies moved closer. They lingered with a soft kiss until the passion began to have its way with them. Allison's arms moved up his chest and shoulders until they reached around his neck and head. She pulled him into her as her hands ran through his hair. The two were worlds away from the airport terminal in which they stood and continued to float further and further away. Ramana's hands moved up her back and pulled her softness into his chest, their bodies becoming one.

Amidst the long kiss, Allison's eyes slowly opened. The eyes before her were full of tears. The moment they looked into hers, they came rolling down his face. Allison whimpered as tears began to fall from her eyes, mixing with Ramana's. Their sadness and tears transported their long kiss into eternity. Unable to control her emotions any longer, Allison's face fell into his chest as she sobbed loudly. He bent his trembling head into her soft hair and gently wrapped his arms around her head, pulling it snugly into his chest. They stood alone at the checkpoint, the security agents the only audience to this touching farewell. They reluctantly pulled away and stared into each other's transformed faces, moistened with their sorrow and joy. No words seemed appropriate after this, their first and last kiss; no words could express better what they felt than the tremors that shot through them at this moment. They seemed to know that this was their moment, that they would never have one like this again. They soaked it up, not even wiping the tears that stained their cheeks and fell from their faces to the floor.

"I love you, Allison . . . I always will." Ramana picked up his bag and took a deep breath.

"I love you too, Ramana. God, I love you so much!" she cried.

He turned and walked toward the agent, handing him the boarding pass and I.D. as the tears continued to flow. Allison watched as he walked down through the metal detector, turning just before he walked away. Ramana realized that this might be his last look as he turned his head. He stopped and focused his eyes intently on the person that had forever changed his life. He tried to take in everything, his senses working to feed this memory all they had. His breath quickened as the moment was burned forever into his soul. She was a part of him now; he would always carry her with him. The sides of her mouth began to rise into a hopeful smile, feeling the depth of his emotion. He closed his eyes and saw the image flashing through the darkness within his own mind as he turned and headed toward his awaiting plane.

Chapter 32

"Do I think faith has a part to play in the pursuit of science? I think that it may have a part to play in self-realization or self-actualization of the individual scientist, but I don't think that faith has a place in explaining the how's and why's of nature."

Allison sat in the back of the dark auditorium on this Sunday morning and watched David address the assembled department. The summer had passed and her thoughts were on her new classes that soon started, but she saw an announcement for this important gathering of the School of Natural Sciences and felt she needed to be there for Ramana. Her attention was suddenly peaked with feelings of empathy for the student who posed the question about faith, and a nervous tension as she felt herself becoming a participant in the discussion.

David continued, "Again I must say it is not my purpose to offend or discourage the beliefs of anyone in this room . . . far from it. But, I have recently had to deal with a clash with the science that we study and the religious beliefs of some of our faculty and students, so I am keenly aware of its implications. But, I believe that since the question has been raised, I must be specific and thorough about my opinion and the opinion of the department."

David Levin, the newly installed Dean of the School of Natural Sciences, stood among his fellow scientists. Arthur Lewis was in attendance also, just arriving back to the university to do a follow up story on the biological research department and Dr Levin's new icon status. David stood at the head of this company of higher minds, charging and lecturing them to rise up and fulfill their destiny as sentient beings. His gaze went to Dr. Green who was sitting in the front row of the auditorium. He had just passed the torch in a simple ceremony. A simple nod from his former boss signaled David to go ahead with his direction. David's mind clicked into gear as he felt the entire crowd urge him on.

"We're all reasoning people here." He smiled as he thought about his words. "And I would say reason is the key. Reason is the beginning and the end of all that we are. It is the only way that we conceptualize and identify what our senses are able to perceive. It is the only way that we are able to acquire knowledge. The natural world exists independent of our reason, our beliefs, and our perception. In other words, the natural world exists whether we believe it or not, whether we perceive it or not. But, by its very nature, everything about it is able to be perceived. Nothing about the natural world can be hidden from us except by our own physical or mental limitations, or in some cases, our willingness not to see it.

For centuries, it seems we have tried to reach beyond the natural world for explanations or a reason for our existence. When, in fact, the answers are out there for our discovery, if we only pursue them. It is my guess that we have created these fantastic stories and myths to help us to better deal with wonder and magnificence of our world. They have helped give to our lives . . . significance when there seemed to be none. These beliefs . . . all of them, have even given us the moral codes that, in the long run, have probably helped us to act in a more civil manner towards one another within those belief communities. Though, in the end, we seem to use these same beliefs to justify horrible atrocities against people who believe differently. My point is, as these myths fade, especially the ones that carry with them ethical implications, it will be the role of science to help reform these and develop a new rational method for addressing the ethical questions of the day . . . to allow all people to come together under a unified truth. It is the natural world, I believe, that holds the key to deciphering these ultimate truths, regarding what . . . I guess you would call the knowledge of good and evil. The forbidden fruit, as it were."

As she listened, Allison pulled out her brand new laptop computer and opened it. Once the computer had fully booted up, she clicked on her email program.

Farther away, her father preached his sermon in the small country church. " . . . More importantly, Abraham began a relationship with God and a spiritual bloodline that would forever change the world, a world hurling through this vast universe four thousand years from that legendary time. A world subdued at last by man's unending quest for knowledge and power, lifting us out of the caves of myth and ignorance that plagued our most early ancestors. We have built machines that have taken us to new worlds and enabled our minds to understand complexities that otherwise would be impossible. Surely in this enlightened era, we have moved beyond the necessity of a whimsical story of a man who obviously didn't have the same information and technology that we have today.

"What's more, Abraham was under the impression that everything that he knew was magically created by this God that occasionally talked to him. He didn't realize that he was the product of an incredible process that we discovered about 150 years ago. Evolution is a wondrous thing. It takes non-life and creates life; it takes simple life and creates complex life. It takes confusion and chaos and creates consciousness and sublime order. No matter how you label it, evolution is a god of incredible power and might.

"Mankind's evolution has taken far beyond the necessity of these myths and legends of Abraham. It seems that credible knowledge comes only from a scientific observation of the facts, an experiment, a clinical trial, a scientific poll with a plus or minus error of 'x' percent. Most educated people seem to have come to the conclusion that the world that we see is a product of this never-ending evolutionary process that sifts out the lies from the truth of our reality. Most people of faith now hold to a reinterpretation of the creation stories in Genesis that use evolution as the tool for what we see and what we are. Now it is science that the world looks to for answers, not faith . . ."

As the two speakers wove their respective sermons hundreds of miles away from each other, Allison began typing an email.

"Ramana,

You won't believe this. I sit in Assembly Hall listening to David's acceptance speech for the Dean of the School of Natural Sciences. He is a pompous idiot!

I am so glad to hear that you took the job at Delhi University. I know that you will do great there. You are the best teacher I have ever had, and your students will love you. I know I do.

I hope you and your family are well and safe. I keep hearing of terrible things happening there and I pray that you can help your country find a way to make peace. My thoughts and prayers are with you everyday. I hope you know that.

I start my first nursing class tomorrow, and I am so excited about it. I swear it is the field that I am supposed to be in. The feeling at the school is nothing like a laboratory (sorry, I know you like labs). It is a true school; it's incredible. I'm not sure I can explain it, but I do know it is where I belong.

Regarding your last question . . . I'm not sure that I can really answer it, but I will try. I get your point about how people naturally are more comfortable with beliefs that they were raised on, and therefore construct a rationality to defend it, whether that rationality be true or not.

Do I think I would be a Christian if I were raised in India or Pakistan? I don't know. I could only wish that someone would force me to examine the heart of what I believe. I've been raised, and even taught by you, to test what I believe, look for the evi-

dence. I think that I have done that, and I think I continue to do it, every day . . ."

Allison was surprised by the sound of someone whispering behind her. "Is that you, Allison?" asked Arthur Lewis.

Allison turned around with a smile. "Hi Arthur."

"May I sit?" he quietly asked while he pulled down the chair next to her and lowered himself. His eyes immediately soaked up the contents of her laptop screen. "I almost didn't even recognize you."

Allison twitched, as her first reaction was to hide her laptop from the reporter. She slowly moved her hand over the top of the computer and closed it. "So what's up, Arthur?"

"So, what do you think about all this, Allison?" Arthur asked vaguely.

She gave him a playful smile. "You mean David's new position? I think it's a perfect fit. I hope they live happily ever after."

Arthur gave her a serious look, trying to decipher her response. "Do you mind if I ask you a few questions, Allison?"

Allison looked around at the ceremonies, realizing that they were coming to and end and said, "Sure, Arthur. Let's get out of here though." She gathered her things and the two walked toward the exit.

Arthur began the interrogation as the doors opened. "You know Allison, there's a lot of talk about Ramana and rumors about how he sabotaged the experiment that you guys worked on. It seems highly probable since he confessed to manipulating the experiment. Do you know anything that can substantiate or contradict these rumors?"

Allison flinched, ready to tell the whole story. Then she thought of Ramana's request not to say anything about what he had done or try to defend him in any way. She stopped walking and wondered about what was going to come out of her mouth. "What makes you think I would know anything about what had happened?"

Arthur cocked his head. "You were writing an email to him inside, weren't you?"

Allison laughed. "You are good, Arthur." She paused. "Let me say this. Ramana is a good man, one of the best men I have ever known. He made some mistakes, I'm sure, but he is a brilliant man. He is the reason the experiment worked in the first place, and I don't think anyone will ever duplicate what he was able to do. The project died when Ramana walked away. I cannot believe that he would ever do harm to the life that he created. It is too important to him." Her mind searched for more words until she forced herself to stop as she instinctively raised her hands. "That is all I will say."

Arthur stood silent for a moment, nodding his head at her. "Hmmm, he certainly has been cast as the sacrificial lamb. I'm sure that there is more to the story here, but I just can't seem to get anyone to level with me."

Allison laughed as she started them walking down the path again. "Come on, Arthur, I don't think that has ever stopped you before. Anyway, if you ask me, I think you missed the real story."

Arthur gave her an indignant look. "What do you mean by that?"

"Well," she started, "I can't blame you for missing it. It wasn't easy to spot. It was about beauty and creation, and life and death; it was about truth and perfection, and love and sacrifice. It was about the God of the universe. You had to look hard to see it, but it was right there for everyone to see; it always is. The trouble is, I think that Ramana and I were the only ones to find it."

Arthur's face softened into a smile. "Well that may be, Allison, but I work for the science desk, not the religion desk."

Allison laughed. "Well, I guess that is part of the story too, trying to figure out exactly who you work for. Speaking of that . . ." She pointed up the façade of the large building that read

"The School of Nursing." " . . . This is where I will be working for the next couple of years." Allison looked down at her watch. "I've got to go now. Good luck with your search, and maybe we will meet again someday. Bye Arthur."

Arthur looked up at the inscription in the concrete with a nod of his head. "It seems the right place for you. Goodbye, Allison. It truly has been a pleasure to get to know you, and good luck with your new venture." As she began to turn away, he decided to say one last thing. "By the way, Allison, I can't get over how much you've changed. You really seem so different now."

Allison smiled as she turned back; her eyes engulfed him in their warm presence. "Thank you, Arthur. I think you're right. I am different now."

Contact G.S. Hentschel
or order more copies of this book at

TATE PUBLISHING, LLC

127 East Trade Center Terrace
Mustang, Oklahoma 73064

(888) 361 - 9473

Tate Publishing, LLC

www.tatepublishing.com